BT
2015

THE LEVINE AFFAIR:

ANGEL'S FLIGHT

LELA GILBERT

WITH **W. JACK BUCKNER**
LTC (RET). SPECIAL FORCES

A POST HILL PRESS book

ISBN (Trade Paperback): 978-1-61868-937-5
ISBN (eBook): 978-1-61868-938-2

The Levine Affair: Angel's Flight copyright © 2014
by Lela Gilbert
with W. Jack Buckner, LTC (ret). Special Forces
All Rights Reserved.
Cover art by Dean Samed, Conzpiracy Digital Arts

Post Hill
PRESS

People sleep peaceably in their beds at night only because rough men stand ready to do violence on their behalf.

George Orwell (attributed)

Chapter One

Even before the sun broke across the horizon, the Nigerian air was thick and hot. A feeble breeze only occasionally rustled the banana leaves. It was deceptively calm and, at least for the moment, Joe Brac had managed to carry himself away, far from Africa. He was remembering the highlands of Vietnam, the jungles and mountains of Central and South America, and the high desert of Afghanistan. He was thinking about how many other clandestine missions there had been. He was wondering if this might be the last.

Snap! The sound of a twig breaking shattered Brac's reflection. He froze, breathless as he peered through the bushes that concealed his position. A bead of sweat trickled down his camouflaged face. A terrorist, or "Tango," as most Special Operations Forces referred to them, broke through the dawn shadows only a few feet away, and proceeded to relieve himself. The short African stood, one hand on his hip and the other holding himself, with the unsteady look of someone who had just awakened a few minutes earlier from a ganja-induced sleep.

As Brac stared, he carefully and silently eased his MP5 submachine gun up to the ready position. It was still thirty minutes before first light and the scheduled kickoff of the raid. This unexpected event threatened to compromise his team and jeopardize the mission. Brac waited, tense with alarm.

Three days earlier, in the darkness of night, a Russian MI 17 HIP helicopter had air-landed Brac's eight-man team several miles from a village in northern Nigeria where Nate

Gregory, an American humanitarian worker, was being held captive. After landing and regrouping, the team had made their way cautiously but steadily toward the village. Always moving under the concealment of night and holing up during daylight hours, they had finally reached a place commonly referred to in military lingo as the Objective Rally Point or ORP. The spot was concealed, easily defendable, and located away from natural lines of local travel. Most important, it was close enough to the village to minimize control problems, providing the team with a good, secure extraction point.

At the ORP, Brac had repeatedly gone over the plan with the entire team to ensure that each man knew his role. Then, accompanied by the sniper and machine gunner, he had proceeded on to the village to conduct his Leader's Recon. Once that recon was complete, the two team members had been left on site to "keep eyes on target" for approximately 24 hours.

Brac had returned to the ORP, where further preparation and coordination had been carried out. The night before, prior to the scheduled morning raid, Brac and three other men had cautiously traversed, in total darkness, the remaining half-mile to the village. They had linked up with the two gunners already on-site and positioned themselves strategically around the village.

By now the team had thoroughly rehearsed every aspect of the operation. They had done a complete map recon, and they had maintained a visual on the village for a full day and night. Each warrior would be armed with an array of weapons—a pistol, grenade launcher, rifle, the works. Every one of them would be outfitted with smoke, fragmentation, and stun grenades, Claymore mines, a CamelBak day pack, a combat vest, night vision optics, an advanced communications system, and a GPS device. The sniper would do his work with a Colt 5.56mm M4A1 assault rifle fitted with an advanced laser hologram site. The machine gunner would rely on an M249 Squad Automatic Weapon (SAW) to get his job done. And finally, just because you never knew what might happen next, a Vang Comp 12-gauge Remington combat shotgun would be slung across one man's back.

Yes, Brac's team was armed to the teeth. They were trained,

focused, and eager. Edgy as he felt, he still knew in his gut that they were ready to roll.

The Tango finished his business, buttoned up his pants, yawned, stretched, all the time staring with unseeing eyes at Brac's hiding place. When he casually turned, sauntered back to a nearby hooch, and disappeared inside, Brac exhaled in relief and lowered his weapon. Twenty more minutes and all hell would break loose. Brac began the countdown, keyed his boom mic, and radioed back to the pilot, who was waiting in a secure location nearby. "Crank it up and prepare for a hasty extraction," he ordered.

Twenty minutes later, it was time to rock and roll. Brac again keyed the mic and all the team members plus the pilot heard the keyword: "Let's party." The sniper was the first to fire, taking out two sentries as they sat half-awake at their posts. A dog barked. The village was just starting to awaken as Brac and his cohort Angel began to move toward the targeted hooch where the American was being kept hostage. Except for the sniper and machine gunner who remained stationary in their posts, the rest of the team crept into the village.

Now other Tangos—some Arab, some African—appeared seemingly out of nowhere. They emerged from doorways and from the windows of huts, from broken-down cement block structures, and from dugouts throughout the village. Someone shouted. Several Tangos got off wild shots, but the rat-tat-tat of the SAW quickly rose above the din. Three Tangos dropped, riddled through, paying with their lives for lax security.

Brac, Angel, and the rest of the team systematically kept moving and taking down "targets of opportunity." The bad guys had been totally taken by surprise and overwhelming firepower. Before long, the Tangos' return fire was practically nonexistent and Brac and Angel charged into the cement structure that imprisoned Nate Gregory.

"Stay quiet!" Angel told the American hostage in a hoarse whisper. "We're going to get you out of here. Can you walk?'

Speechless with shock, Gregory sucked in a deep breath and nodded in the affirmative. Brac and Angel grabbed him by both arms and hurried him through the door while two team members waited outside the door to provide cover. Brac keyed his mic. "Boogedy, Boogedy!" he said. "Let's get the hell out of here!"

The team charged back the way they had come, each member tactically rolling back while providing cover to the others. Brac's men threw several smoke grenades into the village and tossed out a few more along the escape route to further conceal themselves during their exit. Several Claymores had also been placed on the route when the team traveled to the village. Now the last man in the group armed the trip wires as he passed by. The Claymores had been set in a particularly deadly manner, on a tree to detonate shoulder high, and also at ground level, set to blast off additional mines a second or two later.

It was only a matter of time before reinforcements rushed in to take up the pursuit. Time was of the essence. Brac and his team were still a couple of hundred yards from the RP when they first heard the whap-whap of their helicopter. Their pace quickened and just as suddenly they heard the first of the Claymores go off, followed by the screams of men cut to pieces by hundreds of steel balls.

One team member quickly shot two smoke grenades from his grenade launcher in the direction they had just come from, and then immediately followed with a CS grenade. The smoke would conceal the extraction. The CS would water a few eyes and keep the Tangos occupied as they stumbled through the booby-trapped killing field that Brac and his boys had left in their wake.

Brac, Angel, Nate Gregory, and the rest of the team burst into the RP just as the helo appeared over the trees and came in low and fast. Even before it touched the ground, Brac and Angel threw Nate unceremoniously onto the floor, clambered aboard, and within seconds the rest of the team piled in. The pilot wasted no time lifting off. He turned sharply and headed south, smoothly heading back to a safe place.

With any luck, Brac smiled to himself, satisfied with a job well done, *there'll be a nice cold beer waiting for us.*

* * *

The humid air in the cramped cell pressed against Jumoke like a heavy hand. The mud walls seeped with humidity; the prison smelled of garbage and human waste. The temperature was more than 100 degrees. Sweat dripped from her carelessly braided black hair to her temples, mingling with tears that trickled down her dark cheeks. She held her infant daughter tenderly, the child's head pressed against her left breast. Jamoke tried to focus her mind on the child, tried to will a surge of milk into the baby's mouth.

The baby fussed and tugged on the dry nipple. "Abeo," Jumoke whispered, "be patient. It will come."

Jumoke was nineteen-years-old, and not much more than a child herself. She knew that her fear was blocking the flow of milk. To fight the fear away, for the moment, she chanted the child's name over and over. "Abeo, Abeo, Abeo..." she sang.

In their language, Abeo's name meant "Happy she was born," and nothing could have been truer, even though the child's birth was destined to cost Jumoke her life.

In another setting, the graceful form of black Madonna and child would have been beautiful. But in the dank confines of the cell, flies buzzed around the two, drawn to their sweaty faces. Eventually, to Jumoke's relief, she felt the tingling sensation of milk moving into her breasts. Within seconds, Abeo calmed and began to make the gentle sounds of suckling. Jumoke groaned aloud. She was trying not to think about yesterday's courtroom scene, but it refused to leave her mind.

She could still see the judge's hard, angry face as he spat out the words: "In the Name of Allah, Most Gracious, Most Merciful. All praise and thanks are due to Allah, and peace and blessings be upon His Messenger..."

She had been the only woman present, she and her baby girl. Like today, her face had been drenched with sweat and tears. The room had been unbearably hot, made even more stifling by a crowd of Islamic law students, hostile to her case, who filled every available seat in the room. Some stood against the walls, and all of them had rumbled "Allahu Akhbar! Allahu Akhbar!" as the sentence was declared. The judge's voice, which was loud and harsh by nature, had lashed into her body as he spoke:

"I bear witness that you, Jumoke Abubakar, have sinned. You have offended Allah, the gracious, the merciful, by committing adultery. You have disgraced your father, your brothers, and your community. I admonish you that you must repent to Allah for having a sexual relationship with a married man. Turn to Allah and express your remorse to Him. Do not take this issue of repentance lightly, and do not delay in seeking the forgiveness and guidance of Allah.

"Now, in the presence of my brothers, who have taken to heart the Word of Allah, spoken through his messenger Mohammad—peace be unto him—I sentence you for your sin of adultery, Jumoke Abubakar, to death by stoning."

Jumoke had relived the courtroom scene a thousand times in the last 24 hours and she knew very well how the sentence would unfold. As soon as Abeo was weaned, the local Islamic authorities would take the child away. Jumoke would be led to a public square, where she would be buried in the earth, with only her head and chest above the ground. Executioners would assault her with stones. If she was lucky, she would be knocked unconscious early in the process. But in her imagination, she could already feel the blows of rock after rock, striking her head, her nose, her chin. She caught her breath, trembled, and held the child more tightly.

Jumoke was guilty—she had never denied that. She had committed adultery with Abeo's father, who was married to another woman. The child's father was a family friend, and Jumoke had been in love with him all her life. He loved her too, but his parents had arranged his marriage with a woman from a "better" family. The two had tried not to see each other, but late one evening they had unexpectedly run into each other. They had talked excitedly, and wandered off to what they'd thought was a solitary place. Before long, the temptation to make love had been too strong for them.

A few months later, when Jumoke's pregnancy became evident, the wronged wife was informed about the illicit liaison by a village gossip. The wife's brother was a Muslim jurist, and Shari'a law, which governed Abuja State where Jumoke grew up, demanded the ultimate price for such behavior. She wouldn't be the first woman to die for her sexual impropriety, and as long as Islamic radicals controlled the legal system, she wouldn't be the last.

But Jumoke wasn't concerned about legalities. She was a mother with a beautiful daughter—a child who looked so much like her father, the man Jumoke still loved, that she was doubly cherished. He would pay no price for their liaison; in most cases the law punished only the guilty woman. And yes, she was guilty. For years, she had been willing to die for love— nothing else had mattered to her. But now, with this beautiful, amazing child in her arms, Jumoke wanted to live more than she'd ever wanted to live before.

She brushed the flies away from Abeo's face and wiped the sweat and tears from her own. She wanted to pray, but she knew Allah would not hear her—she had offended Him. Another wave of fear rippled through her. She clutched Abeo, cried out in her misery, and wondered—again—what the first stone would feel like when it struck her body.

* * *

Westbound on the Santa Monica Freeway, traffic was crawling from Los Angeles toward Beverly Hills, and it was unusually slow that April morning. An energetic spring storm had blown through over the weekend, leaving behind a rain-washed sky, broken by huge silvery clouds and an occasional squall. It was, for all its inconvenience to rain-wary California commuters, a spectacular morning, the kind of day that announces spring has arrived.

Nonetheless, Karen Burke, acquisitions editor for the fledging New Spirit Press, was in no mood for either rain or rainbows. She had overslept, and as she checked her make-up in the rearview mirror, she confirmed that her eyes were still swollen with sleep. She wearily navigated the Robertson Blvd. off-ramp and pulled into an underground parking structure beneath a high rise bank building.

Karen caught a glimpse of herself in the bank's wall of glass as she waited for the elevator. She smoothed her dark blue dress and readjusted the striped scrunchy that was supposed to confine her wild-looking mane of reddish hair into a business-like knot. It wasn't working very well, but who would care?

"Hi, happy Monday," Karen mumbled to Stephie, the middle-aged receptionist, who doubled and tripled as clerk, intern, and gopher. Her formidable pink-clad bosom loomed authoritatively over a desk-and-computer arrangement. Not exactly what the head-hunters called "front office appearance," but Stephie got the job done, whatever it was.

"Hi yourself," Stephie shot back. "Good morning, New Spirit Press," she continued, answering line one.

New Spirit Press was an imprint of Henry Weiss Book Company, a venerable publishing house in New York. It was a two-year-old experiment, trying to make a profitable foray into the ever-expanding "Faith and Inspiration" book market. As acquisitions editor, Karen Burke was responsible for locating ten or twelve new titles a year, with the hope of expanding to twenty if enough dollars were turned in the process. So far, since the beginning, business had grown steadily. No great best sellers had been launched—no new *Prayer of Jabez* had been discovered; nothing quite like *The Purpose-Driven Life* had appeared over the transom. Still, there was profit, and where there was profit, there was a temporarily satisfied board of directors in New York.

As for the "Faith and Inspiration" side of things, Karen was a cradle Catholic who had on three or four occasions in her life seriously thought that her prayers had been answered. She wanted to believe there was a benevolent Force at work in the world, and it was second nature for her to fit that Force into the grid provided by the Nicene Creed.

On one hand, she often felt defensive when non-believers assaulted the "holy, Catholic and Apostolic Church." She was, however, equally disturbed by religious types who went too far with their assumptions about God and humanity, heaven and hell. She found it difficult to cope with mortals who thought they could understand all mysteries—it seemed a little too pat for her spiritual digestive system. And did she believe the stories she read in the books New Spirit Press published? She wanted to. At the core, she really wanted to. But, at least for now, that was about the best she could do.

She unlocked her office, flipped on the lights, and opened the vertical shades to the cloud-strewn sky. She sighed, wishing she could walk outside. For the first time that year, it felt like spring. There would be no L.A. smog today. She turned on her computer and while waiting for it to boot up, she thumbed absently through a handful of pink message notes on her desk.

Once the server was connected, Karen checked her emails. Nothing from Sid, her erstwhile boyfriend, who, as usual, was on the road with his band. It was no wonder he hadn't written. He was not only computer illiterate, but he was careless about keeping in touch with her when he traveled. In fact, he had only sent her about four emails in his entire life, but she always liked to think there might be another one. Charming as Sid could be, however, and musically gifted as he was, Karen had known for weeks that her interest in him had flickered and was all but extinguished. Too bad, but who needed a relationship anyway?

Pulling her thoughts back to the screen, only one email caught her attention. It was from Frank Goldberg, the Corporate Vice President for Acquisitions in New York: "Let me know what you think of the proposal, Thanks, Frank," it said.

"What proposal?" she answered aloud, shaking her head. "Frank needs to go on a nice long vacation."

"Say what?" A too-cheerful voice drifted in from the next room.

"Just talking to myself," Karen replied to the invisible Jason Prescott, another jack-of-all-trades New Spirit employee who did almost everything except write books himself. "I just got a mysterious email from Frank in New York, that's all."

"Oh, yeah, there's a package for you from him. Hold on, I'll get it."

Jason, a twenty-something black man from West Los Angeles, breezed in and, with a flourish, dropped a large envelope on Karen's desk. "Enjoy," he smiled. *Oh God, how I hate Mondays,* Karen mused as she watched him saunter away like a waiter who had just served up the chef's special.

Something about that email from New York felt like trouble.

Karen ripped the package open and pulled out the contents.

It was a neatly printed, sixty page-book proposal, with a hand-written note from Frank Goldberg, V.P., attached. "Find out if this story is legitimate. If so, I think it has legs. Do a site visit if necessary. It's not us because of the religious material, but it may be a big find for you. Check it out. Thanks. Frank."

Quickly scanning the synopsis and sample chapters, Karen felt a faint ripple of alarm. The non-fiction, news-related story took place in Ogbu, some remote, god-forsaken village in northern Nigeria.

Did he say site visit? In Nigeria? Dear God!

The book proposal was written by an American, Nate Gregory, who had recently been rescued from captivity after being held as a hostage in West Africa. Karen had seen the news reports, and vaguely remembered that Nate had given credit for his rescue to God and some Southern California televangelist. He had also claimed that the U. S. government had completely failed to acknowledge his plight or to assist him in any way during his year and a half of imprisonment.

Noting that the would-be author had been working as a short-term missionary at the time of his abduction, Karen was pleasantly surprised to also note that he had some talent as a writer, and seemed to be well-read, judging from his carefully chosen quotes from other books. She was troubled, however, with his description of his Muslim captors, his somewhat, in her view, colonialist attitude toward the Christian community in Africa, and his eloquent but relentless verbal assault on something called "Shari'a law," the Islamic religious system under which he was held captive. Even a quick scan of Nate Gregory's proposal revealed what seemed to her like outrageous and incredible claims of court-ordered amputations, absurd violations of women's rights, and the burning alive of Christians in their churches.

Great. A religious fanatic finding fault with other religious fanatics. Karen shook her head sadly. What on earth was Goldberg, a notoriously left-of-center New Yorker, thinking?

Staring out the window behind her desk, she debated for a few minutes about trying to contact Frank. She glanced at the clock and calculated: *8:15, so it's 11:15 on the East Coast.* She put her hand on the phone, hesitated, and then remembered the email. It would be easier to broach the subject that way.

"This seems rather extreme," she typed. "Surely situations like this would be front page news in the *Los Angeles Times*."

After clicking "Send" she shoved Nate Gregory's proposal aside and started going through her messages. They were boring, but certainly not as disturbing as the Nigeria material. Surely Goldberg wasn't serious. Within minutes, the email chime drew her eyes back to her computer screen. A rather cryptic response appeared. "KB, Human rights stories don't sell newspapers. Find out what's going on. The book could be huge. FG."

Karen stood up, still staring at the screen, and headed for the office coffee pot. After filling a large I Love LA mug, she headed back to her desk and tried to formulate a strategy. Her first thought was to call all the people she knew who were involved in international affairs, but she was uncomfortable with the story and wasn't ready to talk about it. Much of it was too outrageous to be true.

Instead, she logged on to Google and started checking links with words like "Shari'a" and "Nigeria." There were more than enough postings over the past two years to make her wonder—again—why she had never heard about the threat of so-called militant Islam in West Africa. Of course she knew about ongoing terrorist threats to the United States and various European cities. That hadn't changed since September 11, 2001. And she'd heard occasional rumbles from Sudan and its endless civil war, and from minor blow-ups in Indonesia. But she really hadn't made much of a connection between Islamists and the rest of the world. Now she was a little disconcerted by the number of references to Nigeria, especially on human rights websites. Typical of the reports was one from Humanity.com,

"Islamic militants burnt down four churches and a hotel in the northern Nigerian town of Dutse after a magistrate denied bail to a Muslim youth charged with setting another church on fire, police said on Thursday. Police in the predominantly Muslim state of Jigawa said irate youths went on the rampage late on Wednesday in the provincial capital, southeast of Kano—Nigeria's second largest city where hundreds have died in religious clashes in the past three years."

One horror story led to another, and after an hour or so Karen was feeling a little shaken. By now her phone was ringing with Monday morning urgency. She intercommed Stephie. "No calls, please," she snapped, and hung up abruptly before Stephie could question her.

So maybe Frank Goldberg isn't completely duped after all, she thought, vaguely aware that a rain shower was pounding almost horizontally against her window. *I should know by now that the media usually overlooks Africa. Still this seems pretty important. Did I miss it because I wasn't interested?*

In actual fact, she really wasn't very interested now, except for the fact that the Nigeria story was quickly turning into an assignment, and that meant she not only needed to be interested, she needed to become an expert as quickly as possible.

Karen sighed and looked out the window again, and for some random reason wondered why things hadn't worked out with her and Sid. Her friends, of course, thought that the two of them were completely mismatched—and claimed that she was "superior" to him in intellect and drive. But Sid was talented, and she was so proud of him. Why couldn't he have at least kept in touch while he traveled? There were so many things she'd like to talk about with him. For example, what would Sid say about the strange story in Nigeria?

She shook her head. She could already hear him: "Oh God, Karen," he would scowl, "you should know by now that money, sex, and hate make the world go round. Africans have more than their share of sex and hate, and they'll do anything for money. You know how they are..."

Sid wasn't exactly a racist, but the phrase "small minded" might fit his profile. He certainly was disinterested in international intrigues, and was proud to say that he had never subscribed to a daily newspaper or watched CNN. He liked to think that he kept his creativity unfettered by living in a simple world made up of his musician friends, the crowds that showed up for his performances, and, if it was convenient, Karen.

"What a colossal waste of time he's been," Karen muttered bitterly, picking up Nate Gregory's book proposal to see if his contact information was on the title page. Of course it was—he was Mr. Perfect. She hadn't seen a single typo on the pages she'd read. Faintly disgusted with him for being anal, she also noted that he lived only a couple of hours south of Los Angeles, in Carlsbad.

She was about to call Nate and interview him by phone when the idea occurred to her that perhaps she should arrange a face-to-face conversation with him. It might be a nice change of pace to drive down the coast and meet him somewhere. She could get an idea about his personality, and maybe a better sense about his believability. She opened her date book, assured herself that she had nothing scheduled Wednesday or Thursday, and picked up the phone to call. She punched in his phone number, and after a brief but pleasant conversation, was scheduled to meet with Nate Gregory, aspiring author, in two day's time.

Minutes later, she was printing a map from Yahoo and was about to start a list of questions about the proposal. *It might be a good idea,* she reminded herself, *for you to finish reading it before you make a fool of yourself with the author.* With that, she went to the kitchen to refill her coffee cup, settled into her chair with a stack of Post-Its, a pen, and the proposal, and started through it, line by line. With any luck, she'd find enough holes in the story to sabotage the whole project. She'd get to the bottom of it. Because anything, even temporarily pissing off Frank Goldberg, would be better than making a site visit to, of all places on the planet, Nigeria.

As it turned out, Nate's story was a page-turner. The biggest question mark surrounded his rescue, which he claimed had been masterminded by a San Diego Evangelical pastor. How could such a strategic, perfectly choreographed rescue that seemed to have involved American personnel and a helicopter, be the handiwork of some unknown California preacher? Karen could not comprehend how such a mission could have unfolded. Precise, and not done on the cheap, if it had happened the way he said it did, it was no amateur performance.

Besides, she still thought Nate Gregory had to be exaggerating about the rigorous Islamic law enforcement in

Northern Nigeria. She tried to think of a way to tell Goldberg about her skepticism, but knew exactly what he would say: "I told you to find out what happened. That's your job."

In the couple of days preceding her visit to Nate, Karen researched Ken Wilson, his San Diego pastor. His on-line photograph revealed a pony-tailed, portly middle-aged yuppie. Transcripts of his sermons were posted, but as she looked over one of them, to her theologically untrained eye, he seemed to be parsing some obscure Old Testament Scripture while trying to spin it into a motivational speech. Naturally a touch of morality was thrown in on the side, and the whole thing seemed to go on forever. She shook her head. Although she was anything but a devout Catholic, a fifteen-minute homily by an anonymous local priest seemed far more palatable to her.

"Pastor Ken"—as the website called him—was the senior pastor at an independent evangelical church called Bethany Temple, with a congregation of around 3,000. Judging by posted information, the church seemed to be deeply involved in community work, and also had a message board on international persecution of Christians. As Karen scanned a few threads, she once again found herself reading about events that seemed completely removed from any news stories she had ever seen. How could there be multiple atrocities in places like Burma, Indonesia, Sudan and, yes, Nigeria, with virtually no press coverage? In any case, whatever his game was, Pastor Ken seemed to have his San Diego congregation more than involved in matters beyond their own local sphere.

Two days later, she steered her Rabbit convertible south on Interstate 5, past the last Orange County off-ramp, and through the rolling hills of Camp Pendleton Marine Corps Base. Two Sea Stallion helicopters hovered over a small bay where complex military maneuvers were being enacted, including amphibious landings. A U.S. Navy ship was anchored a short distance away, and Marines were being transported ashore in what appeared to be inflatable Zodiac boats.

Karen's mind flashed back to her father who had served in the Marine Corps during the Vietnam War. He had died the year before. A victim of quickly-moving cancer, he had been a great hero in the eyes of his family and friends. Patrick Burke had been a quiet, intensely private man, and although his many medals and ribbons were still on display in the Burke home, he had rarely discussed his war-time experiences with anyone.

Karen knew her dad had seen hard combat, and at times she had wondered exactly what he'd been through and why he was unwilling to discuss it. He had kept in touch with a handful of veterans, most of whom had settled in the Washington D.C. area and were still involved with the U.S. government. Pat Burke had finished his education after the war and had found a career as a professor of history at California State University.

Karen impulsively picked up her cell phone and pushed the autodial to reach her mother. "Hey, Mom. Yeah it's me," she began. "I'm driving through Camp Pendleton, and they are doing some maneuvers with helicopters and it made me think about Dad..."

"Oh God, Karen. It's always like he's in the next room, isn't it?"

There was silence on the line. Karen's eyes blurred. "I know, Mom. Just wanted to say hi."

"I'm glad you called, honey. But why are you driving through Camp Pendleton? I thought you were at work today."

"This is work, Mom. I have to talk to a guy who wrote a book proposal. He was a hostage in Nigeria, and he got rescued. I have to find out if it's a real deal."

"What's his name?"

"It's Nate Gregory. Why?"

"Because I think our women's group was praying for him when he was still a hostage. Wasn't he doing some kind of missions work?"

"Yeah, he was. Your . . . what group? You mean at St. Vincent's?"

"No, I've been going to a, well, it's kind of a local women's prayer group. Kind of a...Bible study group."

"Are you kidding? You've always hated that kind of stuff. Why on earth...?"

"Karen, when your dad died I started thinking a lot about, well, you know, other things. Spiritual life. That's all. It's not a big deal. Actually, this group prayed for our family while he was sick, and I really appreciated it."

Karen's eyes blurred again. Patrick Burke's death had been

a devastating blow to them both. But a women's prayer group? Time to change the subject. "Mom, I'll tell you more about it after I meet with this guy. I'm glad you've heard of him at least. I should get off the phone now. Love you..."

Karen turned onto a freeway off-ramp and headed for King's Fish House, where she and Nate had agreed to meet. *Mom is still grieving*, she thought as she drove down Paseo del Norte, searching for the restaurant among what seemed like a thousand car dealerships. *But a women's prayer group?*

She shook off her concerns along with the sadness she always felt when thinking about her dad. Instead, she summoned her mind to focus on the meeting at hand. She grabbed her handbag and the leather tote she used for business and hurried toward the door. A man about her age stepped forward. "Karen Burke?" he asked.

"That's me." She smiled. Nate Gregory was considerably taller than her five-foot-five height, and somewhat better looking than the news photo he had included with his book proposal. He had close-cropped brown hair, greenish eyes, and a self-composed style that put her immediately at ease.

They settled into a booth and for some reason Karen was tempted to have a glass of wine. She decided, however, that it was a little unprofessional, not to mention the fact that she might fall asleep driving home. They both settled for iced tea. "So how long have you been back in California?" Karen began.

"I've been home about six months," he explained. "I started writing about two weeks after I got here—I really wanted to tell my story so people would know more about how precarious the situation in Nigeria is."

"You mean politically precarious."

"I mean precarious in every way," he answered. "I assume you've read the proposal. I hope I made the situation clear."

"Yes, you did. Look, I don't know much about Africa or Islam," Karen said. "I've got a lot to learn. To be honest, this book was sent to me by our New York office. Frank Goldberg, our VP back there really thinks it has promise, but wanted to direct it toward our Faith and Inspiration imprint. I'm the acquisitions editor at New Spirit Press, as I told you on the phone, and I want to talk to you a little more about the circumstances surrounding your experiences in Nigeria."

"Of course. What would you like to know?"

Karen Burke was a confident and professional woman, who had interviewed many a prospective author. She also took some pride in her awareness of current issues—she cared about international tensions in the Middle East, confident in her balanced view of that irksome situation. She had worked as an editor on a book about the homeless, and had puzzled ever since about the legal implications of allowing mentally ill people to wander around the streets on their own. She was sensitive to those who pleaded for peace on earth, but because of her father, she had a strong sense that there were times when peace had to be achieved through military conflict—not always a politically correct view, but, she thought, a sensible one. She felt like a reasonable, well-informed person.

But Karen was puzzled about Nigeria. She couldn't equate the horror stories she'd seen in Nate's manuscript, and in some on-line reports, with the silence in the media. She couldn't believe that a great religion like Islam—wasn't it revered as a peace-loving "religion of the book?"—would be violent enough to mutilate burglars, behead blasphemers, or stone adulterers. Was this man crazy? Was he ignorant? Was he part of some weird anti-Muslim movement? Or was he an eye-witness to something unconscionable?

"I hate to admit this," Karen began, her eyes fixed on Nate's face, "but I am kind of in the dark about your situation. My mom told me today that her women's group—*God I can't believe I'm saying this!*—was praying for you during your captivity. But I didn't really know about what happened to you until I got the manuscript, and I still am kind of baffled by the political situation in Nigeria...or is it a religious situation?"

Nate laughed involuntarily. "Sorry," he said. "I'm not laughing at you. I knew next to nothing about the situation when I went over there a year and a half ago. I was between jobs, and to be honest, I was just trying to do something worthwhile for six months. Boy, did I get an education!"

Karen's questions tumbled out over each other in no particular order. "But what about all the things you wrote? The stuff about whatever it's called...Shari'a law? Do you really believe all that? And how could some preacher in San Diego be the brains behind a military rescue? How would he know what to do? More to the point, how would he pay for it?"

Nate shook his head and smiled. "Good questions, Karen. Seriously. Let's just put it this way, if I'd been in your shoes a year and a half ago, I wouldn't have been nearly as tactful as you are. I would have said, 'Okay, Nate, let's be honest. Are you crazy?'"

After a huge gulp of iced tea, which she wished more than ever had been a huge gulp of wine, Karen stared at Nate. "But seriously..."

"Karen," he replied, "I couldn't be more serious. Nigeria is a terrible, complicated situation. And if I can make sense of it in this book, I will. I sure hope, if your guys do decide to publish it, that they'll give me some help with editing. I have no idea how to do this right. But I know...I mean *I know*...that the book has to be written. And if you don't publish it, I can promise you, somebody else will. It's a story that has to be told. And the sooner, the better."

"Why do you say that?"

"Because the longer it takes, the more people will suffer and struggle and eventually die horrible, gruesome deaths."

The two talked for more than two hours. The bottom line was that Nate was actively involved in the defense of a young woman named Jamoke who had been sentenced to death by stoning. "I became aware of the story a few weeks ago," he explained. "I know people who know her, and because of my experiences, I'm in touch with a lot of activists who are trying to help her. There's a lot going on, and I'm not even sure about all the details."

Karen nodded. "That's good, although it's still hard for me to believe something like that could happen in today's world."

Nate's face tightened slightly. "What makes you think that 'today's world' is a humane or safe place? Do you have any idea how many people died horrible deaths at the hand of others in the twentieth century? And let's face it, the twenty-first century isn't looking much better."

He wasn't exactly angry, but Karen could see that she'd hit a nerve. Well, he'd been through a lot, so it was understandable.

"Sorry, I just meant..."

"I know, I know. I used to think the same thing. Look, why don't you find out if your boss will send you over to Nigeria so you can see for yourself."

Oh God, here we go. "I think he actually wants me to do something like that," she answered honestly. "He's calling it a 'site visit.' But it would be pretty hard to figure out where to go and who to see."

"Well, as a matter of fact, I'm going back over there myself in a few weeks. I know exactly where you should go, and could introduce you to people who know a lot more than I do. Why don't you meet me in Nigeria, and I'll take you into the North with me? It means flying into Lagos, connecting in Abuja, and driving a couple of hours into the bush. You'll find out everything you need to know and more."

Karen's heart sank. The words *Worst Case Scenario* were flashing on and off in her mind like a neon sign. "Would it be safe?" she asked lamely, then caught herself. "Well, I know it's not exactly *safe*, but, you know?"

Nate shook his head again. "No, Nigeria isn't at all safe, and you need to know that up front. But we would have people along to keep an eye on us. And if you're interested in international affairs, it certainly will be interesting."

* * *

As first light began to break across the Alabama woodlands, a shadow moved slowly and silently through the trees until it reached one particular spot and eased into position. The shadowy figure might have looked like a random shrub but for the two eyes that peered out near the top, searching the clearing beyond the tree line. As dawn brightened, a doe and two yearlings broke out into the open, their ears erect, sniffing the air. The hunter surveyed the scene, motionless, waiting.

Several more deer appeared—a young spiked buck and two more does. One of the deer lifted its nose and tested the air. Detecting no human scent, it lowered its head and continued to eat. Just then, a huge nine-point buck appeared at the edge of the woods. The does and young bucks had assured him it was safe to enter the field, and he did not sense what awaited him. The shadowy "bush" tensed a little at the sight of the buck, cautiously easing the safety off his weapon and waiting for a close shot.

The huge buck moved within 15 yards of the hunter. The weapon was lifted to a firing position. Again the buck stiffened, ears alert, sniffing the air. The man in the suit had sprayed himself down with a Hawg's scent killer and strategically planted a vial of buck urine in the hunting area; no human odor could be detected in the still morning air.

The hunter gradually squeezed the trigger and suddenly the morning stillness was broken by a muffled pop. At the sound, the buck tensed and jumped straight up. It was too late. A big red splotch appeared just behind the left shoulder. The buck bolted to the right and ran into the woods, leaving behind a trail of red. The hunter remained fixed in his place, waiting motionless for a few minutes until he was certain the large buck was gone. Finally, still clad in his ghillie suit, the man stalked across the distance between himself and where the buck had been shot. He reached down and touched a small red stain on the ground and then lowered himself to one knee. The hunter was satisfied that he had just made a perfect kill...with a paintball gun. The big buck would live to be hunted another day during the regular Alabama deer hunting season. The paintball "kill" would be repeated, but with a more lethal conclusion.

Still edgy and alert, the hunter felt the imperceptible presence of something else. He didn't move, but he knew. He could feel it on the back of his neck. Gradually, he turned his head. The man and a large male coyote locked eyes. For a long moment they stared, transfixed, as each one recognized the other for what he was: a predator.

Two hours later, after cleaning up his paintball gun and placing his ghillie suit in a Scentlok bag, Joe Brac settled down in front of the massive stone fireplace in the lodge's great room, enjoying the scene outside. Leaded windows opened onto 5,000 acres of pristine forest. David Levine's hunting and fishing camp—nicknamed "The L Farm"—was a welcome haven to Brac and his team, who had an open invitation to take advantage of its isolation; not only to hunt but to plan the paramilitary missions that Levine financed and launched from time to time.

To prepare for just such a mission, Joe and the others had just returned from a site survey in northern Nigeria. Later that day, they would gather in a large meeting room and review the information they had gathered. For the next week, they would make painstaking preparations for their next mission. But for now, Joe checked his watch a little impatiently. Just as he glanced at the door for the third time, Kate Slagle appeared— tall, brown-eyed, and as graceful as ever. Kate was a busy lawyer who worked out of Atlanta. Somehow, however, she always seemed to find time to see Joe when he returned to the States. His face brightened at the sight of her. He jumped up and gave her a big hug.

"You made it!" he grinned.

"Of course I made it! I couldn't wait to see you. I'm so happy you're back—and you're here to stay for awhile! Aren't you?"

He chuckled, "Well, you never know about me, do you?"

She looked at him suspiciously. "Are you teasing me or trying to tell me something?"

He kissed her softly. "We're here right now, and that's what's important, right?"

"Right," she nodded, smiling into his eyes.

While she sank into the big leather couch, Joe poured her a glass of chardonnay and popped the cap off a Heineken for himself. He marveled at the way it always seemed as if they'd never been apart. Kate intuitively knew what to ask about and what subjects to leave alone. She genuinely cared about Joe's well-being.

As for Joe, he might be a predator on the battleground and in the woods, but he was no such thing at home. He knew all about the quick flings, the cute tricks in foreign lands, and he longed for something far more substantial. In recent months, he thought maybe he'd found what he was looking for in Kate. She was beautiful, and in wit and wisdom he seemed to have met his match. Laughter came easily to them, as did lovemaking. They were good friends, Joe thought, but so much more. In the six years since his second divorce, Kate was the one woman who had managed to stay on his mind, even though he couldn't always keep in touch with her the way she wanted him to.

Kate had been divorced for several years, too, and she was more than ready to remarry. Joe wasn't at all sure he wanted to go through all that again—his divorces had been painful, prolonged, and costly. He had tried to say so before, but to no avail. Right now, however, the warm glow of their reunion wasn't about to be dampened by talk of an uncertain future. Instead, after catching up for awhile, the two of them responded to an unspoken cue and walked hand in hand to the suite of rooms Joe claimed as his own during his private visits to the lodge.

Behind closed doors, their passion was breathtaking. The frequent separations, if anything, only sharpened their craving for one another. And everything that happened between them that spring afternoon was wonderful. There was no disappointment, no game-playing, no bad timing, and nothing to worry about.

At least not yet, Joe couldn't help but think afterwards, as he felt Kate's naked warmth pressing against him in relaxed satisfaction. He blocked from his mind how soon he would be leaving, where he would be going, and what he would have to do before they were together again.

Focus on the moment, he reminded himself, and let the rest go.

Chapter Two

Alexis Schofield sat with her face in her hands, staring at a poster on the wall of her Washington DC cubicle. Her tiny workspace was cluttered, floor to ceiling, with manila folders, piles of papers, torn-out newspaper stories, and yellow legal pad sheets scribbled over with nearly-indecipherable notes. The walls were covered with poster-size photographs of Africans—most of them graphic and disturbing. Alexis' eyes were fixed on a close-up—a woman's bleeding and swollen back, evidence of a severe lashing. On another poster, a man held out to the camera the stump of his right arm, the hand removed at the wrist; the wound was unbandaged and clearly unhealed. On yet another poster, the head of a man, his eyes still open in horror, lay next to his beheaded body.

It was nearly 10 at night and Alexis had been working since 8:30 AM, tirelessly emailing and faxing press releases, and calling contacts. Her day's focus had been on the impending execution of a young Nigerian woman, Jumoke Abubakar, who had been found guilty of adultery and sentenced by an Islamic Shari'a judge to die by stoning as soon as her infant daughter was weaned. Alexis, who worked for Humanity.com, a human rights group, was trying to publicize Jumoke's story. She and her boss, Emil Carlyle, were hoping to put together a group of activists that would, depending on funding, travel to Nigeria to protest the sentencing and seek Jumoke's release.

The phone rang. Alexis, whose mind was literally thousands of miles away, was startled back into her surroundings. "Alexis speaking," she answered.

"*Well, we've hooked some pretty peculiar fish this time,*" Emil's voice drawled. "*Strange bedfellows, to put it mildly.*"

"How many?"

"*Two for sure.*"

"Two? Only two? After all this work?" Alexis was suddenly weak with exhaustion.

"*Well, don't panic now. There are some other good people mulling things over. But listen to this. We've got a hyper-liberal women's studies professor from Dartmouth, and a hyper-conservative Jewish immigration lawyer from inside the beltway. Those two alone should keep our lives interesting.*"

"Oh my God," Alexis groaned. "A house divided…"

"*No, it's all good. For two people like that to agree about this woman's sentence bodes well for getting the word out about Shari'a. It means we're not just talking to our usual constituents. You're doing a great job, Alexis. Go home now and pick up where you left off tomorrow morning.*"

Grabbing her handbag and heading for the door, Alexis took one last look at the photographs that were attached to the walls with stick-pins. She couldn't help but wonder, in a few months time, if a full-color print of Jumoke's battered corpse would be added to the collection.

"So we've added an uber- feminist and a neo-con to our team. Good times," she muttered to herself, locking the door and heading for the car park.

* * *

What had hit him? His head throbbed and his tongue felt like coarse sandpaper. The taste in his mouth was indescribable. "Ugh!"

Joe Brac, after Kate Slagle's departure, had relinquished his elegant suite of rooms in the main house and was now roughing it with the rest of his team in an old cabin on the L Farm. He eased down the stairs and was immediately overcome by the smell of stale beer and leftover food. Looking around, he shook his head. *Why on earth?* he thought. *Don't I ever learn?*

Joe was too old for this crap and he should have known

better. As he reached the bottom of the stairs, he surveyed the room through blurry eyes. Beer cans were scattered everywhere—on the fireplace mantle, on end tables, atop the rustic oak dining table, all over the floor, and throughout the kitchen. Leftover pieces of T-bone steaks and baked potatoes were still lying on plates, and the guacamole dip had turned black and taken on a life of its own.

"My God....what a mess!"

As he took in the grim scene, he heard a rumbling noise coming from one of the couches, and noticed a lump of clothing with a colorful Afghan draped across it and a tuft of light brown hair sticking out. One of the men, a casualty of the night before, had not made it to his bunk bed and was now lying comatose on the couch, apparently trying to catch flies through his gaping mouth.

Brac stepped over to the couch and gave the lump of a man a good swift punch. "Wake-up, you sorry ass! We're wasting daylight."

"Oh shit, boss. Have mercy, I'm dying..." Angel muttered.

"Mercy is for the *weak!* Get up, wake the rest of the guys up, and be ready in 20 minutes for a good run."

Angel didn't move.

"C'mon now, *get up!*" Brac repeated. "If you're going to hoot with the owls at night, you have to be able to soar with eagles during the day. Let's go!"

Twenty minutes later, Brac and his six men gathered in front of the lodge and were silently stretching, warming up, and doing a few calisthenics. As the sun peeked over the horizon, they took off running down a long dirt road. There was some cursing and grumbling and a lot of huffing and puffing, but as a whole they took to the run with firm determination. Each in his own way was lost in a world known only to him. Five miles later, they were back at the starting point.

Brac looked them over, calculating and recalculating. This wouldn't be their first mission in Nigeria, but this one was far more complex than the last. Of these six, Angel—whose real name was Bill Jones—would be on the ground near Abuja in less than a week's time, finishing up the intelligence gathering that he did so well and taking care of some other details for the boss. Angel was a weathered veteran, about 42 years old, who had served with Brac on and off for more than 15 years. Not only was he a close friend and a peerless intelligence officer, he was also a deadly shooter. The rescue they were planning had been nicknamed "Angel's Flight." Angel would be the first on the scene, and, as always, their number one source of good intelligence.

Jim Amato, whose *nom de guerre* was Rambo, had been indispensable in their first hostage mission in Nigeria. He was a huge, burly type from an Italian home who always looked like he needed a shave. He was already in Nigeria, working with a firm that provided security for oil companies—the few that were still in business—in the Nile Delta.

Mark Steele, "The Judge," had a few grey hairs mixed into his sandy brown buzz, but he was still a lethal, world-class sniper and a compassionate medic. Terry Lambert, "Playboy," whose blue-eyed good looks seemed to attract more women than all the rest of the guys together, did communications and logistics. The rest of the team included a former British SAS commando, and two retired Navy Seals. There would be eight of them when they finally regrouped in Nigeria, and Rambo rejoined their company.

Brac, the oldest, had long been known as "Coyote One." On that morning's run, he had not finished first or last, but somewhere in the middle of the pack. He was pushing 60, and although he could still hang with the best of them, that morning he was hurting, and more than annoyed to be feeling his age. Of course he'd never let on to the rest of the team about his aches and pains—complaining among a group of professionals like these would be considered a sign of weakness. As the leader, Brac had to be viewed as the "best and baddest" of the bunch as well as the most experienced. The experienced part was a given. Maintaining the two Bs took a lot of work.

Joe Brac had never been one to avoid work. And there would be plenty to go around over the next few days. Now that the morning physical training was finished, it was time to brew a big pot of coffee, fry some bacon and eggs, shower, and get down to business. The day before, they had set up a team planning room under the watchful eyes of deer, elk, and moose heads, mounted on the cabin walls on either side of the stone fireplace. The team had worked for twelve hours just organizing the room. Each member had brought his special gift or talent to the process, and each had gone about his tasks with characteristic professional zeal. In fact, so much progress had been made on day one that it had led to a little too much celebrating that first evening.

Today would be different. The initial jubilation of reuniting the team was over and it was time to get into the Who, What, Where, When, and Why. Their financier, David Levine, would join them in less than a week, and he would expect a full fledged mission briefing, including overhead Power Point projections and extensive questions and answers.

Mission planning was something all of them had done innumerable times. They had gathered in similar isolated locations on one continent or another, strategizing all sorts of military and humanitarian operations. Some of their missions had been publicized; others had fallen into the category of "black ops"—top secret engagements no one ever heard about. As they prepared, maps were spread out on tables and taped to walls, photographs were scattered across the tables, a blackboard was already scribbled over with a To-Do list, an easel with butcher's paper sat in the corner, and a sand table had been constructed outside. On the butchers' paper, someone had listed the mission planning format: Situation, Mission, and Execution, which would include Concept of Operation. It was a process that had been ingrained in each of them, originally at Ranger School and the Special Forces Qualification Course, and later on real missions around the world.

The Preparation Phase involved identifying the problem and gathering information. The Decision Phase included developing and listing possible courses of action, analyzing those courses, and selecting the best one. Finally, the Act Phase involved implementing and reevaluating the solution. The mission, enemy situation, terrain, weather, and a myriad of other knowns and unknowns were systematically war-gamed, until all possible contingencies had been considered. Redundancy was built in to every phase of the operation—a back up for every back up.

This hostage mission, unlike their last one a few months before, was far more complicated. The rescue of the young Nigerian girl would be fairly straightforward. But there were other possibilities that might or might not transpire, depending on Intel. Within a two or three mile radius of the hostage rescue, sources on the ground believed there was a cell of terrorists that had been slaughtering entire villages in the most brutal ways imaginable. It seemed to be a single group, probably holed up in some remote compound—no one knew exactly where. These terrorists were said to be like a family living under one roof. If they could be located, it wouldn't be too difficult to neutralize the whole cell.

The third possibility had to do with the disreputable new governor of Abuja, a Northern Nigerian state. David Levine had indisputable evidence that His Honor was on the payroll of Saudi Wahabists. In his relatively short time in office, he had been personally responsible not only for innumerable human rights abuses and other outrages in Abuja State, but also for a good portion of the violence that had taken place in the southern oilfields. And character-wise, he was a duplicitous violator of women—sentencing local girls to death or other vicious punishments for breaking Shari'a law on one hand, and using other local girls for his own insatiable sexual purposes on the other. If the right information became available, Angel and The Judge, the team's snipers, might be able to put a stop to his brutal troublemaking once and for all.

Over and over, Brac, a relentless taskmaster, had each team member rehearse his role in the mission. On maps, on the sand table, and on the actual ground itself, the team was drilled in every aspect of the task: Movement to the objective. Immediate action drills in case of enemy contact. Actions at the objective. Escape and evasion. Plus the usual laundry list of other standard operating procedures. When Brac was totally satisfied with every man's preparation and competency, he assigned to each of them a role in the brief-back they were to give Levine.

The week had been filled with seemingly endless shooting, planning, rehearsals, the inevitable PT, and at times tempers had grown a little thin. After several practice run-throughs, they were ready for the final dress rehearsal. With the exception of a few small glitches, it went off without a hitch. Brac was satisfied. He hoped that David Levine would be pleased, too.

The night before Levine arrived, Brac knew that he and the rest of the men had had enough. It was time to relax. He decided they would all head into town and treat themselves to a few draft Guineses at Bud's Pub and a big dinner at Jubilee Seafood. *Tomorrow,* he told himself as he watched them laughing and talking as if they didn't have a care in the world, *will be another day.*

The next morning, Brac drove to Montgomery Regional Airport at 7 AM and transported Levine to the L Farm. The two men exchanged small talk on the 30-minute drive back. Once they arrived, the rest of the team warmly greeted their financier, whom they genuinely respected. Because of their mutual commitment to the causes Levine embraced and their successful first mission, there was a flurry of handshaking and backslapping. Then, as if on cue, they fell silent, filed into the meeting room, and took their places.

Levine listened carefully. He gave his full concentration to the Power Point, asking questions and nodding in approval at the answers. Finally, he leaned back with his hands behind his head, staring up at an aerial shot of the target village that was displayed on the screen. "You've outdone yourself, Joe. I'm impressed. I've said it before and I'll say it again—you people know your stuff. I feel confident we can proceed with the next step."

The men glanced at each other and at Brac, their expressions subdued. They were pleased, but too professional to look self-satisfied.

"So when do you want me to get the pilot in here?" Levine asked Brac.

Joe thought it over for a moment or two. "Let's get the mock village constructed," he answered, "and make a couple of dry-runs. They we'll get the pilot and helicopter in. Let's say about

5 days from today. My guys can throw a couple of plywood building mockups together, refine their service support annex—ammo, rations, equipment, and so forth—and do some more shooting and walk-throughs. Once the pilot comes in, we will be ready to rock and roll. What do you think?"

"Let's get it going," Levine replied, rising to his feet. "There's someone in that village right there," he gestured toward the aerial shot of the Nigerian village, "whose time has about run out. She desperately needs to be rescued. It's your show, Joe. Get it done".

* * *

The modest three rooms Karen Burke leased in Santa Monica had one notable asset—a stunning view of the Pacific from her living room and balcony. Decorated with the furniture she'd inherited from her divorce settlement—her ex had superb taste—plus a few odds and ends she'd picked up along the way, it was full of color and light. Beneath a vivid oil painting of Hawaii that she had purchased in Maui years before, a collection of multihued glassware gleamed in the late afternoon sunlight. Glancing around the room, she noticed that her telephone's message light was flashing.

She pushed the play button on the recording machine and to her surprise Sid's voice filled the room. "Hey babe, I'm back in town for a couple of days! How about if you come over tonight and we can hang out? Let me know."

After spending two and half hours engaged in an intense conversation with Nate Gregory, and after driving at 80 miles an hour on the freeway for another hour and a half, Karen was more than ready to relax a little. Naturally she was glad to hear from Sid—at least he still knew she was alive. Yet for some reason she was ambivalent about talking to him, and even more so about seeing him.

For one thing, she had tentatively decided to break off whatever was left of their quasi-relationship. But it wasn't just that. At the moment, she was vaguely aware that she wanted to give a great deal of further thought to her conversation with Nate. And she knew very well it wasn't something she could talk over with Sid. For one thing, it would be too much work to bring him up to speed on the background. More to the point, he wouldn't be interested.

By force of habit, however, she immediately returned the call and agreed to drive down to Marina del Rey where Sid and two of his band members shared an apartment. "But I need some time here first," she told him. "I've been away all day and I need to check my messages at work and return some calls. So I'll be over later."

In fact, she did no such thing. Instead, she went out on her balcony with a drink and stared as the sun's orange orb sank into a silver-blue sea. She stared for a long time. She tried to recollect the conversation with Nate but without her notes, which were still in the car, she couldn't quite remember how it had gone. What she did remember was the last thing they talked about—her impending trip. Was she really going to West Africa? What a bizarre twist in her usually predictable life. How had she gotten herself caught up in all this?

After a few minutes, it occurred to her that she was still conscious of Nate's personality, even though it had been more than two hours since they'd gone their separate ways. He had made some kind of impression, that much was clear. And she was well aware that they had agreed to meet again that weekend, to finish up their conversation and discuss their possible trip.

Her thoughts were understandably self-defensive. *I don't want to get sucked into some creepy religious group. Nate doesn't seem weird himself, but that preacher of his could be strange. How could he possibly have put together Nate's rescue? I'm going to make a list of specific questions,* she vowed, *and I will get answers to them all. I'm not going anywhere unless I'm absolutely convinced that I can trust the people I'm with.*

Relieved by her own decisiveness, she went back inside and locked the slider behind her.

The freeway was crowded when she finally left, so Karen took surface streets into Marina del Rey's array of upscale condominiums and townhouses. When she arrived at the complex where Sid lived, it was after seven and she was starving. She ran up the stairs, rang the bell, and he gave her a long hug when he answered the door. As always she was taken aback by how handsome he was—tall, blonde, and a little disheveled, which made him even sexier. She had known him since high school, but they had only started dating two years before. Sid had his faults, but if books could be judged by their covers, he was definitely a best seller.

"You look awesome," he said. "Gorgeous. I love all that wild hair. Drives me crazy."

Karen unconsciously ran her fingers through her long curls, noticing that Sid's two roommates and their girlfriends were slouched in big leather chairs around the living room, watching MTV at high volume. There was a pizza box open on the coffee table and empty Bud Light cans littered the floor.

"Want a beer?" Sid yelled from the kitchen.

Karen hesitated. "Actually, do you have any wine?"

Of course he didn't. Why had she bothered to ask? Beer it was. Can in hand, she picked up a piece of cold pizza and sank into the couch. No one was talking. A barely-clad hip-hop singer was performing on the huge plasma television screen, which had been Sid's Christmas gift from his wealthy parents. One of the girls in the room lit up, and the smoke drifted toward Karen in a blue cloud.

"So how've you been?" Sid asked, patting her thigh.

"Good. Busy. How about you?"

"Missed you, baby," he smiled, looking her up and down.

Karen's response, like everything else surrounding her life with Sid, was mixed. She was flattered. She was so very attracted to Sid, his laugh, his smile, and of course his musical talent. He was an amazing performer. But as she glanced around the room, it suddenly occurred to her that Sid was exactly the same as he'd been at eighteen. He hadn't changed a bit.

"You okay? You want Pammie to put out her cig?"

"I'm fine, Sid. It's good to see you."

He leaned over and gave her a lingering kiss, his hand playing with her hair. "You too," he breathed.

He pulled her next to him and continued to caress her neck and toy with her hair. She tried to think about how glad she was to be with him again, but for some reason she felt uncomfortable. It wasn't so much that there were other people in the room—they weren't paying attention. And it wasn't Sid's immediate familiarity—he was always like that.

The phone rang, and when Sid leaped to his feet to answer it, she was unexpectedly relieved.

She stood up. All at once she was fighting off a strong urge to leave. What was her problem? She hadn't been there ten minutes. Still, she wanted out. What kind of excuse would she use? She noticed that Sid had lowered his voice, and was walking out of the room with the phone. "Yeah, me too," he was saying softly. "You too...I know. I know."

All her female instincts suddenly awakened. She knew beyond the shadow of a doubt that the person on the other end of the phone was a woman. There was no question about it. She knew that Sid wanted to talk to that woman—whoever she was—right now. She also knew that he wanted to make love to her, once he hung up the phone.

No longer ambivalent, she quietly picked up her purse, and let herself out the door. No one even notice that she left. Once outside, she inhaled a huge breath of clean sea air, and walked to her car as quickly as she could. She turned the ignition and left the parking lot, tires squealing, steering with one hand, and turning off her cell phone with the other.

Enough, already, she told herself. *Men! How can they do stuff like that? I swear, I will never understand the way their minds work. Make that their bodies, not their minds. They don't even use their minds...*

When Karen got back to her apartment, the voice mail light on her phone was flashing. She deleted the message without listening to it. She went into her room, determined to go to sleep without wasting another second of thought on Sid. She picked up a bottle of eye makeup remover and a cotton square.

In the bathroom mirror she stared into her own solemn eyes, which were large and grey-blue. They looked lifeless. The mane of red curls—Sid had always loved her hair—was more unruly than usual because she had been nervously running her fingers through it all the way home. She had a pretty face, but it hadn't served her too well as far as romance was concerned.

Her husband of two years had cheated on her with a man.

Her boyfriend was cheating on her with at least one woman. The only good man in her life, her beloved father, had died and left her. She was thirty-one years old and had been alone nearly six years. What was it about attracting good, trustworthy men that she didn't understand?

Although the question remained unanswered, Karen slept more soundly than she would have expected. The next morning, after downing two cups of strong coffee steaming fragrantly in her favorite green mug, she was more than happy to head for the office and plunge into her work. She checked her cell phone before leaving her car in the office parking structure, and found that she had one message. Sid had called about fifteen minutes after she'd left his place.

"Hey, baby, where'd you go? Are you sick? I had great plans for our evening together—we were just getting warmed up. Give me a call, okay?"

She pushed the Delete button and left the cell phone behind.

There were a few emails on her screen from an assortment of people she'd contacted about Nigeria. One was from Frank Goldberg, checking on her progress on the Nigeria project. Another was from someone in Washington D.C. at Humanity.com, writing about a nineteen-year-old woman who had been sentenced to death by stoning in Nigeria. And there was a quick note from Nate Gregory,

"Great talk yesterday, Karen. Can we meet Saturday and finish the conversation? How about Laguna Beach? It's closer for you and a lot more scenic than Carlsbad. Let me know if you can meet me late in the afternoon. We'll have dinner on me. Maybe I can answer more of your questions about my book. Take care, Nate"

First of all, it sounded more like a date than a business meeting, but since Frank was pushing her to move forward with the project, so what? She'd pick up the tab and put it on her expense account. No harm, no foul.

Second of all, after last night she was more than happy to pretend she was having a date with someone besides Sid, even if it was just a business meeting. Sid was history, and in any case, it couldn't hurt to have something else on the calendar.

Besides, Nate was a good guy and Laguna Beach was a fantastic artists' enclave—a perfect place to hang out.

"I have a follow-up meeting with Mr. Gregory on Saturday," she typed to Goldberg. "So far, so good. But I have many questions, most of them concerning his rescue. More later."

"I'll meet you at Splashes bar at 4:00," she wrote to Nate, "inside the Surf and Sand Hotel. It's on New Spirit Press. I'll bring questions. See you there. Karen."

On Saturday morning, Karen called her Mother again. "I'm meeting with Nate Gregory again later today," she told her.

"How was your last meeting?" Ellen Burke asked her daughter. *"I don't think I've talked to you since."*

"Oh, he's got quite an interesting story."

"What's he like?"

"Um...he's nice. He's in his thirties, I guess. Pleasant, not weird. I'm just not sure about all the facts, you know."

"You mean about his rescue?"

"Well, yeah, like who paid for it and who did it, for starters. It's a little confusing to me."

"I thought his pastor did it."

"No way, Mom. The pastor was here the whole time. I checked his website, and he posted sermons and Bible Studies not only that week, but all the weeks surrounding it. How could he mastermind something like that from California any way? It just doesn't add up."

"Maybe he hired somebody to do it."

"Mom, they had a helicopter and a zillion weapons..."

"Oh, that reminds me of your father," she paused. *"And that reminds me—you'll never guess who called me. Do you remember Sean Murray, your dad's old friend from the Vietnam War?"*

"You mean the spook?"

"Honey, he's not a spook. Pat always said that Sean was so grateful to have a nice, steady job with the Defense Department. Some sort of strategy position."

"Okay, whatever. I'm glad he called. What'd he say?"

"Oh, he was just checking on us to see how we're doing. He said to tell you hi, and if you're ever in D.C. to please contact him. He'd love to see you."

Karen tried to picture Sean Murray in her mind. She remembered him as tall and angular with glasses. It had been several years since she'd seen him, so long ago she couldn't remember when. "It would be fun to talk to him. Maybe he'd tell me a little more about Dad's military career."

"I didn't know you were interested in that, Karen."

"Oh, you know, I'm just curious. Dad was so closed-mouthed about it all, I can't help but wonder what happened. Anyway, Mom, I've got to go. Love you. Talk to you soon."

Later in the afternoon, Karen Burke pulled into the Surf and Sand hotel and handed her car over to the valet. "Are you checking in with us?" he smiled.

"No, just having dinner."

"Don't forget to get this validated," he said, handing her a small card with her last name scribbled across it.

She met Nate at Splashes Bar, which was dominated by large breakers flickering with glass-green light at the curve, and pounding against the sand just a few feet beyond the glass walls. It was a spectacular view. She had been there before, but had forgotten how dramatic it was. Once they had exchanged niceties and marveled over the beautiful setting, their conversation picked up more or less where it had left off before.

"So what exactly were you doing in Nigeria?" she asked, referring to the list of neatly bulleted talking points she'd brought along. "I know you told me before, but somehow I lost track of that part of the conversation."

Thankfully, this time they were both far more relaxed, due in part to the glasses of Chardonnay they both ordered, and the soothing surf in the background. Karen's agenda was fairly straight forward: she hoped to get enough information to make her site visit to the Nigerian hinterlands unnecessary. Nate seemed more than happy to answer her questions, far less uptight than before about whether his manuscript was acceptable or not.

"I went to Nigeria to do a short-term missions project—it was supposed to last about two and a half weeks. Ended up being just short of a year—but most of it was spent in a filthy hole somewhere around the village of Ogbu, which is a couple of hours outside Abuja. Anyway, we were trying to help the local people rebuild their church. It had been leveled by some Muslim extremists..."

"What exactly do you mean by leveled?"

"I mean *leveled,* as in burned, and then blown up with grenades and anything else they could find. It was just a shell, three walls, and part of the foundation. That's it. So we were going to rebuild it. Our church does projects like that, and of course we took some medical supplies and clothes in to the people, too. They are super poor. So anyway, we'd been working for about a week and a half when I got picked up."

"I know you said in the proposal that you had gone for a walk or something. But tell me what happened. Did you know it was an unsafe area?"

"Just about every place in that part of the country is unsafe in one way or another. But yeah, I'll tell you what happened. That night I couldn't sleep. Four of us were sharing a room, it was really hot in there—no air conditioning of course—and one of the guys was snoring so loud it was driving me crazy. My stomach wasn't feeling great, either. I hadn't really adjusted to the food.

"So anyway, I got up, put on my shoes, and went for a walk. We were inside a walled area, but it wasn't locked or especially secure, so I didn't feel like going outside the gate was a particularly big deal. It was a Friday night, and I found out later that a firebrand preacher at one of the mosques had given a call for jihad earlier that day. But I'm not so sure that's why it happened.

"In any case, I walked by a few houses, and then I kind of felt the presence of someone behind me. It was actually four guys. I couldn't see their faces—their heads were covered except for their eyes. They had handguns—I think one of them had an automatic rifle.

"Anyway, I turned and started to speak to them, when one of them grabbed me, shoved the barrel of his pistol inside my mouth and covered my face with some kind of a hood. I think they must have knocked me out after that, because that's all I remember until I woke up in a hellhole somewhere. I was tied up, gagged, and had a raging headache. But once I made some noise, they came in and gave me some water and bread of some sort. They ungagged and untied me." Nate was lost in some unpleasant memory that caused him to fall momentarily silent.

"Did they...were they abusive?"

"Oh, yeah. At first, they were very abusive. It was...bad. I've written that part in more detail now—I didn't do it very well in the proposal. I can show it to you."

Karen nodded. "I can't even imagine what you went through. And I've never questioned that part of the story. I guess it's the rescue I don't understand, Nate. I don't doubt your story at all—please don't misunderstand me. And I know we started to talk about this before. But you give credit to your pastor, and yet judging from what you wrote, and from what I've read elsewhere, there's no way some middle-aged preacher in Southern California put that rescue together."

Nate raised his eyebrows and looked at the ocean for a few seconds. "There's a lot I don't understand either. And to be honest, that's my biggest concern about the book. I realize that there's more to what happened than I know. The truth is, once I got here, I was unable to find out much more than what I wrote. Pastor Ken isn't talking. He just clams up and says, 'Just praise the Lord, Nate. Don't thank me.' Anyway, you're right. It doesn't all add up."

"Is that one of the reasons you want to go back to Nigeria? To see if you can find out what really happened?"

"That's one reason, yes. Another is that I want to overcome my fear of the place. But the most important reason is exactly what I told you—I want to help finish the work I started. From what I hear, the church could be rebuilt in a couple of weeks if enough of us helped out. Also, there's that case pending in the courts—I told you about it before."

"You mean the woman who's supposed to be stoned to death? I got a press release about that yesterday."

"Yeah, I was asked to be in a meeting there—some group is planning to send a delegation to talk to her family, and then to plead for her life with the state and national governments. They figured I could help because my name was in the media and I'd been through some things myself."

Much as she second guessed herself, Karen was

increasingly intrigued. For just a moment, her mind drifted back to Sid's apartment. She glanced around at her present surroundings, feeling an unexpected surge of hope and anticipation.

"Can you tell me about the rescue?" she asked. "You didn't include that chapter with the proposal."

"No, I didn't. I really wasn't ready to write it yet. That and the abduction were kind of hard for me to remember. But now I've spent a lot of time thinking about it all and I think I'm pretty clear about what happened."

Just as he began, the hostess interrupted. "Gregory? Party of two? Your table is ready."

They got up and followed her to a small table that was situated next to the water's edge, with only a pane of glass between them and the surf. Although it was still light, a candle flickered on the table and a menu awaited their perusal. Neither of them looked at it. "So go on. Please," Karen said.

Nate sat quietly for a moment, gathering his thoughts. His face, which to Karen had always looked calm and at times even serene, appeared tense and drawn. He took a deep breath, as if he were about to jump into a deep pool.

"I guess you could say that by the time it happened, I had nearly given up hope. I'd prayed and cried and raged, and by then I had reached a point of resignation. There was nothing more I could do except wait and see. One day I felt hopeful, the next day I felt the darkest kind of despair. But somewhere in the depths of my being I guess I really thought I'd make it out alive. And so I tried to hang in there and keep my mind busy, remembering places I'd been, trying to envision people I knew, things like that. I played a lot of mind games with myself and tried to do some exercises, but it was all pretty pathetic.

"That night I must have been pretty soundly asleep—even though it was never comfortable, I got used to sleeping on a thin mat on a concrete floor. I remember praying, as usual, for patience and help. I think I prayed for my parents, too. And I dozed off.

"I woke up to the sound of shooting close by—intermittent gunfire. Then I heard somebody coming into the cell I was in— of course at first I thought it was my guards, but it wasn't. It was two Americans, dressed in military camouflage. One of them said, 'Stay quiet. We're gonna get you out of here. Can you walk?'

"I was really stiff. I also must have been in shock—shaking all over, and for a few seconds I thought I was going to pass out. But I got hold of myself and said, yeah, I could move well enough to go with them. They took me by the arms, one on each side, practically dragging me. A few times they actually had to lift me off the ground to keep going. They got me outside the structure, which looked like a rundown barn. I saw four other soldiers covering the entry way with automatic weapons. They told me they had a helicopter not far away. As it turned out, it must have been more like half a mile from there. I don't know. I was just so weak and out of it, I don't even know if I was conscious the whole time. Anyway, eventually I saw the helicopter and the next thing I knew, they'd thrown me inside. I really don't know how they did it. It all happened too fast. "

"So were any of the guys that came for you Africans?"

"No, none of them were African. They were mostly American, maybe a couple of Brits or South Africans—I couldn't tell what kind of accent. But I know they were fully equipped with all kinds of hi-tech gear, radios, earphones, and I don't know what else."

"Have you had a chance to look at the menu?" a waiter ventured into a break in Nate's story. "Anything from the bar?"

"No, thanks, give us a few minutes," Nate said, "unless you want something, Karen."

"No, not yet. Please go on. So you got into the helicopter, and the four guys that were behind you got in and you took off, right?"

"Not exactly, no. While we were running to the helicopter, I looked behind us a couple of times and saw two or three guys running backwards, facing the village, covering us. Then, all of a sudden there was a burst of machine gun fire from inside a building. Our guys opened fire. About that time I noticed there were two more of them running with us. I think there were a total of eight of them plus the helicopter crew.

"So by then I was beyond terrified—all the running and sound just about pushed me over the edge. Don't forget I had been sitting for months in almost complete silence. But those guys had it covered. After the last of them got to the helicopter, there was a series of loud explosions behind them—between them and the others. They must have booby-trapped our exit route. I heard screaming, and... Anyway, within seconds we were lifting off."

"Weren't you afraid someone would shoot you down? Or were you too numb to care?"

As Nate talked, his eyes moved back and forth, as if he were watching a movie on an invisible screen slightly above Karen's head. He seemed almost to flinch from time to time.

"I was scared. I was excited. I was confused. All of the above. I saw some shots coming our way, and there was a lot of yelling and some pretty intense radio contact going on. I will tell you this—the guys on the ground were no match for those commandoes. To this day I have no idea who they were, but I can tell you that they knew exactly what they were doing."

"Did you ask them if they were with the Army? What did they say?"

"No, they weren't with the Army—for one thing they didn't have regulation U.S. uniforms on. No names, no badges. When I asked, 'Who are you guys?' they just said, 'We're your friends. We're happy to see you alive.'"

"That's it? No other information?"

"No, they didn't do much talking—just gave me some bottled water. They offered me half a sandwich, but I couldn't eat anything. Afterwards, they just talked among themselves. They seemed to be in high spirits. I remember being wrapped up in blankets and still violently shivering. One of them must have been a medic, because he checked me over as well as he could and stuck an IV in my arm. I was filthy and I know I smelled terrible. Anyway, they took me to an airfield somewhere, got me into a shower—I really don't remember much about it. There was a change of clothes there—some gray sweats.

"After I got cleaned up, I was transferred to a small private jet. It stopped once for refueling, but I was asleep during most of the flight and still don't know where I was. They may have given me some kind of a tranquilizer—I kind of remember taking a pill or two. I ended up at Stansted Airport north of London, where one of the men from our church met me and took me to a hospital. The doctors put me on another drip and kept me over night. Next day we flew back to L.A. on a British Airways flight—first class. My first and last first class flight, but it was sweet."

With the relived rescue operation behind him, Nate exhaled loudly and smiled. His face visibly relaxed. "Maybe we should look at the menu. I've done enough talking for awhile."

"Nate, don't you hate those men that robbed you of so many months of your life?"

He shook his head. "I really don't know how I feel—or how I should feel." He stopped and thought for a minute. "I sure didn't mind knowing some of them were getting blown to hell that night, and if I'd been in better shape and had a gun, I would have helped get that job done. No problem. But on the other hand, I don't have some huge desire for revenge, either. I guess I just don't want anyone else to go through what I've been through, that's all. And that's why I want to help that girl. You know, the one who's supposed to be killed for adultery."

"Yeah, I know." Karen nodded. "I'd like to see her get some help, too."

Karen studied Nate's face for a moment as he read the menu. It occurred to her that she knew almost nothing about him—his background, his family, his education. She hadn't asked because his personal history outside the hostage story didn't directly relate to his book proposal.

Besides, the one thing she was pretty sure about was the Nate Gregory was single. *Keep it professional,* she told herself. *But if there are any good men in the world, he's a good man.* Dismissing the thought as quickly as possible, she picked up her own menu and tried to focus her attention on its very chic, very expensive selections.

* * *

Venice's Grand Canal quietly lapped against the Gritti Palace Hotel's outside restaurant as four men sipped their espressos and concluded their lunch conversation. It was an idyllic scene: gondolas, water taxis, and vaporetti plied the green water beyond the hotel's waterfront terrace, while the Church of *Santa Maria del Salute* shone in pale marble splendor against the lapis sky. The eyes of a few wealthy tourists, who occupied a handful of surrounding tables, were drawn to the group primarily because it included a Saudi Arabian shiekh, his head draped in a traditional red and white ghutrah. Seated with him were a former U.S. Secretary of State and two oil company executives.

"Forgive me for repeating myself," the American diplomat said, "but do keep my words in mind. There are many voices calling for a stronger U.S. military presence in West Africa. Even now American Special Forces are training locals there. I refer you, again, to the white paper published by the African Oil Policy Initiative Group, calling for a large regional command post. They are recommending something similar to our configuration in South Korea. The violence in Nigeria and the slowdowns at the oilfields are setting off alarms, and I needn't mention the religious conflicts. There are those," he made brief eye-contact with his Saudi host, "who claim that some of the Muslim attacks on Christians are being incited by Wahabists, and..."

The Saudi nodded silently, eyes hooded, wiping his lips with his napkin as Phillip Taylor, a self-made Texas oilman interrupted, his blue eyes glittering in irritation. "Who the hell is stirring all this up anyway? The religious right?" Along with several other multi-national corporations, Taylor's company was deeply involved—by any means necessary—in developing a successful Nigerian oil export franchise.

"Yeah, sure, there are always a few born-again wackos raising money with their newsletters," the former Secretary responded. "But they aren't the only ones in this case. There are even some feminists getting on their high horse about women's rights in Muslim states. My issue is, don't underestimate these people—they've caused all kinds of trouble in Sudan. Remember the Talisman oil fiasco?"

Steven Goldman, Phil Taylor's colleague and close friend, shook his head. "Lunatic fringe," he declared. "Look, our people in D.C. are fully apprised of the situation. We have excellent contacts within the administration, as you well know. There will be no, I repeat, no American military adventures in West Africa."

"The neo-cons may not agree with you, Steve," the former secretary warned.

"There will be no U.S. military intervention in West Africa." Phillip Taylor repeated Goldman's statement. He made eye contact with his Saudi host, as if the two of them shared some special understanding. "The neo-cons are losing their influence even as we speak. They've got more than enough egg on their face after all the confusion in Iraq." He paused and glanced at each of the others, then pushed back his rattan chair. "Let's resume our conversation at dinner. Now if you'll excuse me, I have some phone calls to return."

Chapter Three

It was daybreak on Sunday morning, and the little village of Agalaba, near Kano, was beginning to stir—women were making their way to the well and stirring the fires near their homes. It was a Christian village, so many families were preparing themselves to attend services at the local church.

The quiet was broken by the sound of dozens of male voices shouting, "Allahu Akbar! Allahu Akbar!" The dull thudding of feet running, the louder thunder of horses' hooves, and the shouting grew louder by the second.

The villagers froze in their tracks, paralyzed by fear. They knew very well what the sound of the voices meant—Islamic jihadist warriors. When they finally began to move, they moved quickly. Those who weren't inside their homes frantically returned to be with their families. Those inside their thatched mud huts tried to run into nearby bushes.

Screams of horror, children wailing, groans of agony filled the air as the jihad warriors, armed with machetes and swords, began to hack the fleeing villagers to death. The ratatat of automatic gunfire could be heard sporadically, although the villagers themselves—all of them civilians— were almost entirely unarmed.

The primary victims of the warriors were young men, and they were left to die in pools of their own blood, their arms or legs sliced off, some of them beheaded, others slashed in the belly and disemboweled. A few lay dying, gurgling out unfathomable words in the last moments of their lives.

"Go to your church and you will be saved," some of the

warriors ordered the women, children, and elderly. In their panic, frightened church members rushed inside the large, open structure where the pastor courageously stood by the door. Most of them saw him gunned down in a hail of bullets, and his terrified parishioners stepped over him as he died, tripping helplessly over his body.

About 20 villagers gathered inside the church, huddling near the altar at the front, mute in their fear. They could hear the mayhem outside, the crackle and roar of burning houses, as the warriors torched them, one by one. The chaos of sound and smell was indescribable. Women clutched their babies and tried to comfort their sobbing toddlers. Old people sat in shock and resignation, preparing themselves for the worst.

And soon it came. Two jihad warriors charged into the church, one with his Kalishnikov firing, mowing down the refugees. The other rushed to the front with a machete, randomly slashing at both the living and the dying. Minutes later, several other warriors appeared at the entry and shouted, "Get out!" As the two killers rushed for the door, the others sloshed several cans of gasoline over the bodies and the church's interior. They, too, ran out after igniting the fuel in several places.

Two hours later, the entire village of Agalaba was burned to the ground and only a handful of villagers, who had fled, were left alive. One of them, a young mother, was mortally wounded and died in her children's arms.

Two of the survivors were twelve-year-old boys. In better days, they had spent many happy hours exploring the local countryside. They knew their way around and were acquainted with some of the local militiamen. These well-intentioned warriors, with their outdated weapons and obsolete communication equipment, had tried to organize themselves to provide some protection for several villages.

Running, literally, for their lives for more than two miles, the two boys found their way into a small cluster of buildings where a few militiamen were stationed. "Uncle!" they both shouted, their young voices shrill. "Uncle! jihad warriors have attacked our village. They are killing everyone! Everyone is dying! Uncle, help us. Please help us."

By that time smoke was billowing on the horizon. The boys suddenly noticed that there was a white man standing with the militiamen. As the Africans scurried around to gather their weapons, he spoke to the boys, "Do you speak English?"

One of them nodded, not sure whether to be afraid of the American or not.

"My name's Billy. I'm a medic from America. You know what a medic is?"

"You are a doctor?"

Billy answered solemnly, "Yeah, I'm a doctor. I came here to help you and I won't hurt you. But let me ask you something. Do you know where those jihad warriors came from?"

"Yes, Uncle, they have a camp. I can show you."

Billy squeezed the boy's shoulder. "That's what I want you to do—I want you to show me where their camp is. But for now, you two stay put right here. A few of us are going to see if we can help the people in your village. As soon as we come back, then you can take us to the camp. You understand?"

"Yes, Uncle, we will take you there."

"Don't you leave here, you hear me? These two will keep an eye on you," he pointed toward a trio of young Nigerians who were serving as sentries.

The oldest boy fought back tears. "We will be here."

The other boy nodded in agreement and watched as Billy and a handful of Nigerian militiamen piled into an old Land Rover and headed toward the massive funeral pyre just across the way.

* * *

Sunday morning found Nate Gregory in the contemporary sanctuary of his church, Bethany Temple. Light poured in from several skylights, and a set of gelled spotlights illuminated the carved wood cross behind the pulpit. Nate was seated in a green velvet theater seat—the room could accomodate1,500— where he listened to Pastor Ken preaching about Christian responsibility to the less fortunate around the globe. He reminded the congregation of their own church's activism.

"You *know* that we care about the poor and the oppressed.

You *have watched us* getting our hands dirty in the world, reaching out to those who cannot help themselves. You *are well aware* that by God's grace, I was able to see that our brother, who is with us this morning," he motioned toward Nate, who smiled uncomfortably, "was released from the clutches of the enemy. We are engaged in the world, and we want to see you join in the battle, too. 'What can I do?' you ask? I'll tell you what you can do. You can pray. You can volunteer your time. And, brothers and sisters, *you can give from your abundance.*"

Nate squirmed a little, feeling embarrassed and uneasy. It wasn't the first time Pastor Ken had implied that he had personally been responsible for Nate's dramatic rescue from his Nigerian captors. Nor was it the first time he had tied it into an appeal for money.

At first Nate had been more than happy to give Pastor Ken all the credit he seemed to richly deserve. But after working on his book for months, after thinking deeply about the events surrounding his captivity and release, and after trying to answer Karen Burke's many inquiries, Nate had more questions of his own than he had answers. He was no longer convinced that this man had been directly involved in his rescue. Pastor Ken may well have made some contact with someone. That seemed more likely than not. But by now Nate realized that the local clergyman was neither connected enough, rich enough, nor clever enough to have orchestrated such a finely tuned rescue mission.

But that raised even more questions and one specific question in particular. If not Pastor Ken, then who?

Nate tried to distract himself by looking at the view beyond the sanctuary's side windows where a lovely garden, lush as a rain forest, flourished inside a climate-controlled glass solarium. It was all very soothing, but Nate was feeling a rush of nervous energy. He couldn't sit still. His skin felt prickly and tight. He wanted to walk out, but didn't dare.

In the six months since his return from captivity, he had fought a battle with depression and anxiety. After several sessions with a psychiatrist, he had been prescribed an anti-depressant, which had brought a measure of relief to him. But the trauma he had endured at the hands of his captors had done considerable damage. He had gone to Nigeria a calm, easygoing man with a prestigious college degree, a great career in communications, and a positive attitude. He had returned to Southern California sleepless, fearful, unable to focus on his work, and indecisive about almost everything.

Nate's mind wandered from the sermon to the strange course his life had taken. He thought about his marriage—the happy years he'd spent with Suzanne, the birth of their beautiful daughter, and then the news from the doctor. He could still remember how he'd felt when he first heard those three awful words—metastasized breast cancer. Suzanne had died a year later—three years ago—and their daughter Chelsea was now five.

Nowadays Nate and Chelsea lived with Nate's parents in an apartment built over their garage. Chelsea—his beautiful little blonde angel—had been staying with her grandparents when Nate made his mission trip to Nigeria and was subsequently kidnapped. During those months the school community had reached out to her, and she felt very close to both her teachers and classmates. Once Nate returned home, there had been no reason to put her through any more upheaval, so he had stayed with his parents.

But it wasn't a comfortable situation. Nate loved his mom and dad, but somehow living there made him feel like he wasn't an adult anymore. He had the sensation that somebody had pushed a hold button and his life was going nowhere. Everything seemed to be waiting for something else. He was waiting to finish his book until he returned from Nigeria. He was waiting to find out if New Spirit Press wanted the book before he shopped it around more. He was waiting to get a steady job until he got back from Nigeria. He was waiting until he felt more at ease with himself, more settled and adjusted emotionally, to look for a new home, a new life, maybe even a new woman.

Letting go of Suzanne's memory, not comparing her with every other woman, was very difficult for him. Her death and his months of captivity had beatified her in his mind, placing her on a pedestal of perfection, beyond reproach. And because his normally active sexual nature had been shut down by the trauma he'd been through, he had no particular drive to get beyond the past.

All this left him feeling exceptionally uneasy. His present circumstances were like a poorly fitted pair of shoes—never quite comfortable. He fixed his eyes on a large tree fern outside the sanctuary window, breathed deeply, and waited impatiently for the sermon to end. He wanted to talk to the Missions Pastor about his forthcoming trip. He wanted to let him know that Karen Burke would be involved in it. Most of all, he wanted out of there.

At about the same time that Sunday morning Karen was on the phone with her friend and physician, Dr. Ray Martin. Dr. Martin had been the Burke's family doctor for years. He had seen Ellen and Karen through Pat Burke's death, and had known Karen since she was a small child.

"West Africa?" he was saying. *"Are you sure you want to go to West Africa?"*

"No, I'm not at all sure I want to go," Karen told him. "In fact I'm fairly sure I *don't* want to go—and am looking for all kinds of reasons not to."

"Well, let's start with political reasons," the doctor said. *"The Israeli Palestinian situation is causing all kinds of anti-American sentiment. Aren't there travel warnings about U.S. citizens going to Nigeria?"*

Karen paused, "Maybe so. I haven't checked."

"And then there is the jihadist movement. Of course, you know, Karen, that I personally believe that God is bringing history to a close and that all this turmoil is leading to a huge conclusion. Have you read any of the Left Behind *books?"*

Oh God, Karen thought. *Here we go again.*

Dr. Martin was a bright and delightful friend. But he had long been inordinately interested in the end of the world—at least that's how Karen interpreted his curiosity about ancient Biblical prophecies and how they might be tied into current events.

"No," she said cautiously, "I haven't read them. I didn't know they had anything to do with Nigeria."

"They don't," he laughed. *"But the way things are going in the world, you can count on there being more conflict, more*

danger, more threat to our personal safety, especially if the U.S continues to support Israel. One of the signs of the times is that there will be wars and rumors of wars."

"So do you think I should stay home?" Karen asked hopefully. Surely if that was her family doctor's view, it could be the deal breaker. She'd just tell Frank Goldberg that her physician felt it was too much for her. She was already constructing the conversation, "Too much for my mother, too. You know my father died recently," she would say.

Dr. Martin didn't miss a beat. *"No, I think you should go, Karen. It's important to keep doing what we're supposed to do. And the book this man is writing sounds like it could make people far more aware of radical Islam and how it's spreading."*

"So you think I should go?" she repeated lamely.

"Right. That's what I think. Just let me take a look at the Center for Disease Control's website and see what kind of shots you need for that part of the world. I know you'll need anti-malarial medication. Let me see what else. We'd better get started soon—some of the shots may have to be given in a series. Anyway, I'll find out what you need. Just come in Tuesday or Wednesday afternoon."

Karen hung up the phone thoughtfully. She looked out her window at the sparkling ocean. What a perfect day for a long walk on the Santa Monica beachfront. Karen was restless, feeling a measure of inner turmoil. A score of conflicts were fighting for her attention: fear and excitement, caution and hope, curiosity and cynicism. Maybe walking would help her focus.

She went into her room, pulled on her running shoes and socks, tied back her hair, and started trying to find her sunglasses. The TV was on in the living room, and she could hear a breaking news story on CNN about a church being burned to the ground somewhere in Africa. She glanced at the screen and saw a map of West Africa and a small photograph of the CNN reporter, who was on the phone from Lagos, Nigeria.

She froze, watching as the first reports came in: a village invaded by armed killers, civilians mutilated, a church congregation burned alive. Where was this happening? Northern Nigeria, of course. The reporter was carefully using words like "alleged" attacks and "unconfirmed" atrocities. The conclusion was that "ethnic violence had troubled the area for years."

After locating her sunglasses, Karen turned off the television and more or less fled her apartment. She remembered her conversations with Nate Gregory, and his rather passionate belief that the problems in Nigeria were religious, not ethnic. In his view—and he certainly had paid his dues in forming his opinion—radical Islamic jihadists were systematically taking over village after village, slaughtering people and livestock, while their political counterparts were imposing medieval Muslim laws on entire populations, whether Muslim or not.

As she headed for the beach, she mused that Nate Gregory and Dr. Ray Martin would agree on many points. And in fact, she almost wished they could meet and she could listen in on their discussion. On the other hand, she wasn't quite prepared for Dr. Martin's "last days" interpretation of events. Even if people were burning other people up in their churches, wasn't talk about the end of the world a little over the top?

She walked as fast as she could, a brisk wind in her hair, the taste of salt on her lips. She went from walking to jogging to running, trying to maneuver around rollerbladers and other human and canine obstacles. At the same time she was also trying to outmaneuver the thoughts that were racing one against the other in her head.

After 45 minutes of fast-paced movement, she returned to her apartment, grabbed a bottle of water out of the fridge, and collapsed on the couch drinking it. Breathing heavily and damp with sweat, she felt calmer than before, although nothing had really changed. She clicked on the news, but there was nothing more on the Nigerian story. It seemed to have been pre-empted by some kind of a congressional scandal, and a leaked report that tax-dollars were being used to fly wealthy oil-company executives to world-class resorts for clandestine meetings.

She impatiently turned off the TV, and glancing across the room, noticed that her message light was flashing. Almost automatically she listened to the one voice-mail message: *"Hi,*

Karen, Nate Gregory here. I had a meeting today with our church's Missions Pastor, and it looks like my trip to Nigeria is scheduled for the 20th of April, about ten days from tomorrow. I guess it would be best for everyone on this end if you could get there sometime in late April or early May. Is that possible? You'll just have to get yourself from Lagos to Abuja, and I can meet you there. Anyway, give me a call and let me know what you think about all this."

Nate left his number and the recording ended. So he would be leaving in a week and a half. And now she was supposed to go in just over two weeks. She began to panic. Shots. A Nigerian Visa. Clothes. Logistics. Background reading. Could she really do all that in three weeks time? The way Frank Goldberg had sounded last time they'd talked suggested that she could either make the trip happen or die trying.

* * *

The fully loaded 747 screamed across the Atlantic toward Germany. From there Joe Brac would board another Lufthansa flight to Nigeria, but meanwhile his thoughts transported him to another time, and another journey that had taken place just a year before.

In his mind, he was in Istanbul. Dawn was breaking, and the smells of Turkish coffee and fresh-baked bread wafted through the air. He stood on the roof of the Four Seasons Hotel overlooking Istanbul. The first of five daily calls to prayer, *Sabah*, echoed across the city from loudspeakers atop minarets, and as he gazed westward, Brac could see two of Istanbul's most venerable monuments, the Blue Mosque and Hagia Sophia, facing each other across the Sultanahmet Square. The view had been breathtaking. Brac, from his seat on the plane, recalled taking a moment to savor it. He remembered reflecting on the previous four weeks, which he had spent traveling throughout Turkey.

Brac had provided the security for a band of pilgrims who had visited various places like Ephesus and Aphrodisias— historic sites that the Romans and Byzantines had endowed with beautiful architectural masterpieces. He had crawled with the travelers through the underground cities and caves of Cappadocia, had stood in silence within the cave church of St Peter in Antakya—ancient Antioch—and had visited a small cave in Sanliurfa which was said to be the birthplace of Abraham. Brac had accompanied his clients as they viewed cobalt blue and white Iznik tiles, admired the flowing arabesques painted onto the interior of the domes of the Blue Mosque, and had stood in awe beneath the vast nave and mosaics of the Hagia Sophia.

The next day, he planned to take them on a hectic trip to Istanbul's Grand Bazaar to buy up any last minute collectables for the trip home. Then he would take the clients to the airport and return to the hotel for a well deserved rest, massage, and one last dinner in Turkey before his scheduled flight back to Alabama.

In his memory, Brac recalled descending the interior stairs of the Four Seasons, crossing the carefully tended outside garden located within the walls of the hotel, and entering the lobby. It was hard to believe that such luxury and elegance had once been a Turkish prison. Some poor soul had even carved the date of his incarceration on one of the columns in a hallway, or at least, that's what the head-of-security had told Brac during their tour of the premises.

As he headed toward the dining area, a voice startled him, calling out, "Mr. Brac, Mr. Brac!" One of the hotel personnel rushed up to him, announcing, "Sir, I have a message for you," and handed him a brief note scribbled on hotel letterhead.

The message read, "Mr. Brac, I'm in town for a few days and would like to meet with you. It will be worth your while. I'm staying here at the Four Seasons, Room 403." It was signed, "D. Levine."

While Brac ate a traditional Turkish breakfast of yogurt, feta-type cheese, tomatoes, olives and cucumber, along with bread and butter, honey and jam, all served with tea, he read the mysterious message several more times. He didn't like the fact that someone he'd never met or heard of was so familiar with him and his whereabouts. This was no chance meeting, and Brac did not believe in coincidences.

Well, I guess I'd better find out what this is all about, Brac told himself after signing the breakfast bill and returning to his room. He picked up the phone and called Room 403. On the second ring a man's voice answered.

"Is this Mr. Levine?" Brac inquired.

"Yes it is. How may I help you?"

"Mr. Levine, this is Joe Brac. I have a message here, saying that you want to talk with me".

"Oh, yes! Good morning, Joe. Thanks for calling me back so promptly. We have mutual friends, and you have come highly recommended to me for some work I have in mind. I'd like to get together with you at your convenience. Maybe we could have dinner and discuss something I think you will find interesting. What's a good time and place?"

There was a long moment of awkward silence while Brac gathered his thoughts. "Today won't work. And tomorrow morning, I have to accompany some folks to the airport," he replied. "I should be back in the hotel sometime after 2 PM. Then I want to get in a good workout. So, why don't we plan on meeting downstairs in the bar at about 6 tomorrow night? Maybe we can drink a couple of Efes lagers together and then walk over to the Kathisma restaurant, over by the Blue Mosque. How does that sound?"

"That sounds fine to me," replied Levine. *"I'll see you at 6 o'clock."*

Brac put the phone down thoughtfully. *Who in the hell is this Levine guy?* He asked himself, realizing that the name sounded faintly familiar. *And where does he get off calling me "Joe?" We haven't even met! Hopefully tomorrow will shed some light on what he's up to. In the meantime, I'll make a few inquiries myself.*

Setting his curiosity aside for the time being, Brac went about the business of readying himself to accompany his clients to the Grand Bazaar. He knew enough already to brace himself for the tangled maze of streets and alleys, the crowds, the noise, and the constant movement throughout thousands of booth-like shops. That, coupled with the carefree unpredictability of shop-till-you-drop civilians would surely make for a very long and trying day.

Oh well, that's why they pay me the big bucks, he reminded himself, glancing in the mirror to make sure he looked presentable. He stared at the brown-eyed, lanky man who looked 15 years younger than his legal age. He was still strong, still quick, still ahead of the game, and still curious about what lay ahead of him. Were his days of action really over? *My job is simple,* he told himself. *Keep them safe, keep them out of trouble, keep them from doing or saying anything stupid. Not the most exciting stuff after 30 years of killing bad guys, but it's a living.*

He had come a long way since his first days in the Army.

He stared out the window of the 747. The memory of his time in Turkey and his recollection of meeting Levine bled into an even earlier memory.

Summer, 1965, Joseph Brac had entered the U.S. Army as a young Second Lieutenant Infantry Platoon Leader, where he had first gone through a gambit of military schools at Ft. Benning, Georgia, including Airborne and Ranger School. He had then been sent as a replacement to the 1st Cavalry Division in Vietnam. His first trials by fire had come under the command of the infamous LTC Hal Moore. That had strengthened his character and tempered his soul for a journey that, over the next 30 years, would see him in actions throughout Central and South America, Asia, and the Middle East.

As a Special Forces officer assigned to a special anti-terrorist unit, C Company, 3rd Battalion, 7th Special Forces Group, he had been instrumental in training and advising a Colombian unit that had ultimately tracked down and killed the elusive and ruthless leader of a major Colombian drug cartel, Pablo Escobar. These types of "black" operations were the trademark of Brac's military career. Even during a handful of years during which he had taken a break in service, he had involved himself in contract work with the CIA and other agencies. However, the *esprit de corps* and camaraderie always drew him back to the military and Special Operations. His final claim to fame had come in the mountains of Afghanistan, where he'd coordinated all Special Operations against the Taliban and Al Qaeda.

Over the years, Brac had accumulated a box full of medals, including the Silver Star, Legion of Merit, two Bronze Stars, two

Combat Infantry Badges, and sundry other awards and decorations from both the United States and foreign nations. He had even received awards for actions that were not included in his official record.

Thirty years later, after two divorces and a lot of fire fights, for more reasons than he could list, Brac had finally called it quits. He had been in excellent physical shape, used to going 24/7, but by the time he reached his late fifties, he had given up his Green Beret and had entered the civilian sector. From there, he went to Istanbul and found a job as a security consultant for VIPs, celebrities, and philanthropists who wished to travel the world—in that particular case, Turkey.

The food had been invariably fantastic. The accommodations were always world-class. The people? Well, they were... anything but ordinary.

As the airplane drew closer to his destination, Brac's thoughts jumped ahead again. In his mind, he had just met with Levin in Turkey. He recalled changing his mind and becoming very interested in hearing what Mr. Levine had to say.

* * *

After a fitful night, Karen headed for her office the next morning with a clear list of things to do. As she rushed past the front desk, she told Stephie to hold all calls until further notice. Sinking into her chair and waiting for her computer to boot up, she punched Nate's number into her phone. But before it rang, she hung up and called her mother instead.

"Mom," she began, trying to keep her voice as calm as possible, "it looks like this trip to Nigeria is happening in about two and a half weeks. I thought I should let you know."

"Oh, Karen, I'm so glad you called. I knew about your trip. Ray told me yesterday—we went out to dinner and he said..."

"Ray?"

"Ray Martin, Karen. Dr. Martin."

"You went to dinner with Dr. Martin?"

"I go to dinner with him almost every Saturday. I thought I told you that."

"Mom! Are you dating Dr. Martin?"

"Of course I'm not 'dating' him. We're just, you know, old friends."

Oh my God.

There was a significant pause. Then Ellen Burke, who seemed to be a fountain of information that Monday morning, continued. *"I called Sean Murray yesterday, too, and I told him about your trip. I hope you don't mind but I gave him your work number."*

"I don't mind, but why would you give him my work number?"

"Because he wants to talk to you before you make any plans about Nigeria. He said he 'urgently' wants to talk to you. He sounded worried, honey."

Karen inhaled deeply. "Mom, I have to make my travel arrangements this morning. He better call me right away or there won't be time for me to talk to him first."

"Okay, I'll get the number."

After finishing up the call with her mother, she quickly called Nate. "Are you serious about my going to Nigeria? Is this a real deal? Because if you want me to go in less than three weeks, I've got to get busy."

"I couldn't be more serious. I've already talked to everyone on this end and they'll make sure you have a place to stay. Now we're not talking about five-star hotels or restaurants, Karen."

Karen's voice was a little sharp. "Of course not. I'm not like that, Nate. I wouldn't expect to be pampered."

"I didn't mean that you would. I just want you to know that for a few days you're going to be roughing it. Be sure and talk to you doctor about medications, too."

"I already did."

"Sorry, I know you're a professional. I..."

Another call was coming in, and Karen could see on the caller ID that it was a Northern Virginia number. "Nate, not to worry. There's no problem. I've got to take another call, but I'll talk to you later. She clicked off Nate, and clicked on line two.

"Karen Burke."

"Sean Murray here," said a faintly familiar voice. *"I hear you're planning a trip to Nigeria. Do you have a few minutes to talk?"*

Warm-hearted and sentimental about his friendship with Karen's father, Sean Murray was clearly uneasy about Karen's assignment. He took copious notes on their phone call, and promised to call her back in a few hours. Assuming he would be over-protective of his old friend's daughter, Karen was 99% sure he would insist that she not go. Instead, when he called back, he patched her into a three-way connection with David Levine, a global entrepreneur and billionaire. Karen faintly remembered hearing about some of Levine's shadowy international exploits, including a few brash and, some thought, too risky hostage rescue projects.

"David Levine knows Nigeria very well," Sean Murray explained before Levine came on the line. *"He knows where the bodies are buried, so to speak, and he knows what's out there for the future. There's absolutely no one better for you to talk to..."*

David Levine was in New York, en route to Jerusalem via London. *"Ms. Burke, I don't know you, but Sean Murray is a good friend. And because he's brought me into the loop here, I'm going to be blunt with you. Under no conditions should you travel to Nigeria without talking to me first, face to face, not on the telephone. I'll be back in London on the 20th of April. I'll be at Claridge's Hotel. Two days is all I need with you. But you're taking your life in your hands if you don't take me up on this,"* he said flatly. *"You can fly direct to Lagos from Heathrow. On your way, you spend a couple of nights at Claridge's and I'll foot the bill since you're a friend of Sean's. There are some things you need to know."*

He hung up, and forty-five minutes later a sober Karen called Frank Goldberg. "Are you sure you want me to go to Nigeria?"

"Well, let me ask you this, Karen. Are you convinced that there's enough of a story there to make a best-seller out of this proposal?"

Now was her chance to squirm out of the deal. "I think..." she paused, but in a split second realized that she *had* to go. It was a foregone conclusion. "Yes," she said with as much confidence as she could muster, "I think it's a powerful story. I think the political situation is far worse and far more significant than most people realize. I think Nate is a good writer. I think there's more to be learned about his rescue, which may make the story even more powerful. But it's a dangerous trip, and a friend of my late father's wants to be, um, a little bit involved in my plans."

Goldberg thought for a moment. *"What do you mean, involved? He wants to go?"*

"Oh God, no. He's got a full time job. It's just that, well, I think maybe he works for the U.S. Government. Actually I know he does. And I think he knows quite a bit about West Africa, and he wants to take some security measures."

"Like what?"

"No cost to us, he told me. But he wants me to meet with David Levine in London so Mr. Levine can brief me on the region. And he wants to arrange for a security person to meet me at Lagos and go with me to Abuja. Someone he knows, I guess."

"David Levine? *What in the hell does David Levine have to do with you?"*

"So you know who he is?"

"My God, Karen, don't you know who he is? Don't you think I read the newspaper? Of course I know. He's a heavyweight mover and shaker." He stopped momentarily to breathe. *"Look, if I don't have to foot the bill and this guy doesn't demand a piece of the action, that's fine. He may have some solid background information. I just don't want anyone running off with the story or trying to influence it or anything like that..."*

"That's not his concern," she interrupted. "I've already talked to David Levine. He's not interested in book publishing." She was both annoyed and defensive. She hadn't, until that moment, realized just how amazing the unfolding scenario really was.

"You've already talked to David Levine?" He really sounded impressed. He also sounded nervous. *"All right. Let me think. Okay, you're going to have to talk to our legal department. We will do all we can to make sure you're in good, safe hotels and have the right documentation. But we can't guarantee your safety. You understand that, right? So you'll need to sign some release forms. Are you willing to do that?"*

"Whatever. What about a visa? Sean Murray said I need to

apply for a visa right away—that the process can be a little slow. And I'll have to stop for a couple of days in London on the way to meet Mr. Levine. He'll pay for the hotel, or at least that's what he told me. Claridge's Hotel."

"My God! Not on my nickel! Look, just find out if Levine knows who really got Nate Gregory out of captivity and we'll all win this one. Okay, call legal. We'll take care of your expenses—except for Claridge's—and, look, I appreciate your willingness to go. Just make sure you keep everything confidential. Like I said, this could be one helluva book. Let my assistant know your itinerary, and you can contact me directly by email while you're over there. Keep me posted."

After consulting again with Sean Murray, and reviewing the visa requirements of the Nigerian High Commission in Washington D.C., Karen downloaded a visa application. Once she had completed it, she arranged with the New York legal department to fax her an official letter, spelling out the nature of her business and verifying the Henry Weiss Book Company's commitment to provide sufficient financial support for her during her visit to Nigeria. Another call to Nate assured her that his church would also fax a letter to her, formally inviting her to their mission in Abuja. A travel agent in the building ticketed her flights, and she photocopied the return flight coupon.

By 4:15 the next day, she shoved the required letters, the return flight information, and her passport into a white, purple, and orange FedEx envelope and sent the whole pile of red tape to Washington D.C. She would be leaving Wednesday, April 25, and would return on May 11. She watched the FedEx courier walk away with her passport and documents, went to her office, and picked up her purse.

Next stop, Dr. Ray Martin.

"Karen, your mom told me that Sean Murray is helping out with your trip arrangements," he said cheerfully, after he breezed into the little medical cubicle with a tray that was bristling with needles.

"Well, it's nice to know you're up to date on my plans," she said dryly, wondering momentarily if he was going to wind up being her stepfather. Not such a bad idea, really, but she was still shocked to know that he'd been taking her mother out to dinner for months without her knowing it.

"I hope all those needles aren't for me," she said, suddenly aware of the immediate threat to her person.

"Yep, all for you. Let's see, we've got Hepatitis A and B, Yellow Fever, Meningitis, Typhoid, and a tetanus/diphtheria booster. Oh yes, and I need to give you prescriptions for Cipro, anti-malaria and diarrhea meds, and an antibiotic in case you get an upper respiratory infection. Do you need sleeping pills?"

Karen stared at Ray Martin as he scratched away on his prescription pad. She was overwhelmed with the realization that her life had just spun completely out of control. She was about to answer when her cell phone rang. Without checking the caller ID, she answered.

"Karen Burke."

"Karen, it's Sid. I'm back in town for the night. You want to hang out?"

"You have got to be kidding!" she almost shrieked. "Sid, I am so over hanging out with you—you have no idea! Lose my number, for God's sake!" She pushed End, and turned off the phone.

"Yes, I think I do want some sleeping pills," she answered meekly.

He smiled, nodded, and murmured, "Ambien, 10 mg." He wrote out one last prescription, then turned his attention toward the tray of needles. "Okay, now let's get the rest of this over with."

* * *

"Jumoke," the woman whispered. "It's me."

"Mama, I'm so glad to see you!" Jumoke's voice was hoarse. "How did you get in here?"

"Nasir knows one of the guards. You know Nasir, from the mosque. He told me I could bring you some food and some clean clothes."

The woman looked around at the filthy dirt cell where her daughter and granddaughter were being held. Two blankets lay on the earthen floor next to a damp wall. A reeking hole in the corner served as a toilet. "I can only stay a little while. Here, let's get your clothes changed."

She took the baby, who was wrapped in rags that were soaked in urine and waste. She gently disrobed the baby, wiped her emaciated body off as well as she could, and rewrapped her in fresh cloth.

"She is very thin," the grandmother remarked, trying to keep any note of alarm out of her quiet voice.

"I don't have much milk, Mama, but if I stop nursing her..."

"Maybe you could give her a little banana, too. Will she take it?"

"Mama, I'm so scared. I think she is sick." Jumoke's face was wet with tears. She, too, was shockingly thin.

"I am trying to get help for you," the older woman whispered. "There are people from America and England who have sent letters to me. And a man came to see me last week. He says he's a medic or a doctor. I am not sure who he is."

"Oh Mama, be careful. They will arrest you! What will I do if they arrest you, too?"

"Jumoke, don't worry about me. Let me worry about you. The man who came wants to help you. He asked me to tell him exactly where you are. He helped me draw a map for him."

"A map? Of what?"

"Of the inside of this building. So they can find you."

Jumoke put her hand over her face and caught her breath! "Shhh...someone will hear you, Mama! Be careful!"

The grandmother held Abeo while Jumoke quickly changed into a clean bubo and wrapped a freshly washed iro around her narrow waist.

"Here's some fruit and flatbread," her mother said, setting a basket next to the crude bench where Jumoke spent her days sitting, rocking her baby, and fretting as the child seemed, lately, to be withering before her eyes.

"Mama, if she dies, they will kill me."

"I know. That is why I have to help you both, even if it is dangerous. What could be worse than losing both of you? Don't you think it will kill me if they kill you? My heart would be broken."

The women sat in silence for several minutes, each trying to keep her fear and agony to herself.

"What else has happened, Mama? Is everyone else all right?"

"Everyone but a young girl from Katsina. She was lashed for having sex."

"Was it true?"

"She was raped, and when she went to the Shari'a elders to tell them what happened, they arrested her. They said she's a whore. No one would defend her, and the man who raped her got his friends to say that she seduced him. Now she's pregnant with his child, and her back is covered in sores from the beating. She is very sick."

Jumoke stared at her mother, then looked at Abeo who was listlessly rooting for her breast. "Those men are crazy," she said quietly.

"It was never like this before," her mother said. "There are foreigners stirring up trouble—Arabs from Sudan. Someone told me there is a mullah from Saudi Arabia at one of the mosques in another village. What do they know about us? What do they care about our tribes and our people?"

A man's voice startled the two women, "Time to go. Now. Before someone sees you. Go! Get out!"

Mother and daughter quickly embraced. "Try giving her bananas," she whispered, kissing Abeo on the head and rushing away.

As Abeo slept in her arms, Jumoke tried to imagine what would happen if someone tried to rescue her. She wondered who would do such a thing. She looked around at her cell and could not envision anyone but her mother coming to her aid. The afternoon was quickly fading into shadows, but her mind was alight with ideas. Would they come at night? Would they somehow deceive her guards? Where would they take her? Was Abeo strong enough to withstand the harsh handling that might happen if someone came for them? The horror that always accompanied thoughts about Abeo seized her like cold fingers around her spine.

She thought about the young girl from Katsina. For a time, before she was sentenced to stoning, Jumoke's greatest fear had been the lash. How unbearable to be sick with early pregnancy, shamed and terrified, stripped to the waist, tied to a post, and whipped. Someone had told her once that the usual sentence was 140 lashes for sex out of wedlock.

She closed her eyes, trying to blot out the violent images that were playing out in her imagination. Men in courtrooms. Men with angry faces. Men with guns. Men with machetes. Men with whips. Men with stones.

She wondered if she'd thanked her mother for coming. Then she remembered the bananas. She leaned over, picked one out of the basket, and peeled it. She tried to mash it in her fingers without waking Abeo. She would hold it in her hand until it was warm. Maybe the hungry baby would eat it. Maybe she would like it and smile. Maybe it would save her life.

Chapter Four

They were a regal looking pair, the governor of Nigeria's Kaduna state and the Saudi sheikh. Both were robed in white, and both wore crimson head gear—the Nigerian a colorful, embroidered abeti-aja, and the Saudi a characteristic red and white ghutrah. The two men sat comfortably in a breezy, open room overlooking a well-tended garden just outside Abuja, sipping tea and discussing their common interests. A fountain sparkled and splashed as they carried on their conversation in Arabic.

"The work of our brothers in the south is progressing well," the Nigerian smiled. "We have carefully followed your plan and have already completed two mosques—one in Aba and another near Port Harcourt."

The Saudi nodded. "It is very important that we keep to a very clear path. It is even more important that we should be patient. If we are wise and honor the words of the Prophet, peace and blessings be upon him, true Islam will unroll like a glorious scroll from the top of the country to the bottom, west to east, north to south. Your great nation will be blessed by the pure faith and...by a great abundance of oil. You will become one of the greatest nations in the world. And you, my friend, will be a wealthy and famous man!"

The Nigerian's dark eyes glittered with joy. The prospects for a great and glorious tomorrow were very real to him. And his association with this powerful Arab had already opened doors he had never envisioned even five years before. But the path wasn't without obstacles. "One of the problems we face, as well you know, is the outrage of the Western infidels when they are exposed to the purity of Shari'a law. There are many complaints in the global media."

"Much of what we do will never be reported in the media," the sheikh said mildly. "We can accomplish a great deal with our warriors by removing the infidels from key areas. Destroying them and their churches is an essential part of our work here. The more of them that are removed from the country, the more Wahabism can flourish."

"There is talk in the south," the governor pointed out, "about American oil companies and their subsidiaries trying to reopen some of the closed facilities in the Niger Delta. We do not want them in our country. I'm sure you understand that they are very powerful and have excellent security systems. They are nothing short of surrogates for the U.S. Government and the American military. We must prevent them from re-establishing themselves in areas where we have already driven them out"

"I have heard about these new efforts. As a matter of fact, I spoke to an American oilman in Venice who has dreams of just such an enterprise. Of course, I promised to assist him."

The two chucked amiably. "And do you expect him to take action?"

"Perhaps," the Shiekh smiled. "But if he does, I will be one of the first to know. He deeply trusts me, you see. I have been filling his pockets with loose change for years."

"You will keep me informed?"

"It goes without saying," the Saudi replied. "We are brothers and fellow-warriors, you and I. We will celebrate every triumph together. The holy jihad in your great country is only beginning."

* * *

Around 8 PM, six Americans and a Briton, most of them in their mid to late 30s, gathered at Nnamdi Azikiwe International Airport in Abuja, Nigeria. They had arrived on three separate flights. Even after they caught sight of each other and nodded slightly in greeting, they didn't say a word as they made their way through customs and immigration control and out into the main terminal.

Joe Brac was already on the ground in Abuja—he'd been there two days—and he watched thoughtfully as the others walked toward him. One by one Playboy and The Judge and the others caught his eye and then casually glanced away. They were his long time comrades-in-arms, and they didn't have to say a word to communicate with each other. The other three, less well known to him, were an impressive looking trio in their own right. He'd worked with them only once before and had been very pleased with their professionalism. Overall, he was happy with the team. If only Rambo were with them today, everything would be perfect.

Shaking off scores of omnipresent "guides" and "cab drivers" who were frantically hustling business, the team gathered momentarily outside, where sweltering air pressed against them like a heavy weight. Suddenly an African man caught their attention, smiled, and signaled thumbs up. He spoke quietly to Brac, and the group of seven followed him into a small building adjacent to the airport terminal. There the African quickly distributed two guns and several rounds of ammunition to each of the seven. They quickly holstered Russian pistols under their shirts or at their waists, and loaded AK47s and ammo into their luggage. No more than three minutes later they climbed into a couple of well-worn Isuzu Troopers, and their local drivers headed northwest through the twilight.

Little was said on the journey—only small talk about the heat and the surroundings. Finally, a couple of hours later, the vehicles pulled onto a rutted dirt road and into a nondescript compound, which was surrounded by an eight-foot chain link fence, topped with four strands of razor wire. It was too dark to see more than the closest structures, but inside the fence—which extended for more than six miles around the property's perimeter—were four warehouses, a large, one-story house, a handful of Quonset huts, and a well-worn airstrip. The buildings that had been painted at all were a drab grey-green, intended to blend in with the countryside.

Brac, at Levine's instructions, had arranged for their team

to lodge and train there, at what was officially known as Feeding the Hungry Care Center, International/West Africa Section. It was located just over 100 kilometers from Abuja, and its warehouses stored more than a million US dollars worth of donated food, medical supplies, and used clothing. But that wasn't all. It had a long-abandoned airstrip that was in surprisingly good condition—it looked like it had been recently renovated. And among its outbuildings, surrounded by half a dozen colorless acres of dry grass and rocks, was an old aviation hangar in which were stored several containers full of brand new, state-of-the art military materiel and communications technology, courtesy of David Levine.

By the time they arrived, Brac's men were tightly wound and wary. It was their job to be cautious, and throughout the ride, they had silently wondered if they would make it to their destination without incident. Even now, although they had passed through the center's rolling chain-link gates, they remained on guard. Was this isolated outpost secure? Or had they been led into some kind of a trap? They barely glanced at each other; instead they kept an eye on Brac, checking for telltale signs of trouble on his impassive face.

They were driven to a remote Quonset hut, far away from the central buildings and not far from the old hangar. It, like the hangar, looked like a vintage WWII relic, and its aluminum surface apparently hadn't been painted since then. As they were unloading their gear, two other Westerners arrived. One was Angel, who had been on the ground for several days. The other was a middle-aged man with a slight foreign accent. "Good to see you, boys," he said.

He was David Levine's representative, and he shook hands with each of them, thanking them for participating in the mission.

They immediately grabbed their bags and followed him into the darkened building. He flipped a switch and the light revealed bunk beds at one end of the structure and a makeshift office at the other. Although the furnishings were plain and unquestionably utilitarian, the floor was swept and there was no dust in the air. Someone had made preparations for them.

"Everything on track?" Brac asked the man.

"We're all set." He nodded. "You know what to do. You'll be working in a 10 or 12 mile radius of this location. Of course you've seen the maps—you probably know more about the surrounding villages than I do. The girl is northwest of here, and several of the villages surrounding hers have been attacked. Some of them have been completely gutted and everybody slaughtered. As you've seen, the city of Abuja is a two hours drive away. Hundreds of people, mostly Christian villagers, have died in Abuja State over the past three years, thanks in large part to the governor's duplicity." The man took a breath and concluded. "In any case, Mr. Levine is delighted to know you are here, and he sends his best regards."

Fifteen minutes after the men's arrival—as they were stowing their kits, arranging the office to suit their needs, hooking up their computers, and testing their phones' reception—someone knocked on the door. With some reluctance, Angel let in two Nigerians dressed in military camouflage and a third man wearing a clerical collar. By now it was after 11 PM and most of the travelers hadn't slept for nearly 24 hours.

"Thank you for coming," one of the Africans said in heavily accented English. "We have very much looked forward to your return."

"We're glad to be here," Brac said with a courteous nod. "Thank you for coming out to say hello. It's nice to see you two again," he smiled at the soldiers, "but I don't think we've met," he said to the priest, extending his hand.

The cleric, bowing slightly and shaking Brac's hand, spoke very formally, "Gentlemen, my name is Pastor Benjamin Onu. On behalf of our Christian community here in Abuja State, I welcome you. We are very glad and grateful to you for coming to us. Your help is a great gift to us and our people. It is an answer to prayer. We believe that together we can change the history of our country, and perhaps of the African continent."

As Pastor Onu continued to expound on Nigeria's troubles, Brac's mind wandered. Onu's words reminded him of his own first conversation with David Levine. It had taken place in Istanbul over a dinner of lamb and rice, cucumber and tomatoes. "I intend to put together a small paramilitary unit that can perform surgical military strikes, rescue hostages, and deal with tyrants." Levine had told him. "I believe that it's time for some of us to rise to the threat of jihad."

Brac had frowned slightly. "Isn't that the Army's job?"

Levine's eyes locked onto Brac's. "It used to be. And even now, in some cases various governments will step in. But there are many places in the world—a growing number of places, I'm sorry to say—that will never receive help from the Americans, Brits, Aussies or anybody else. Think of places like Sudan, for example. And Nigeria."

"And parts of Indonesia," Joe had added. "I see your point, Mr. Levine."

"Call me David, please."

"Okay, David. Anyway, from what I've read, these terrorists aren't thinking of themselves as citizens of separate nations."

"That's right," Levine had eagerly continued. "In their minds they are all part of one pan-Islamist nation that has no borders. And they've declared war on the rest of the world, especially on Jews and Christians. Have you heard some of the sermons in their mosques? Unbelievable hatred! And in some areas they're killing the so-called infidels by the thousands. As I'm sure you know, a lot of the violence goes unreported, and even if it is, no one lifts a finger to help. I think the time has come for private individuals to get involved. We have to fight for the sake of the oppressed," Levine had concluded, "because no one else will fight for them."

Brac had nodded, "I'm sure you know that our motto in the Special Forces is *De Oppresso Liber*—to free the oppressed. That's what a lot of us have been doing for decades."

"I know that." Levine smiled. "That's why I tracked you down, Joe. I think it's serendipitous, perhaps even providential, that we are both in Istanbul tonight. Look, I am a very wealthy man, and I have the resources to create a crack paramilitary group. I can afford whatever it takes to get the job done right. But I need you to help me. I want to hire you to put my team together, to train them, and to lead them on our missions."

Joe looked at David skeptically. "But I'm retired. And every day that goes by, I'm further out of the loop."

"Well there's more than one loop, Joe. Look at it this way.

You may have retired from the U.S. Army," Levine said with a slight chuckle, "but to paraphrase another great American military leader, 'You have not yet begun to fight!'"

Brac had laughed out loud, and the two men talked late into the night. They shared the same concerns about militant Islam—Levine as a Jew and Brac as a Christian. As it turned out, they knew many of the same people. They shared stories and remembered fallen heroes. Both men knew more than their share of background information—deep intelligence that was not available to the general public. More to the point, they had both seen for themselves the indescribable horror and despair terrorists inevitably left in their wake.

After mulling their conversation over for 24 hours, Brac had called Levine and accepted the job. In subsequent weeks, he had assembled an eight-man unit along with a handful of back-up operators who were of the same mind, and willing to do whatever Levine wanted done. And now they were here, on their second assignment to Nigeria, ready to make their next move.

Brac refocused his attention on Pastor Onu, and cast a sidelong glance at Billy Jones. He thought he could detect just the faintest hint of impatience in Angel's voice. "Yes, sir, we're glad to help out. Thanks for the opportunity. Just as soon as we get some sleep, we'll get things moving."

The Nigerian bowed again and smiled. "You are more than welcome. Of course you are all very weary, and I will not waste any more time talking. We have talked more than enough in this country. You see, it is time to *do* something. I think you have a saying, 'Actions speak louder than words.'"

"We like to think of ourselves as men of action," Brac told him, "and we'll do our best to get things done."

Brac, Angel, and the others shook the pastor's weathered black hand and watched through the doorway as he and his two companions climbed into an ancient military vehicle and waved goodbye. Beneath a broad swath of silent stars, with the sound of a million insects choiring in the background, the old jeep pulled away from the Feeding the Hungry compound and rumbled into the West African darkness.

* * *

April 25th dawned fair and bright enough, but five minutes after pouring herself a cup of coffee and clicking on the TV, Karen stared bleakly at the screen while one of CNN's early morning business reports was repeatedly interrupted by news bulletins: Intercepted communiqués from the Middle East and "chatter" indicated that some unspecified international flights from the U.S. to Europe were at risk for terrorist attacks. Just to be on the safe side, or so it seemed, the Department of Homeland Security had once more raised the terror alert level from yellow to orange.

Well, at least the flight to D.C. isn't international, she told herself. *And Sean Murray will tell me what to do about the British Airways flight to London. By the time I leave Dulles, the whole thing will probably be cleared up.*

For days she had focused her attention of clothing, toiletries and the kinds of things that she might need in Nigeria—things she couldn't pick up at the local Nigerian pharmacy or department store. A look at her list of skin care products, cosmetics, shampoo and conditioner, and assorted other self-care items told her all she needed to know about her own personal vanity. *Better to be prepared,* she consoled herself, *than stuck somewhere without mascara or lip gloss.*

Karen had traveled extensively during her career in the publishing business, but primarily in the United States and Canada. And what few international junkets she'd made had been to Westernized Asian and European cities. This journey was, to say the least, a new experience. She reviewed her list, made sure she had a change of clothes and basic necessities in her carry-on bag. She checked and rechecked and double checked her passport and tickets, assuring herself that there would be no unpleasant surprises—at least not any that were due to her poor planning.

When the Super Shuttle driver knocked on the door an unprecedented five minutes early, she was ready to go. She clicked off the TV, glad to be rid of the constant recaps of terrorist warnings and the overly-excitable news reporters who seemed to revel in every emerging crisis. Meanwhile, what was she supposed to do? Cancel her trip? She was determined to go—to get on with the project and get it over with and done—but the news had injected an extra dose of anxiety into her otherwise upbeat mood. She wasn't really scared, but there was a rising tide of worry rippling not far beneath the surface. She realized just how edgy she was when she was jolted by her cell phone's ring. She caught her breath.

"Karen Burke," she snapped, answering far more sharply than she meant to.

"Hi, honey, it's just me." Come to think of it, her mother's voice sounded a little stressed, too.

"Hi Mom, I'm in the shuttle and on my way."

"You'll tell Sean hello for me, won't you? And be sure and ask him what he thinks about these terrorist warnings."

"If he's worried, he'll bring it up, Mom," Karen said, trying to sound calm. Why was her mother's concern always so irritating?

"There no reason for you not to ask him, Karen."

"Mom, stop worrying. I'll be fine."

"I'm going to my prayer group today. We'll have special prayer for you, honey."

"Thanks, Mom. Just don't give them every personal detail of my life, okay? You and I both know how much those women love to gossip. Look, I'll try to call from London. Love you, Mom. Bye."

Karen hadn't flown out of LAX for a few months. As the shuttle made its way to the United Terminal, it was evident that there were more police cars and vehicle inspection checkpoints than usual. Still, because it was mid-week, the lines didn't look too bad. *So far, so good*, she told herself. She checked in, took off her shoes and belt, and walked through the security check without setting off any metal detectors or raising other alarms. After putting herself back together, and downing a Starbucks cappuccino and scone, she walked through the jetway and found her seat on the airplane.

The five-hour flight to Washington-Dulles was blissfully uneventful. She slept, read, and tried to imagine what it would be like to meet David Levine. Once the plane was on the ground, she boarded a big transport trolley to the main terminal. Karen quickly sighted a tall, wiry man with horn-rimmed glasses and a worried face.

"Sean Murray," she said with a smile.

He took her in his arms, and for some reason the warm embrace of her father's old friend brought with it an unexpected surge of emotion. She swallowed, fighting off the tears that stung her eyes.

Sean wasn't a talkative man by nature, and he didn't say much at first. "Let's get you checked in and then we can have a nice visit," he suggested after they had made their way to the British Airways counter.

But once she and Sean found their way into a booth at T.G.I.F., neither Sean's reserve nor Karen's efforts to remain cool and aloof lasted long. He began their conversation by reaching into his pocket and handing Karen a chain strung with a military ID tag. *Burke, Patrick Brendan* the imprinted dog tag read, followed by her father's Social Security Number, Type O, and the words *Roman Catholic.*

"It was your father's tag from Vietnam. He sent it to me when he realized he was dying," Sean said quietly.

Tears streamed down Karen's face as she clutched the silvery metal necklace in her hand. She was speechless, shaking her head slowly, then studying Sean's solemn face.

"He and I shared some combat experiences that no one who wasn't there will ever understand," Murray continued. "I can see by what you're doing that you've got a little of your old man's courage, so I want you to take this with you to Nigeria. In the meantime, I'll do all I can on this end to make sure you're safe. I can't do everything, but I can do something."

What Sean Murray actually did for the Defense Department Karen would never know for sure, but he lived in an environment where warriors still mattered and where military brilliance and bravery still shone brightly against the backdrop of what seemed to be an ever-darkening world. In the short time they had together, Sean told his old friend's daughter some stories about her father—stories she'd never heard before. He told her about the anguish of Vietnam, the deaths, the fears, the loneliness, and about Patrick Burke's personal courage and heroism.

Karen was deeply moved. It wasn't just that her father had been a brave Marine or even a hero. As Sean talked—and his words were carefully chosen—a curious awakening dawned within her. It was somehow, someway related to her present journey and the lessons she was learning from Nate Gregory's story. Listening to Sean, she caught a glimpse of something she'd barely noticed before. Maybe she had first sensed it on September 11, 2001, but now it was more clearly defined.

Along with love for her father—who had been a steadfast pillar of affirmation, affection, and admiration in her life—and with a wave of renewed sorrow at his loss, she also began to feel something else. It was at first inchoate and visceral; she ✓ was beginning to recognize it as a defiance against abuse, loathing of inhuman atrocities, rage against arrogant killers who shed blood without mercy. Whatever the political subtleties may have been in Vietnam, Patrick Burke had believed until he drew his last breath that justice and truth were worth dying for.

Did she believe it too? Karen Burke pulled her father's military ID chain over her head and tucked his dogtag inside her silk shirt. Somehow, unfamiliar as the idea was, she thought maybe she did. One thing she knew—she wasn't about to ask Sean if she should turn back, considering the threats. She was going to Nigeria, come what may.

Still, saying goodbye to Sean Murray was difficult. He looked a little forlorn as she walked away from him, and he seemed like a part of her family. For more reasons than she could enumerate, she didn't really want to leave him. Perhaps to make their parting a little easier, he'd become more businesslike as it came time for her to walk away. He assured her that she would be quite safe in David Levine's very capable hands. He said that his "friends" would be aware of her movements. And, without the slightest embarrassment or hesitation, he said, "I promise to pray for you every day you're gone, and will light a candle for you at every mass I attend."

Karen turned and waved at him one last time. Seeing his lean frame silhouetted against a sea of strangers, she choked up, but managed to make her way through security anyway. Ever efficient, she located her gate and settled down there until

BA flight 216 was ready to board for its 6:50 PM departure.

According to her calculations, Karen had about fifteen minutes to wait. She looked around and noticed that several people had gathered around a television monitor that was tuned into CNN. She picked up her carry-on bags and made her way to where she could hear. With a sinking sensation in her gut, she listened to the latest breaking news report: three British Airways flights had been specifically named as targets for a terrorist attack that evening. One of them was BA 216, Washington-Dulles to London-Heathrow.

Karen checked her watch more often than she needed to while keeping an eye on the gate. There was no movement whatsoever to indicate that boarding was eminent. The BA ground crew was not giving anything away, but they were clearly tense. Half and hour passed, then an hour. Karen couldn't help but notice a small group of devout Muslims standing together. While one man read from a small booklet aloud—presumably the *Qu'ran*—the veiled women who accompanied him looked around uneasily. They seemed embarrassed. Were they part of the security problem?

Karen brought herself up short—she instantly realized that she was judging an entire family based on nothing but their so-called racial profile. But still—wasn't it a bunch of Muslims that had started the whole terrorist problem in the first place? *Oh God,* she thought. *How could I do that? Those poor people are probably just as nervous as I am.* She took a deep breath, tried to readjust her anxiety to a less politically incorrect level, and walked to the other side of the gate seating area.

Just then a team of grim-looking security personnel punched a code into the gate keypad, filed through the door, and disappeared onto the jetway. They returned half an hour later, looking somber, not saying a word to each other or anyone else. Almost immediately the phone rang at the counter, and when the attendant answered it she spoke in a low and muffled tone, her back turned to the crowd. After less than 10 seconds, she hung up and clicked on the microphone. "We regret to announce," she said in a monotone voice, "that for security reasons, Flight 216 to London Heathrow has been canceled. We will attempt to reschedule passengers on a later flight on a first come, first served basis."

The announcement, of course, launched a surge of shoving and elbowing malcontents. Scores of angry and frightened London-bound travelers rushed the counter, trying to talk themselves onto BA flight 292, which was supposed to depart at 9:25 that same night. Because of her fortunate location in the gate area, Karen managed to find a spot close to the front of the line and, to her amazement, was given a seat assignment and a boarding card. It looked like she was going to London after all. Better late than never.

But by now a deep uneasiness had crept into her mind and spirit. The Muslim family had been given boarding cards, too, and to her dismay she was consciously wishing they weren't on her flight. Her reaction troubled her, as did her circumstances. She tried to call her office, hoping they would notify David Levine of the flight delay. She couldn't reach them—in fact she couldn't get a signal on her cell phone at all. She thought about trying to call Sean Murray from a pay phone, but people were lined up six and seven deep at every telephone in sight.

Taking a few deep breaths and trying to calm herself, she went back to the monitor to see what was going on with the other targeted British Airways flights. All had been grounded, and a fourth Air France flight from Paris had been escorted into JFK by fighter jets. A note, written in what appeared to be Arabic, had been found in the plane's lavatory. There was no information, as yet, about what the note said.

Exhausted, impatient and restive, the passengers who had boarding cards watched and waited as the minutes ticked by. At long last, an hour after its scheduled departure time, Flight 292 finally began to board. By then the people who weren't stretched out trying to sleep on the terminal floor were both hungry and resentful. Everybody's nerves were seriously on edge. Anxious as they all were to complete their journey, no one really wanted to get on the aircraft. Still they lined up, found their seats, and buckled their belts. Some of them closed their eyes and moved their lips. A couple of Italian looking women quietly fingered rosaries. Karen impulsively pulled her father's dogtag out of her shirt and clutched it in her hand as the plane rumbled down the runway and slowly, heavily lifted off.

But something wasn't right. The big plane was circling above the airport at a low altitude. Karen's heart pounded in her ears. There was not a word from the cockpit, and she desperately stared at the flight attendants, searching for a clue. They glanced at each other inquisitively and looked almost as nervous as she felt. Not one of them made a move to get up and move around the cabin. Three times the aircraft banked and circled. Meanwhile, turbulence rattled trays and shook open a couple of overhead compartments. Karen's deeply disturbed state of mind increased with every passing moment. Her heart was beating so fast she could hardly breathe.

After an agonizing fifteen or twenty minutes, the plane's nose finally began to rise, gradually at first, and eventually everyone felt the welcome thrust of the engines. The aircraft finally seemed to be gaining altitude and speed and heading...was it northeast? But what had happened? Were they safe or was someone taking the plane for a ride to an unplanned destination? Not a word was spoken in the cabin. For almost an hour, the flight attendants remained belted in place. Finally, inexplicably, one of them snapped open the buckle on her seatbelt, got up, and headed for the galley. The others soon followed.

For the duration of the flight there was no announcement about the plane's strange take-off, no explanation, no indication from anywhere that all was well or that anything out of the ordinary had happened. The flight crews' response to what had seemed like a terrifying episode was absolute silence. For the entirety of the six hour flight, Karen Burke's body and soul were on full alert.

Twice, she unsteadily got up and went to the lavatory. Trying to calm herself, she drank two bottles of horrific red wine that should never have been allowed outside of France, and ate nothing but the bread that was served with her dinner. As she battled for self-mastery, two things came into her mind—her mother's annoying little prayer group and Sean Murray's unexpected promise to light a candle for her at mass. For once, both seemed like reasonable ideas. In fact, for perhaps the first time in her life she was, in her own way, pounding on heaven's gates too. Granted, it was a silent prayer, maybe even less a prayer than an inner cry for mercy. But she consciously felt that she was in need of help from, as they say, "a Power greater than ourselves."

An eternity later, after a bumpy landing, Karen gathered up her carry-on bags. Emotionally shattered and weak with relief, she somehow managed to walk on rubbery legs off British Airways Flight 292, alive and unharmed. Into the benign English Thursday morning, she took with her the awareness that she and her fellow passengers had suffered a great wrong; that the threat of violence she had just experienced had no rightful place in the civilized world. Again she felt the unfamiliar surge of defiance she had experienced at Dulles. She touched the cold metal of the dogtag that hung on the outside of her shirt, strangely comforted. For some inexplicable reason, her anger told her that what had been someone else's battle yesterday had become her battle today.

* * *

Nate Gregory had been back in Ogbu, Nigeria for three days and was engaged in what seemed to him to be a full-fledged assault on his sanity. He had seriously thought he was losing his mind during the last two long, hot nights in the sleeping area he shared with several other men. The rest of the time he had remained focused on the physical work he'd gone over there to complete. Meanwhile he was making whatever arrangements he could to be sure there were some meetings scheduled by the time Karen Burke arrived early the following week.

Returning to the sights, smells, and sounds that were associated with his abduction had stirred up his worst fears, boiling over into all sorts of anxiety, uncertainty, and depression. He had been warned about the "triggers" that were hidden in his five senses, sure to fire off unpleasant memories and unwelcome emotions. He had been cautioned about the possibility of Post-Traumatic Shock Syndrome, and how it might affect him. But nothing had really prepared him to revisit the heavy hot air, the smells of hot earth, charcoal, and rubbish that never quite left the atmosphere, the occasional and random sound of automatic gunfire, and of some distant muezzin's call to prayer. Taken together, they had nearly overwhelmed him.

Meanwhile, during the past two nights, his sleep interrupted by jet lag and worry, Nate had seriously questioned whether it was a good idea to include Karen Burke in this insane attempt to bring closure to his nightmare. Sure, he wanted to get his book published, and that was her reason for making the trip. But he felt like she was an intruder in his private hell, and he wasn't so sure he wanted to open himself up enough to let her in.

As was his habit, he allowed his thoughts to return to his beloved Suzanne, and he imagined the comfort and compassion she would have offered him. What would she say to him if she were here? He tried to remember the sound of her voice, and realized that along with that, he had also forgotten the contours of her face. He could no longer see her in his mind's eye. Why did he have to face this alone? As always, the "why" questions remained unanswered, no matter how many different ways he turned them around, puzzled over them, or tried to wash them away with his tears.

Once he got out of bed on his fourth day in Nigeria, however, Nate was aware that his heavy spirit was beginning to lift a little. Maybe this would all turn out for the best. At least he knew Karen would have a security person with her, and that would be good for him, too. *Nothing like a security person when you're feeling insecure.* He smiled ruefully.

As he and his co-workers labored long hours on the church reconstruction, Nate felt more of his stress and fear dissipate with every stroke of the hammer, with every moment of heavy lifting. He was sweating, breathing hard, but the job was getting done. That alone was rewarding.

"Hey, Nate," Ryan, a team leader from the San Diego church called out, "here's a fax for you."

Nate laid down his hammer, brushed a couple of persistent flies away from his wet face, and walked across the cement floor. "What's up?" he asked, glancing at the paper.

"Looks like it's about the woman who is supposed to be

stoned to death. That group of human rights people is arriving in Abuja next week, hoping to appeal to the Governor of Abuja and the President of Nigeria. They're going to meet over in what's left of Agalaba village—you know the one that got burned down where everybody died inside the church? I guess they just want to confirm that you'll be there to tell them about your hostage experience. You knew about this, right?"

"Oh yeah, and I'll definitely be there. Of course I'll have Karen Burke with me by then, and her security person. Can one of you guys drive us over there? How far is it from here, anyway?"

"Not far. Half an hour's drive, maybe. Sure—we'll make sure you get there."

Nate walked with Ryan toward the ramshackle room that the ministry was using as an operations center. The small area was unbearably hot, and whatever breeze might have stirred the outside air never seemed to reach the little office—its two small windows were nailed shut. A fax machine was hooked up to a cellular phone, and a laptop was jerry rigged with a wireless connection to the Internet. It all worked at least part of the time, thanks to a small generator and a couple of resourceful techies who had come along.

Nate wrote out a confirmation on the fax, and sent it back to the U.S., confirming the arrangements. He glanced at the laptop screen, which was open to the BBC news website. Two more kidnappings had taken place in Iraq. Nate's heart sank. He was in Northern Nigeria, far from the Middle East and any of the conflicts there. Still the story made him feel like it was happening to him all over again. He took a couple of deep breaths and tried to slow his racing pulse. At the very least, the latest abductions served as a chilling reminder of his own ordeal and of the ongoing risks Americans faced in many parts of the world. But more to the point, two men were bound and gagged in a filthy corner somewhere, going through an ordeal all too similar to his, and there was nothing he could do to stop it. Where would it all end?

"Mind if I try to get into my email?" he asked Ryan, attempting to change channels in his brain.

"That's what the computer's there for." Ryan shrugged. "Go

for it."

Sandwiched between short notes from his parents and lame jokes forwarded from a couple of friends, he noticed a message from Karen Burke titled "Hello from London."

He opened the file and read the short memo. "Well, I got this far in one piece," she wrote, "despite every kind of terrorist scare you can imagine on one flight! I hope all is well with you and expect to see you in a few days. Best, Karen."

"Thanks," Nate mumbled to Ryan. As he walked back to the building site, he wondered what kind of terrorist threats Karen was talking about. At the same time he tried not to think about what the kidnapped Americans in Iraq were facing right then. "It should be an interesting week," he said to no one in particular.

* * *

Considering all the confusion surrounding her flight, after clearing passport control, Karen was surprised to see her luggage tumble onto the carousel shortly after it began to turn. She lifted her garment bag and suitcase onto the cart and tried to figure out what to do next. Sighting a sign that said "Nothing to Declare," she headed in that direction. Smiling politely at the customs officers inside, she passed through the hallway without incident. Seconds later she emerged into the bustling arrivals terminal, where she caught sight of a young man holding a neatly printed sign that simply said "Ms. Burke."

"Hello, I'm Karen Burke," she said to him, hoping she was the only Ms. Burke in need of transportation.

"I'm Tom." He smiled. He took the luggage cart from her and led her to the parking area, where he opened the rear door of a black Mercedes with tinted windows. The Times was folded on the leather seat, beside a bottle of water. She settled into the plush car while the driver loaded her luggage into the trunk. She checked her watch. It was 10:35 AM GMT when they pulled out of Heathrow and onto the motorway to London.

The driver was polite but taciturn. She looked around as they drove, but by then exhaustion had robbed her of her natural curiosity. She longed to enjoy the sumptuous ride, but her eyes kept closing. She dozed off, awoke with a start, and dozed off again. She opened the water, drank a little, and drifted away once more. She might as well have been in an L.A. Super Shuttle for all the pleasure she gained from the European luxury vehicle.

When they arrived outside Claridge's—because of her arrival so early in the day—she had already resigned herself to the prospect of sitting in the lobby for several hours until official check-in time. She walked through the revolving doors into the reception area and was immediately overwhelmed by the historic hotel's elegant art nouveau interior. At the reception counter, she smiled at the polite young man in uniform and said, "Hello, I'm Karen Burke, and I'm sure I'm far too early to check in."

Thankfully, after briefly checking his records, he said with a warm smile, "Your suite is ready, Ms. Burke. My colleague will escort you there now. Just leave your bags, and we'll bring them up to you momentarily."

Her host had reserved for her a "Junior Executive Suite," which amounted to two full-size rooms, one a bedroom and one a study. The office area was outfitted with a desk, CD player, fax machine, and Internet connection. A plasma television screen filled the bedroom wall, and the young Claridge's employee showed her how to send and receive emails by using a small keyboard. As if by magic her in-box came to life on the huge screen.

The suite's décor was a lesson in understated elegance, tinted teal and soft blue, while the bathroom looked like a mini-spa. On the hardwood desk was a gift basket containing fresh fruit, three French cheeses, water biscuits, a bottle of Spanish red wine and a note. "Welcome to London," it read. "I look forward to meeting you at 7:30 PM for dinner at Gordon Ramsey. Enjoy your day. David Levine."

Karen glanced at her watch again. 11:15. She had almost eight hours until dinner. She stifled an unrealistic impulse to walk around London. Instead, she pushed the Do Not Disturb button besides the door, sank into a hot bath, and drifted asleep several times while floating dangerously in the fragrant bubbles. Minutes later, scented with the luxurious body lotion she found on the marble counter, she wrapped herself in a soft terry cloth robe and collapsed on the bed. She slept, dreamless and undisturbed, for five hours.

Once awake, and longing for coffee, she happily remembered room service.

Within minutes a steaming cappuccino accompanied by complimentary cookies were presented to her with almost royal aplomb. With an unspoken Thank You to her host, she signed the coffee to the room, and tipped the young server generously. Inhaling the coffee's aroma and sighing deeply at her good fortune, Karen slowly summoned her mental faculties and began to get her thoughts in order for the evening's conversation. As she thoughtfully nibbled on cheese and crackers from the gift basket, she wondered yet again what it would be like to have dinner with David Levine. Ready or not, she was about to find out.

Two hours later, she brushed her mane of reddish hair into a pony tail and fastened it with a beaded black barrette. She took extra care with her make-up. She pulled a long-sleeved black sheath over her head, hooked pearl drops through her ears, and slipped into some radically chic Jimmy Choo shoes that cost more than all the rest of her clothes put together.

Feeling better than she'd dared hope, she took the elevator to the lobby and found her way into the Lobby Bar. While waiting to be seated, she stared at the spectacular Dale Chihuly light sculpture that gleamed and sparkled above the room, trying to comprehend how many galaxies away her small Santa Monica apartment was from such a place. It was 7 when she ordered a gin and tonic. By the time she had half finished it, she was nearly over the jittery feelings that had persistently accompanied her thoughts about the inevitable meeting with David Levine. Instead she was beginning to feel very good indeed about life and her momentary good fortune. The terrors of the flight to London were fully eclipsed by the hotel's lovely ambiance.

Promptly at 7:30, the hostess very courteously asked if she, Ms. Burke, would like to join Mr. Levine for dinner at Gordon Ramsey. She sipped the last of her drink, signed the check, and walked across the bar to the restaurant's entryway. She recognized her host, thanks to a news photograph of him she had finally located and downloaded from the Internet.

Research had proved to her that there weren't many photos of Levine to be found. But now she was looking at the genuine article. He was just under six feet tall, somewhat hefty, his face scarred on one side as if it might have been burned. His fine wool suit was slightly rumpled, and the knot on his blue tie was off-center. His graying hair was bushy, as were his eyebrows, contributing to his unkempt appearance. But keen intelligence sparked in his blue-green eyes, and he moved with unexpected grace as he showed her to their table.

"Karen Burke," he said, "I am so glad you could join me for dinner." She was surprised to hear that he had a noticeable foreign accent. Until that moment, for no particular reason, she had assumed that he was a native New Yorker.

As they sat down at a table, Karen's appetite was quelled by an appalling relapse of nerves. She tried to control the slight trembling in her right hand as she reached for her water glass. But it wasn't long before Levine had put her at ease, telling her about his good friend Sean Murray. She even found herself showing him the dog tag she had received from Murray the day before. To her surprise, Levine seemed genuinely moved by the story. At one point, he almost seemed to have tears in his eyes.

Before long, however, the subject changed from friends and family to Nigeria. Karen explained to him her skepticism about the story. "I found it hard to believe that things like stoning and beating women for so-called sexual crimes and massacring villages could be going on without being front page news. And, to be honest, the anti-Islam angle seemed kind of, well…" She struggled to find the right words.

"Politically incorrect?" Levine smiled. "I don't think being anti-Islam and opposing injustice in the name of Islam are the same at all," he told her. "Islam has 1.2 billion followers around the world. Probably no more than 10 percent of them are radicals. Let me ask you something—how much do you know about Shari'a law? Have you had a chance to do any reading about it?"

"I've seen the term mentioned, but no, I don't know anything about it," Karen said, trying to remember what she'd read. Stuck somewhere between jetlag and nervousness, her brain was not working very well.

"Shari'a law is, generally, an Islamic rulebook for all aspects of life. It's not just about religious practice. In recent years, a very strict form of Shari'a called Wahabism has begun to be enforced in Saudi Arabia. You probably know about it because its most famous promoter is Osama bin Laden. Anyway, in 1999, the Governor of Zamfara State in Nigeria proclaimed that Shari'a would be the rule of law in his state. Since then, nearly a dozen other Nigerian states have made the same decision."

"So the stoning and beatings of women are the main problems with Shari'a?"

"Hardly," David Levine answered with a humorless chuckle. "It is a cruel, barbaric system, with amputations, beatings, and beheadings imposed as penalties for crimes. Men and women have no equal rights—they are not even allowed to ride in the same buses or taxis. Women are forbidden to ride on motorcycles—in fact at least one woman has been stoned to death for doing so."

"For riding a motorcycle? Are you serious?"

"I could not be more serious, Karen. The hands of thieves are cut off at the wrists. Women are flogged for wearing trousers. One man had his eye cut out because he had injured a friend's eye in a fight. A pregnant teenaged girl was sentenced to 180 lashes for having sex with her boyfriend. I could go on and on."

Karen put her hand over her mouth and stared, wide-eyed, at Levine. What could she say? She couldn't dispute his statements—she'd seen enough evidence herself to believe him. As he related to her one horror story after another, Karen tried to appreciate the gourmet fare and the pale apricot-hued ambiance in the world famous restaurant. But it was no use. She was so appalled by David Levine's statements that she was unable to get her head around everything he was saying.

Nonetheless, a few things were exceptionally clear. Within two days she would be in a hellhole where women, children, and men were being burned alive for their religious faith, where jihad warriors were carrying out brutal raids on innocent and unarmed civilians. In the name of their God and his Prophet, radicalized Muslim fighters were decimating communities, leaving behind an unthinkable residue of mangled bodies, and burnt out villages.

Then Levine turned his attention to Jumoke Abubakar. With more detailed information than she could have retained after all her research, he retold the story of the young woman who had been sentenced to a brutal execution by stoning for adultery.

"She will die an agonizing death if somebody doesn't intervene. There is no hope for justice in Nigeria," Levine explained quietly, "unless good people take matters into their own hands. No nation on earth will defend the Nigerian Christian population when there are endless political layers and oil reserves at stake."

"Are you...a Christian?" she asked Levine.

"No, I am not a Christian, I am a Jew."

Oh God, I should have known that, Karen cringed.

"My father and most of my relatives died in the holocaust," Levine continued. "Only my mother survived, and she is still living in Jerusalem. I fought for many years in the Israeli army. I do not speak as an uninformed bystander."

"Karen, there are a few things you must understand about this so-called 'war on terror.' The war, in the minds of our enemies, is a war against the infidel—you and me—for the sake of establishing a pan-Islamic state. This isn't just about Nigeria. It is a global threat. In the minds of the jihadists, there is no difference between Christians and Jews and, really, all non-Muslim Americans. As a matter of fact, there are reports of books in mosques throughout America, calling for the death of Christians and Jews."

"In America?"

"In America. Some reports say that 80% of the mosques in America are financed by Saudi Arabian Wahabists."

"So they are telling American Muslims to kill Christians and Jews?"

"That's what some of their publications say. Karen, in their view, we are their mortal enemies because America supports the existence of Israel, and America does embrace radical

Islam's geo-political ambitions. As you probably know, I have been very fortunate in my business and am privileged to do what I can to protect and assist innocent people in difficult circumstances. On several occasions it has been necessary for me to provide rescue and relief for certain individuals when they have run out of options."

She nodded. "I'm sure there are many stories yet to be told."

"Yes, that's true. It is also true that some stories must never be told," he said levelly, looking directly into her eyes. "The battle is just beginning. We must be wise and strategic in all we do. I know I can count on your confidentiality in certain matters."

Are you sure you should be saying all this to a book publisher? Karen thought momentarily. But this was no ordinary business conversation—not with Sean Murray involved. She went on to explain the purpose of her trip, telling Levine about Nate Gregory's captivity and rescue, about his book, and about the human rights organizations that were trying to help Jumoke Abubakar by pleading for her pardon at the highest levels of the Nigerian government. "My primary mission is to confirm the facts in Nate Gregory's story," she explained, "and to help clarify some ambiguities. My publisher thinks it is a very important book," she added.

Levine nodded but did not comment. He listened carefully, taking what Karen thought were unusually extensive notes in a small book. After telling her how to connect with the bodyguard who would meet her at the Lagos airport, Levine told her he would speak with her once more the following morning. And he asked her to return to Claridge's on her way home. "I want you to come back and tell me all you've learned."

"I'm scheduled to arrive in London on May 8," she said. "So shall I stay here instead of at the airport hotel? Is that what you'd like me to do?"

"Yes, of course. Stay a few days extra if you like and enjoy yourself," he added. "But please bring Nate Gregory with you. I've been wanting to talk to him."

"So you already knew about Nate?" she asked, suddenly puzzled. Somehow she had assumed that Nate's story was too obscure for Levine to have been aware of it.

David Levine gave Karen a look that revealed something between condescension and pity. "Let me explain something to you, Karen. Nate Gregory is free to write the book you're concerned with because of the efforts of some very brave men. And, at least part of the time," he paused and sipped the last of his wine, "those men work for me."

* * *

Phillip Taylor's private jet had been on the ground less than thirty seconds at Port Harcourt, Nigeria when a convoy of three white SUVs manned by former American Special Forces Operators and Nigerian nationals rolled onto the tarmac. Quickly and efficiently, Taylor and his luggage were situated in the second vehicle, and the three Suburbans headed directly toward Tumo Oilfield. The now-empty facility had been shut down by Shell Oil since 2003 in the wake of violent clashes between the Ijaw and the Itsekiri ethnic groups in the area. Those deadly confrontations had threatened the operations of several oil companies.

But undeterred by past bloodshed, Taylor was convinced that he could make a fortune by cutting a deal with Shell and reopening the closed Tumo field. He had been working long and hard at some under-the-table arrangements with a Saudi Arabian sheikh, who was an oil tycoon and whose radical Islamic connections would help to protect the operation. The sheikh explained to Taylor that he had several projects in the works. For instance, he had arranged for a group of Saudi Wahabists to make their presence felt in Nigeria's southern states by constructing two new mosques and recruiting local poverty-stricken youths into their conservative ranks.

The Saudi tycoon had explained that his view of Islam brought strength and discipline to otherwise aimless young men. Taylor knew nothing about religion except for the Southern Baptist churches he'd left behind in the hot Texas dust decades before. As far as he could see, all religion was good for people who needed it. He figured the arrangements he had made with the Sheikh offered a win-win situation to all concerned.

Uneasy as he may have felt about the trek across the Niger Delta region, Phil Taylor was equally energized by the prospects of opening up a huge, lucrative oil refinery and production facility for petroleum products. In his imagination, his courageous move would teach a few Shell executives a thing or two about the kind of edgy, innovative leadership the energy business would need in the 21st century. Some of them had been a bit condescending to him in the past. He smiled quietly, envisioning the expressions on their faces as they read the news about his new venture and his smart, savvy relations with the Saudis.

Seconds later, the news story Phil Taylor was composing in his head was blown apart by two deafening explosions. The blasts rocked the convoy, obliterating the first and third vehicles along with everyone in them. The number two Suburban rolled over, and was quickly pried open by several heavily armed terrorists, their identities hidden beneath black ski masks.

Taylor's face, shredded by shattered glass, was bleeding heavily. Half a dozen of his ribs were broken, and his body was severely bruised. But he was dragged alive out of the vehicle, roughly blindfolded, and shoved into a waiting Pathfinder. All but two men in Taylor's highly professional security detail were either killed by the explosive devices or shot on the spot.

Those two, however, managed to crawl away, injured but alive. They radioed for help, and an hour or two after the Pathfinder's departure, they were quietly extracted from the carnage by a local military vehicle.

The following day a news story, released by Reuters, was short and succinct: "Phillip Taylor, an American oil executive from Midland, Texas was abducted by armed militants in the Niger Delta near Nigeria's oilfields. His whereabouts are unknown and there has been no word from his captors." The story was accompanied by a photograph of a blue-eyed, middle aged man, a little heavy in the jowls, wearing a silly grin and a Dallas Cowboys cap.

Chapter Five

For the next two days, at Mr. Levine's suggestion, Karen slept late, ate well, and did a little sightseeing in London. The day she was to leave for Nigeria, she woke up at 4 AM, far too early for her liking and too late to take another sleeping pill. Frustrated in her attempts to doze off a little longer, she finally got up and walked the streets around Claridge's. She found an open coffee bar, devoured a cappuccino and croissant, and was back in her room by 6 AM. Her flight was to leave Heathrow at 12:05, and she had agreed to meet David Levine in the lobby at 9 for a few final instructions.

After checking out, she left her bags with the bellman and walked into the Lobby Bar where breakfast was still being served. She ordered another cup of coffee, and as she stirred it, she watched Levine finish up a conversation on his cell phone as he made his way to her table.

He greeted her with a warm smile and a few niceties. Then he said, "Do you have an international mobile phone?"

"No," she told him. "I only have a U.S. phone."

Levine reached into the pocket of his baggy tweed jacket and pulled out a case that contained a phone, an extra battery, and a wall charger. "There will be more than a few dead spots in Nigeria," he explained, "but it will work in many places. This way you can keep in touch with me and with Sean Murray. I've written some numbers here." He handed her a small card with his name embossed on the front, and three telephone numbers written on the back.

"What's the third number for?"

"It is the number of the man who will be meeting you at Lagos. His name is Joe Brac. He works for me and just happens to be on his way to Abuja, too. He'll go with you that far. Then another security person—someone who knows Joe—will escort you the rest of the way. He'll make sure you get safely back to Lagos."

"What's his name? Does he speak English?"

"Oh yes, in fact you'll find that many Nigerians speak English. But Billy Jones is an American. He's a former Special Forces soldier and nowadays he does some international work for us. I wouldn't be surprised if Nate recognizes Billy, although he had a full beard and long hair the night of Nate's rescue. And needless to say, Nate wasn't in the greatest of shape."

Karen was intrigued, unsure about what was confidential and what wasn't. "Should I say anything about that to Nate?"

"No, there's no reason for you to get involved. If Nate recognizes Billy, that's fine. Otherwise, let's leave things as they are until he comes to London. I'd like to talk things through with him myself. There are some things that should be clarified."

Karen smirked. "Like the fact that the pastor of his church didn't really rescue him after all?"

An amused expression flickered across Levine's face. "That's quite an interesting story, isn't it?" He smiled.

Just then the driver who had met her plane the day before appeared at the table. "Good morning, Mr. Levine, Ms. Burke."

Levine nodded. "Good morning, Tom,"

Tom glanced at his watch. "I hate to interrupt, but it would probably be wise for us to leave for the airport a little earlier than usual. Security is rather tight this week, as you well know."

"Of course. Thank you, Tom. We'll be right with you."

Tom went to retrieve Karen's bags from the bellman while David Levine paid the bill. "Anything else you would like to know?" he asked Karen.

"I can't think of anything," she said. "But I am really glad to have the phone. It makes me feel a lot better, just knowing I can get hold of someone if I need to."

"Well, don't give up if it doesn't work the first time. Just keep trying. All the code information is inside the carrying case. You'll be fine. You're in good hands."

As she and Tom pulled away from the hotel in the Mercedes, Karen wondered whose hands Levine was talking about—his own, his mercenary soldiers', or some other source of protection that hadn't come up in their conversations. And that reminded her of Sean Murray. She pulled the world phone out, checked the dialing instructions, and called Sean's number.

"Karen!" he said, sounding a little groggy. "Are you safe and sound in London?"

"I'm just leaving for Nigeria. It's a little after...Oh, Sean, I just realized that it's way too early for me to be calling you! I'm so sorry!" Karen closed her eyes and shook her head in dismay. *What an idiot!* She chastised herself.

"Karen, I get calls at all hours of the day or night. Don't worry about it."

I had dinner with Mr. Levine the first night I was here. He talked about you a lot."

"He's a good man," Sean replied. "And a very interesting one," he added more cautiously. "He'll do what he says he'll do, no matter what it takes. You're in good hands, Karen."

"So he tells me—his exact words, in fact. Anyway, that's good to know. Thanks for setting it up, Sean. You've taken such good care of me. And I really appreciate all your good advice."

Sean chuckled. "You're about to begin the adventure of a lifetime, Karen. One way or another, you'll never be the same once you get home. And please call me when you get the chance, especially if I can be of any help. Call me day or night."

"Sean, I'm so sorry. Next time I'll do the math *before* I dial."

"Stay safe. You're in my prayers."

* * *

The two bedraggled strangers who arrived at the Feeding the Hungry Center were detained at the gate. When they asked to see Joe Brac, no one in the guard house was familiar with his name. After placing several phone calls, the guard realized that they were talking about the lean, tanned American he'd seen coming and going a few times—the one who called himself

"Coyote."

A runner was sent to the remote area where Levine's team was staying, and before long a British man jogged up to the gate to retrieve the pair. He nodded to them as if he knew them, and the three sauntered off together. They had, in fact, met before, in the ragged mountains of Afghanistan. They were all Special Forces Operators who had fought side by side in the Afghan War. Now an unpleasant turn of events had brought them together again.

When they finally reached Brac and the others, a subdued reunion took place. They were, in some ways, the best of friends; all brothers in an elite fraternity. Still it was hard to feel elated, no matter how much camaraderie they had enjoyed in the past, when they were there to talk about Shadow, and to report to the others the way he had died.

"Just exactly what went down that day?" Brac asked the thirty-five year old redheaded Staff Sergeant he knew best as Shotgun. Shotgun's companion, Blue Note, an African American, wore a bandage on his left hand, and his left ear and neck were badly burned.

Shotgun described the convey of white Suburbans that had been escorting Phil Taylor on his trip to the oil refinery, and he described the sudden ambush. "There were seven or eight of them," he said. "They had on ski masks, but we could see them clearly from where we were."

"How did you get out of there?"

"We crawled away from the explosion before they saw us— once the area was cleared out, the boss sent a truck for us."

"You guys were all working for Triple C Security?" Brac knew the private contractor well. They provided armed protection for corporations, diplomats, and sometimes even State Department missions. He had turned them down for several jobs himself.

"Yeah, Triple C sent us out with the Taylor convoy. That bastard had so many enemies. He's got even more now."

There was a lapse in the conversation. Then Brac quietly asked, "So Rambo got blown away in the explosion?"

"He was in the passenger seat of the lead vehicle." Blue Note's voice was tinged with bitterness. "Blown to hell. At least it was quick."

Again, silence. "Anything else we should know?"

Shotgun nodded. "Yeah, we found out there was a little celebration afterwards. Two guests of honor. Some Saudi son of a bitch was parading around in his raghead outfit. Him and his new best friend, who comes from right here in Abuja."

"You mean the Saudi's friend was from Abuja?" Brac scowled. "Who is he?"

"The honorable governor."

"The governor of Abuja flew down there to hang out with a Saudi prince?"

"Yeah, and to celebrate the kidnapping."

" Well, now isn't that special," Brac said in a mocking tone.

"Yeah, it's real special. At least that's what we heard from our local friends down there. Do you know anything about the governor?"

"Hell, yes. At least I know enough not to be surprised by what you're telling me. For now, let's just say the bastard's first term of office may not last quite as long as he expects it to."

* * *

As Karen's plane soared into the early afternoon sky, Nate was hard at work on the new church. His clock was set only an hour ahead of London time, even though he was in a radically different world. He knew Karen was probably on her way to Nigeria by then, assuming British Airways flight 75 hadn't been visited by any unwelcome circumstances. After wrestling with his attitude about Karen's "intrusion," he was actually starting to look forward to seeing her again. The group of men he was working with were nice guys, but he had little in common with them. It seemed to him that they kept him at a distance, treating him as some sort of hero, and were reluctant to engage him in any meaningful conversation. At least Karen knew something about what he'd been through. And besides, she was an attractive woman. Not that he was interested, but at least she wasn't hard to look at.

He glanced at his watch, laid down the tools he'd been working with, and walked over to the little office. "Can I check my emails again?" he asked Ryan, who shrugged and gestured toward the laptop.

"Hi Karen," he typed, "I hope you're safely on your way to Abuja. If you get this before you head north, just know that my thoughts and prayers are with you."

Nate paused, trying to figure out what else to say. "I'm looking forward to seeing you..." he went on, then paused again.

"Best regards," he typed, then deleted the words. *No, Too cold.*

"Warm regards." He deleted that as well. *What are regards anyway?* Nate groaned. He hated quibbling with himself about words. He thought about Karen and her willingness to make the trip at all. She had a lot of courage. But he didn't need to tell her that right now.

"Your friend Nate," he typed and immediately deleted.

What is your problem? He asked himself. "Thanks so much for making the trip, Nate."

He typed the words and hit "send" before he could think about it anymore. It occurred to him that for the last 36 hours Karen had been on his mind more than he might have expected. In a flash of insight, he thought maybe he'd given her more room in his thoughts after realizing that Suzanne was starting to fade from his memory. A wave of sadness washed over him as he walked back toward the building area.

I wonder if grieving the loss of a memory is different than grieving the loss of a person. Probably so, Nate sighed. *I'll never forget Suzanne. I refuse to.*

He glanced at the others, who were drilling, hammering, sweating in the midday heat. A couple of weeks before, the area they were working in had been nothing but a charred concrete slab. Now it was quickly changing into a small chapel. The people in the little village would never forget what had happened there, but everybody knew that rebuilding would help heal their broken hearts. "*Beauty for ashes*" someone had carved on the little church's new crossbeam. *Beauty or no beauty,* Nate thought, *sometimes it's just really hard to say goodbye to the ashes.*

* * *

The flight touched down in Lagos, Nigeria on time, before 7 PM. It was still unbearably hot in the city, and as Karen made her way into the terminal, she was hoping with all her heart that her baggage had arrived, too. She'd heard several horror stories about disappearing bags in Africa, and she was so focused on finding them that she completely forgot about the man who was supposed to meet her. What was his name again?

Just then she noticed that someone had fallen in step beside her. "Ms. Burke?"

She hesitated for a couple of seconds, "Yes?"

"I'm Joe Brac, Ms. Burke," he began.

"Please call me Karen," she interrupted. "And thanks for meeting me."

"Glad to be of help, Karen," he smiled. "Let's get your bags and get ourselves to the gate for the next flight."

"I tried to fly all the way through on British Airways," she explained, "but all my travel agent could find was Bellview Airlines. I hope it's safe!"

"As safe as anything else in this country," Joe said, moving quickly toward the next gate. "We need to move to make that flight—we've only got about 30 minutes."

Joe Brac proved himself to be a man of few words, at least as far as conversing with Karen Burke was concerned. Once they strapped themselves inside the blue and white aircraft, which bore the hopeful logo of two birds soaring across the sky, they settled in for the one-hour flight. They were seated next to each other, and Karen, who was certainly curious about Joe's work for David Levine, tried to start a conversation with him. She was rewarded with a friendly smile and some very short answers. Joe seemed intent on consulting his laptop computer and reading his dog-eared spy novel.

By that time, Karen was feeling the unexplainable exhaustion that comes with flying. She had been sitting six hours on her way to Lagos. She hadn't done one thing all day but sit, and yet she was weary. Thankfully they were heading for a hotel—the Abuja Sheraton. It certainly wasn't going to be anything like Claridge's, but it was reportedly clean and safe.

They were to spend the night there, then leave the next morning in a vehicle David Levine had arranged for—a Land Rover, he had told her, that would be able to cope with washed out African roads and other unforeseen hazards.

The plane landed uneventfully in Abuja, and their luggage arrived with them. Brac had arranged for a local vehicle to drive them to the hotel which was a peculiar looking structure, featuring two ten-story towers that appeared to be leaning toward each other. Karen's room was fairly well appointed, and—most importantly—the sheets on the bed were spotlessly white.

"I'll call you at 7:30," Brac said as they headed for their rooms, "to make sure you're up and around."

She was irritable, and for some reason she got the feeling that Joe Brac thought he had to make sure she kept on schedule. "I'll be in the coffee shop by then," she replied, perhaps a little shortly. "Don't worry about me. I'll be ready."

"I'll make sure you get into your room all right," he answered. She bristled a little at that, too, but then remembered that David Levine was doing his best to make sure she was safe.

"See you tomorrow, Joe," she said as she opened the door.

"See you tomorrow. Get some sleep."

Once inside, Karen looked around the room distractedly. Tired as she was, she felt restless and unable to relax. She decided what she was going to wear the next day, pulled it out of her suitcase, shook it out, and hung it in the closet. Glancing out the window, among the city lights she could faintly see the outline of a mosque on the horizon, and she recalled David Levine's grim stories about Nigeria's radical Islamists. *What kind of a mosque is it?* she wondered. Only in the last two weeks would it have occurred to her that there might be different kinds of mosques and different kinds of Muslims. She shivered, took a deep breath, and wondered if this trip really might turn out to be dangerous.

It's probably not that risky, she thought. *I'll be fine.* But as the next few minutes ticked by, Karen began to feel a strange sense of alienation from everything she knew, from everyone she cared about. She longed to talk to somebody, but the one person in the hotel she might have had a conversation with was Joe Brac, and in her opinion he had proved himself to be distant, inaccessible, and uncommunicative. She would have loved to disappear into the oblivion of sleep, but there was no way that was going to happen—at least not right then. She decided to see if the hotel's business center was open. Maybe she could get online and check her emails. Come to think of it, there might be an important message waiting for her. There might even be something urgent, something she really needed to know.

She got back on the elevator and went to the front desk. She bought the lowest priced Internet access card she could get, and made her way to the cramped, smoky room that offered photocopy service, fax, and—supposedly—internet access. The computer's operating system was some ancient form of Windows that barely functioned. The "high speed" access to the internet was a prehistoric modem, glacially slow and hopelessly prone toward error messages.

A European sat at the other desk. He had connected his laptop to the modem and was making bitter comments in a language she didn't recognize about the results of his efforts. Karen smiled at him and watched her screen as the machinery laboriously tried to find a server. Finally the password page appeared, and to her amazement she logged on. There was another interminable delay. Then she watched as her messages—12 of them—scrolled down the screen.

Nine of the twelve were spam from various news services and consumer outlets. Two were from friends at her office, one forwarding an unfunny joke she'd seen three times before, the other kindly wishing her a safe trip. The last one was from Nate Gregory. She read it quickly, caught off guard by the "looking forward to seeing you" line. She was about to see what else he said when the room went suddenly pitch black.

"Oh God!" she burst out, feeling more alarmed than she probably should have.

"Welcome to Africa," her cynical companion muttered in heavily accented English. "The power will be on in a few minutes, but you'll have to start all over again.

Just as predicted, seconds later the lights flashed on and off two or three times in a row. "Maybe they'll stay on," her companion said, "and maybe not."

In any case, whatever had caused the power failure seemed to have affected the modem, because no matter how many times Karen tried to get back on line, it was a lost cause. "This page cannot be displayed" messages appeared no matter what the e-address, and after ten minutes of frustration, she finally gave up.

Back in her room, she found herself feeling lonely again, and before long she was thinking dark thoughts about her life. Why was she always alone? She clearly was romantically challenged. She chastised herself yet again for the stupidity of her marriage to a gay man. She castigated herself for the absurdity of dating a flake like Sid who obviously had a woman in every major city in the U.S., not to mention the American heartland's suburbs and small towns. Now here she was half a world away from home, wanting nothing more than to share her rather unusual circumstances with a man who cared about her. She was longing for nothing more than two strong, warm arms to hold her while she fell asleep. And what did she have? Nothing. Nobody. Not a chance.

Too tired to allow herself a complete emotional meltdown, Karen wiped away a tear or two then organized her possessions so she could make a hasty exit in the morning. No way she was giving Joe Brac—*that cold-hearted bastard,* she scowled, knowing very well that she was being unfair—the satisfaction of seeing her show up late. She requested a wake-up call. She set her alarm clock in case that failed. She crawled into the bed, first checking for bugs at the foot of the bed simply because of a nasty article she'd read in a travel magazine.

She stretched out and sighed. "Looking forward to seeing you soon..." Nate had written. That didn't sound like a business-like remark. Or did it? Of course she had no idea what he wrote after that because she'd never been able to get back online to find out. Since day one she had carefully avoided any sort of personal ideas about Nate Gregory, not to mention romantic ones, to enter her mind. She was a professional, and professional women knew where the boundaries were. But what about Nate? Wouldn't he be as careful as she would? Or would he?

"Story of my life," Karen muttered bitterly, groaning aloud and rolling over in disgust.

She was just starting to get drowsy when she remembered the Ambien in her overnight case. *No way I'm staying awake all night,* she thought defiantly. She got up, downed a 10 mg. tablet with a huge gulp of bottled water, and climbed back into bed. The pill had no time to work. She had no opportunity to grieve over the caring arms that weren't there to embrace her. She was asleep in less than 30 seconds.

The next thing she knew her alarm clock was buzzing, the phone was ringing, and the droning voice of a muezzin was calling Abuja to prayer. As first light dawned across the face of Aso Rock, Karen Burke was startled awake to her first full day in Nigeria, West Africa with a jolt of unholy cacophony.

* * *

Nate awoke several times during the night to gunfire—the popcorn sound of automatic weapons. During his first trip to Nigeria, he had learned that it wasn't unusual to hear various weapons firing at night. No one ever seemed to know who was shooting or why. But now the noise was closer and more urgent. And it played havoc with his anxiety.

He rolled over in his bed and opened his eyes. "Hear that?" he said quietly, unsure whether anyone else in the bunk area was awake.

"Maybe it's a wedding," one of the guys answered hopefully.

"No, it sounds like somebody's returning fire."

"Oh, somebody's stealing a car or something. Nothing to worry about."

Nate started to point out that there was a lot to worry about, and he could prove it, but he remained mute. Sleep was out of the question, however, at least for the moment. He tried to think about something pleasant, but his fears were very much in charge of his thoughts. Remembering that Karen Burke was supposed to arrive the following day, he became even more anxious. What if some kind of an armed conflict was breaking out? What if she got caught in the crossfire? With every passing minute, his suggestion that she visit Nigeria and see the situation for herself seemed more ridiculous and, well, self-serving.

In the distortion of late-night reflection, Nate began to blame himself for the disaster that was sure to follow her arrival. He didn't give a lot of thought to the reality that she, an adult who appeared to be of sound mind, had decided to make the trip. Or to the involvement of her publishing company or David Levine. Lying in the shadows, listening to the pop-pop-popping of guns, Nate Gregory slipped back into the intense uneasiness he had felt upon returning to Nigeria. He was near despair.

He tried to picture Suzanne, but once again her face was obscured by time and forgetfulness. Then he tried to remember Karen. All at once he could almost see her, looking as she had in California, sitting beside the ocean at Splashes Restaurant. In that moment, he realized that she had been beautiful in his eyes, but he had refused to see her that way. In his loyalty to the past, he had blocked out any trace of future hope. He groaned, turned over, and tried to sleep, reminding himself that if she really was beautiful, if he wasn't just fantasizing because of his loneliness, he would know for sure in less than five hours.

* * *

Karen could see Joe Brac standing outside the hotel, talking to some men in a late model Land Rover. Three of them were African, the fourth looked like an American. She rolled her bags outside and approached them. Joe looked her up and down briefly. "Isn't that shirt a little bright colored?"

Karen glanced at her green shirt then eyed him uncertainly.

"Didn't anyone tell you not to draw unnecessary attention to yourself when you're out here?"

"No one told me anything about what to wear or anything else," she answered shortly.

Joe simply shrugged. "Well, here's your ride to Ogbu," he said. "I'm not going that direction right now, but these gentlemen will make sure you get there in one piece. You'll be back here by the weekend, correct?"

"Yes, as far as I know, Nate Gregory and I will be back here on Thursday to meet up with the human rights delegation."

"I'll make sure you've got safe transport. See you later, Karen."

"Great." She nodded, then turned to the men in the Land Rover. "Hi, I'm Karen Burke."

The Nigerian driver nodded and smiled at her. One of the other Africans took her bags and stowed them in the back. "Hello, ma'am, I'm Billy Jones," the American said. He was dressed in civilian clothes. His short-cropped hair and clean-cut appearance made him look a little younger than his 42 years. "I work with Joe, and I'll be keeping on eye on you for the next few days."

Karen nodded. Billy was seated in the front passenger seat. *Shotgun position*, she thought, wondering if he was armed. All things considered, she hoped so. She was soon seated between the other two Nigerians in the middle of the back seat.

"How far do we have to go?" she asked Billy.

"Depends on how long it takes us to get through a few roadblocks, ma'am." He smiled. "Ogbu is kind of out in the middle of nowhere, but it shouldn't take us more than two hours."

After Brac said a couple more quiet words to Jones, the vehicle pulled out of the hotel complex and onto the road. They passed a large, gold-domed mosque with four imposing minarets as they made their way out of town. "Is that an important mosque?" Karen asked.

"It's the national mosque," the driver told her.

"Is it old?" she asked.

"No, it was built in the 1980s. It isn't old, but it is an important building in the community."

"Of course," she said lamely, wondering whether she should keep her thoughts to herself until they got to the village where Nate was working.

The morning light was still faintly pink in the clouds above Aso Rock as the sturdy SUV headed north and then east. As they rolled along through the countryside, Karen grew drowsy.

She dozed off several times, but she was awakened suddenly when Billy Jones muttered, "Oh shit," and the car began to slow down.

Ahead of them, an ancient-looking military truck was pulled across the road at an angle, and several armed men in a variety of ragtag camouflage uniforms and carrying automatic weapons stood on either side of it. One of them held up his hands, ordering them to stop. It didn't look to Karen as if they had much choice. The road was blocked, squared off by barricades and the truck, and those formidable looking guns seemed to caution all concerned against thinking outside the box. She tried to ignore the sick feeling in the pit of her stomach.

"So they've set up a new one," Billy grumbled. "Never a dull moment with these bastards."

"Looks like locals to me," the driver said. "Probably just after money."

"Let's hope that's all they're after." Billy glanced at Karen, who was immediately conscious of her too-colorful shirt. It seemed to be growing brighter with every passing second.

The driver stopped. He and Jones both got out and went to talk to the soldiers who were manning the road block. Karen nervously tugged at the chain around her neck and held the dogtag between her fingers. *Oh God, get my out of here alive,* she silently pleaded.

After watching the inaudible conversation for what seemed like a very long time, to her relief Karen saw Billy Jones pull what looked like a couple of American greenbacks out of a pocket inside his shirt and hand them to one of the soldiers. There was a nodding of heads, the hint of a smile, and within minutes a passageway had been cleared between the military truck, the barricades, and the soldiers guarding the road. They were on their way again.

Karen exhaled heavily. "If they wanted money," she asked, "why did it take so long to talk to them."

"You can't rush things with people," Billy said. "You have to take the time to listen and get a sense of what's going on. Some people want money, some people want something else, and they'd be insulted if you offered them money right up front."

"Oh..." she replied, wishing she were anywhere else on the planet but here.

She watched the brownish green, rolling landscape flow by, marked by dusty bushes and dirt roads that seemed to lead nowhere. They passed through two more roadblocks—these were more permanent and did not come as a surprise. Karen checked her watch as they left the third one. It was a little after 9:30 in the morning. They had been on the road just over two hours.

She was beginning to wonder how female travelers took care of their personal bodily functions when she noticed some activity ahead. A military vehicle of some sort was perched on the side of the road and a handful of soldiers were rushing around, a couple of them shooting automatic weapons into a ditch.

The driver glanced at Billy Jones, who hesitated only a moment before he quietly said, "Keep rolling." He reached inside his polo shirt collar and pulled out a small handgun. Without a word, the men on both sides of her slung the AK47s that had been resting on the floor around their necks and rolled down the windows.

Karen's mouth was dry and her pulse was pounding in her ears. She wanted to ask a thousand questions, but had enough sense to keep quiet. She really didn't want to hear the answers anyway. The driver floored the accelerator. The Land Rover roared forward. As they flew past the roadside incident, one of the men turned his gun toward them. A Ping! rang out from the rear. The big vehicle swerved.

"He just hit the bumper, that's all," Jones said, watching the mirror on his side of the vehicle. "Just a punk kid with a gun. Good thing he can't shoot straight. We're okay now."

Less than ten minutes later, they turned onto one of those seemingly aimless dirt roads with no sign, and no distinguishing landmarks around it except for a couple of boulders to the left. They headed across the empty countryside, leaving a huge dust cloud billowing behind them. After skirting potholes, slowing for a few stray goats, and turning again on an even narrower roadway, Karen saw just ahead a cluster of building in various stages of disrepair. Near the center was a construction area and a couple of vehicles, which were fenced in.

"Well, we made it safe and sound," Jones said cheerfully. "None the worse for the wear. Welcome to Obgu, Abuja State, Ms. Burke." His mouth curved into an ironic smirk. "Hope you enjoy your stay here in Paradise."

The Land Rover rocked up the rutted road and braked just long enough for a young African boy to unlock the compound's chain link gate and swing it open. The small village of Obgu amounted to little more than a scattering of dwellings, some with corrugated steel roofs, and others thatched. The construction site was set apart from the rest of the little community by chain link. Even from inside, it was impossible for Karen not to notice the village's poverty level. What was life like for the people there? For that matter, Karen couldn't help but wonder what life held for her in the next few days. Just then she saw Nate Gregory walking quickly toward the vehicle. She took a deep breath, stuck a few stray curls behind her left ear, and smiled at him.

When Nate opened his arms to welcome her, she didn't draw back. For once she wasn't overly concerned about professional etiquette. She was more than happy to be on the receiving end of a brief but strong embrace. In fact she actually felt, for a moment or two, dangerously close to tears.

"So you made it!" Nate laughed. "It's a long way from California, isn't it?"

"It's definitely a world away from any place I've ever been," she agreed, glancing around at their battered-looking surroundings.

"How was the drive from Abuja?"

"Um...we only got shot at once." Karen pointed to the rear bumper.

A troubled look crossed Nate's face. "I'm sorry."

"Hey, we made it. It wasn't a big deal. Honestly. Anyway, it looks like your construction job is coming together."

"It really is," he said, warming to the change of subject, "when you realize that two weeks ago they started with just a cement slab, it's really pretty impressive. The biggest job, however, is going to be dealing with those human rights campaigners. Some of them are supposed to get to Abuja in a couple of days or so, and they are coming for a site visit. We aren't exactly equipped for entertaining big shots. And we're kind of afraid they'll draw a lot of attention to the village. If they do, the terrorists may just get the idea that they should come back."

"So what did you hear about . . . what's the girl's name who's supposed to be killed?"

"Jumoke. I haven't heard much more since I got here. She's still imprisoned, her baby is sick. That's about it."

"And how are you doing? What was it like coming back here?"

Nate hesitated. He looked into Karen's face as he tried to find the right words. It occurred to him that he had been longing to talk to somebody about his feelings about returning to Nigeria. Yet, now that he had the opportunity, he wasn't at all sure what to say or how to say it.

"It's been pretty interesting. I've been...well, trying to adjust. I'll tell you more about it later on. Right now let me show you where everything is, starting with what isn't exactly a 'ladies' room.'"

Karen noticed that Billy Jones was walking with the Nigerian men she'd been riding with, and for the first time she noticed how tall and muscular they were. The three of them headed toward an outbuilding carrying Billy's kit bag and an automatic weapon. Meanwhile, Nate took her bags and led her into a large, carefully swept room with several cot-like beds, each hung with mosquito netting. A young African girl was standing near the door wearing a huge smile. "Welcome, Auntie," she said with a bow. "You are welcome in our village."

Karen smiled back at the girl, and glanced at Nate. "Auntie?" she said quietly after the girl bowed slightly and left.

"Don't worry, it's a term of respect, not a case of mistaken identity," he told her with a grin. "Anyway, here's your bed. There'll be a bowl of water for washing up every morning and evening. And some towels."

He set her bags down and led her outside. "Sorry about this," he said, pointing toward an odiferous latrine. "I guess it'll just have to do..."

"Actually, I'm more than happy to see it. It was a long ride," Karen told him as she quickly disappeared inside.

When she returned, she found Nate staring in the direction of Billy Jones, who was standing a distance away talking to one of the burly Nigerians.

"Do those African guys work here?" she asked.

"They're hired guns," Nate nodded. "The people that did the contracting for the new church hired them. I think they are in the Nigerian Army, or at least they used to be. But I'm trying to place that other guy, Billy Jones." Nate's eyes narrowed with concentration. "He got here last night—said he was here to provide you with security protection. It's strange, but I feel like I've seen him before."

"You'll figure it out eventually," she said matter-of-factly, remembering David Levine's last minute instructions. "Maybe you knew him at home. Anyway, what else is around here?"

The compound beside the church construction area amounted to three wings surrounding an open courtyard. One wing contained the project office and a small eating area, sparsely furnished with two tables and a dozen folding chairs. A makeshift counter held a couple of camping stoves and a coffee-maker. To the side was a small refrigerator; just outside was an electrical generator. Across the courtyard were sleeping quarters and the chemical latrine. On the open side was the construction area and beyond that stretched the gate, which was locked and guarded.

Nate showed Karen around, and for the next few hours, they talked non-stop, listened carefully to each other, and smiled more than they might have expected. He told her about the people working on rebuilding the church, and about the local people who worked for them preparing food, cleaning, guarding, and driving. She told him about the terrorism threats that shadowed her flight to London, and a little bit about Sean Murray. She said nothing about David Levine.

They were both vaguely aware that the loneliness each of them had experienced in recent days had demolished their usual defenses, so they were quite happy to be together. The sequence of events that had caused their paths to cross in the first place now provided them with common ground for conversation. Despite the limited time they had spent together, and regardless of their differing life experiences, they had lots of things to discuss—things that really mattered, if for differing reasons, to each of them.

They were sitting in the room that served as a kitchen and dining room. Nate was leaning back on a folding chair at the end of a table, and Karen, who was sitting next to him, had fallen silent as she stared incomprehensibly at two Humanity.com news releases about the conference that was supposed to begin in a couple of days. As the heat increased and the air pressed against them like a heavy hand, Nate glanced at his watch. It was nearly 2:30. "Do you want to lie down in your room and rest for awhile? It's cooler in there."

Karen never hesitated. "No—I'm fine here. I'm enjoying this, heat and all. I'll read this stuff later." She shoved the papers into her purse.

Nate turned to look at her and their eyes met and held for just a few seconds longer than either of them might have intended. Karen looked away, feeling a catch in her throat and wondering why.

"I'm glad you came," Nate said softly. "It was pretty terrible when I first got here, and I had second thoughts about dragging you into all this. But now that you're here, I know it's the right thing. I'm really glad you could come."

Karen nodded, looking at her hands for a few seconds. "I'm glad I could come, Nate. And I'm sorry it was hard for you, but I'm not surprised. What exactly happened?"

Nate inhaled deeply and whooshed the air out of his mouth. "I don't even know how to describe it. Close to a very long, very intense panic attack, I guess. Even when it wasn't that severe, I was fighting some serious anxiety. It went on morning, noon, and night for the first two or three days."

Almost involuntarily, Karen put her hand on his arm. "What a nightmare," she said quietly, "coming back to the same place."

"There are a lot of triggers." He laughed at the worried look that flickered across her face. "I mean figurative triggers, but there's a lot of gunfire at night, too. You'll hear it tonight."

"Who's shooting?"

"Who knows?" He shrugged. "Bad guys vs. other bad guys I

guess. Anyway, it's okay. I'm okay now. And you'll be okay, too"

She nodded and moved her hand away from his arm, perhaps a little reluctantly. "Well, I'm glad I'm here, too. I think it's important—maybe for a lot of reasons." She paused. "And I think it's what my father would want me to do." She had been fingering the chain around her neck. Now she pulled the dog tag out of her shirt. "I should tell you about this."

"This is a GI dogtag, isn't it?" Nate reached over and examined the tag. "Was it your father's?"

"An old friend of his—an ex-Marine who fought with him in Vietnam—gave it to me on my way here. It's kind of a long story." She glanced at him, not sure if he would be interested. Sid certainly wouldn't have been. The look on Nate's face, however, told her that he was very interested indeed.

"We've got all the time in the world." He smiled at her. "So tell me about your father. And after that, tell me about yourself."

* * *

David Levine had just hung up a secure phone in his office after a forty-five minute briefing during which Joe Brac had updated him in detail about the paramilitary team's preparations in Nigeria. Levine was about to order lunch in when his cell phone alerted him to a text message from his personal assistant, "ed friedman on line 1 says it's urgent."

Levine shook his head in frustration and called his assistant immediately. "Of course it's urgent," he told her irritably. "Go ahead and patch him through."

After a couple of beeps, he said, "Hello Ed, what can I do for you?"

"*Mr. Levine, thank you for taking my call.*" Friedman sounded unusually nervous. "*I...I'm calling about Phil Taylor. I guess you heard?*"

"Yes, I heard about the kidnapping. I'm sorry to hear about it. But he was in a rather vulnerable spot driving around out there in the oilfields. There's a very good reason no one is working down there."

"*Phil is a visionary, Mr. Levine. He had a brilliant plan for putting those refineries back online, and he felt like he had to move forward, even though there were some naysayers among the Shell people."*

"Forgive me, Ed, but those naysayers apparently have a lot more common sense than Phil did."

"It's true that sometimes, because of his creativity, he may step across the normal parameters."

"He's an *asshole*, Friedman," Levine interrupted. "Face it! He's a greedy asshole. And now he's about to get his throat cut by those bloodthirsty bastards. He had no business going in there. You know that as well as I do!"

Friedman was silent for a few seconds, unsure whether he should hang up or finish what he'd started. He drew in a deep breath. *"Mr. Levine, I was calling to find out if you'd be willing to help get Phil out. I know you're well connected with the Saudis. Hell, you're well connected with everybody. So I'm sure you've heard that they're involved in this."*

With every passing second, Levine was losing a little more patience. "Ed, what exactly do you want me to do?"

"Mr. Levine, I... was hoping you could talk to them. I guess I thought you could negotiate with them—make some kind of an offer. A little money. A bargain of some sort. Maybe we can find out what it would take to get Phil out of there."

David Levine closed his eyes and rubbed his forehead with the palm of his hand.

"I will not negotiate with the Saudis, Ed. I cannot and will not cut deals with them."

"But it could be a matter of life and death!"

"Of course it's a matter of life and death!" Levine exploded. "Of course it is! Look, you're a Jew," he reminded Ed Friedman. "You're a Jew and I'm a Jew. Don't you know that every time you get in bed with Saudi Sheikhs you get in bed with the Wahabists? And don't you know that they want nothing more than to kill Jews."

"But why do they want to kill us?" Friedman was bewildered. *"It's illogical."*

"Ed, for God's sake don't talk to me about logic! What planet do you live on? I want you to tell me something. What is it about jihad that you can't quite figure out? Just exactly what is it about an Islamic declaration of 'holy war' against Jews and Christians that you don't understand?"

Chapter Six

Jumoke awoke with a start. Her arms tightened around Abeo, and she pressed the sleeping baby's head against her breast. It was dark and she could barely see, but she could feel that someone else was in the cell. She shivered in terror and a tiny sound of fear escaped her lips.

"Shhh...don't be afraid. I'm here to help you," said a man's voice nearby. He was whispering, but it sounded as if he had a foreign accent, maybe American.

"Who are you?" she whispered back, still trembling.

"I'm a medic. I just came by to see how you're doing."

"How did you get in here?" she whispered.

"It wasn't so hard—not nearly as hard as getting you out will be."

By now he was close beside her, resting on one knee. His blue eyes were scanning the room. He had a small device in his hand that looked like a cell phone, and he was punching a series of numbers into it.

"How's your baby doing?" he asked.

"She's..." Jumoke caught herself. She didn't want to talk about Abeo's illness. What if her captors took the sick baby away from her? She loved Abeo too much to let her go. Besides, the child was her lifeline—once she was gone, Jumoke would face her death sentence. They would dig the hole. They would bury her in it. The stones would fly at her face, her head.

"Fine. She's fine," she said in as firm a voice as she could muster.

"May I see her?" he asked, reaching for the infant.

Hands shaking, Jumoke handed her daughter over to the man, who was wearing desert camouflage BDUs and a backpack. He took the limp, feverish child in his hands and looked at her closely. He ran his hand across her hot, nearly bald head. Abeo did not wake up, even after he gently returned her to Jumoke's arms.

"She's not doing so well, is she?"

"She's getting better," Jumoke whispered quickly. "She's better every day."

He nodded solemnly, rose to his feet, and strode across the cell to look out its one small, barred window, visually investigating the area outside. Jumoke noticed that a square of moonlight was faintly gleaming in the distant sky.

"I'm going to leave now, but I'll be back in a few days with some friends. We're going to try and help you. But do not tell anyone that I was here. Do you understand me? Do not tell a soul."

Jumoke nodded. "I understand. I will not tell anyone, not even my mother."

"Good girl. You take care, now," he said, disappearing out the cell's door and relocking it behind him.

* * *

Nate was up before dawn the next morning. The sound of guns had awakened him an hour or two before, and he had been listening and thinking ever since. There was definitely more gunfire than before, and it seemed closer. He almost imagined that he heard shouting, too. He thought about Jumoke, the young woman whose prison cell was no more than two miles away. He wondered if someone had rescued her the way they had rescued him. Maybe that's what the shooting was all about.

As dawn's pastel colors deepened into day, Nate pulled himself out of bed, threw his clothes on, and headed for the compound office. He tapped his thumb against the laptop's mouse a few times until the computer woke up and the British Broadcasting Company's red and white news banner appeared across the top of the screen. Nate yawned and stretched, wondering if there was any fresh coffee in the galley.

He glanced back at the screen, catching his breath as he read the BBC's breaking news crawl: "Outbreak of inter-religious violence in Northern Nigerian village. More soon."

Nate jumped to his feet and rushed outside, listening, looking around, fighting the fear that gripped him. It was so quiet he could hear his pulse beating in his ears. There was no sound, no movement, not even the whine of a plane or the distant drone of a highway. The world was silent. He looked outside the gate at the horizon. Nothing unusual there, either, except perhaps a faint blur of smoke in the north. But even that was to be expected as villagers stirred their fires back to life.

He breathed deeply, inhaling the warm morning air and trying to breathe out the feelings of dread that were still stirring inside him. He went back to the computer and clicked on the breaking news ticker, but it did not link to a story yet. He tried to find other news sources, but there was nothing about Nigeria anywhere else—not even on Al-Jazeera.

Just then he saw Billy Jones striding across the compound. He knew Jones was there to keep an eye on Karen, so he rushed out to meet him. "Have you heard anything about the shooting last night?" he asked, assuming that Jones had his own private communications link to the rest of the world.

Jones nodded. "I heard the gunfire, too, and it wasn't that far away. But nobody's talking to me about it—at least not yet. I'll check in with my people again in an hour or two. Everything's quiet now anyway, so I wouldn't worry. Whatever it was has probably died out."

"I'm worried about Karen being here."

Jones nodded. "Yeah, it's just as well we get her back to Abuja as soon as we can. She's supposed to leave day after tomorrow. Maybe we can do it tomorrow instead."

"That's a good idea. I'm going with her, you know. There's a conference at the hotel there."

Billy Jones nodded. "We should go as soon as possible. It may get worse around here before it gets better. See you later."

Nate walked away feeling less than satisfied with Jones' enigmatic words, still feeling sure that they had met before. He had unconsciously added that mystery to the list of things that were making him uneasy. Of course things were never especially good in this part of the world, but what exactly did he mean by, "It's probably going to get worse?" Was it just an expression he liked to use? Nate shook his head, and went to search for something to eat. He could see Billy Jones talking on a cell phone in the distance.

* * *

Sean Murray's home phone rang early in the morning, just as he was getting out of the shower. He answered it and found himself talking to David Levine. *"Have you heard what's going on in Northern Nigeria?"* Levine asked.

"Not in the past couple of days," Murray said. "Why? What's up?"

"I'm getting some pretty sketchy reports right now, but it sounds like another Christian village was attacked in the middle of the night. Three of the local church elders were shot, execution style. It happened less than three miles from Ogbu."

"Is Karen still on the compound there?"

"Yes, and I've got a man there with her. But it's heating up. That's good in terms of our plans, but it's bad in terms of Karen's personal safety."

"Have you talked to her?" Sean frowned. "Is she afraid?"

"She's got her phone turned off. I guess I should have told her to leave it on. I'll tell her security man to pass the word to her. I want to be able to contact her myself."

"Well, she can't be very scared if she's not calling either of us."

"Well, that's true enough. Look, what do your people hear about the big picture over there, Sean?"

"You've seen the report on the oilfields, haven't you?"

David Levine squinted at his laptop screen, looking at the files he'd saved in the past few days. *"I see that there have been some demonstrations down there, which were pretty clearly orchestrated by the radicals. Any word on Phil Taylor? Has that hit the news yet?"*

"Not a thing that I've seen or heard. But news coverage or not, I doubt very much if anyone is going to go in after him. Of course the radicals will use the news about him to stir things up. And now we've got these human rights people flying in. Some of them understand the realities down there, but the others are both naïve about the Islamists and negative about anything but peace initiatives—you know, heart-to-heart 'dialogue.'"

Levine snorted. *"What a load of horse shit. I'll be very glad to have our little mission accomplished. That will clear the air considerably."*

"How does all that look?"

"My man on the ground says they are ready to roll. Just waiting for the go ahead."

"Do you think they could move early if they have to?"

"You bet they could."

"All right, I'll keep you posted, David. If you get in touch with Karen, tell her I said hello. And, if you don't mind, let her know that I kept my promise to her on Sunday. She'll understand."

"I'll tell her. And I'll be in touch."

The phone clicked off and Sean Murray glanced outside as he slipped the receiver back into its cradle. The lilac bush next to his bedroom window was heavy with pale, fragrant blossoms. The lawn glistened with dew, and birds were singing everywhere. Northern Virginia was as peaceful as Heaven. Sometimes it was hard to believe that elsewhere in the world, at that very moment, people were shedding blood, enduring torture, living in terror, and dying in agony. He rubbed his face with a towel, put his glasses on, and clicked on CNN. He wished with all his heart that his old friend Patrick Burke's daughter was anywhere on the planet but in Nigeria.

* * *

Karen had found it difficult to get to sleep. Her mind had been on Nate. She had tried for awhile to push the thoughts away, but before long she had given into the slightly intoxicating sensation that something was happening between them. It was a wake-up call, a stimulating rush at least for awhile, but thanks to her doctor's pharmaceutical expertise, she had slept well anyway. She'd been oblivious to the gunfire and awakened with an optimistic feeling about life.

After taking a sponge bath and putting on clean clothes, she headed out the door for the galley, feeling sure that at least one of the men at work there drank coffee in the morning. Inside the little dining area she saw Nate eating with several of the other workmen who were rebuilding the church. He didn't see her at first—he was talking rather earnestly to someone.

She poured herself some coffee, sat down, and seconds later Nate made his way over to her table. He looked worried. "Did you sleep alright?" he asked her, studying her face.

"I slept very well, thank you!" she told him with a warm smile.

"So the gunfire didn't bother you?"

"I didn't hear a thing. Was there gunfire again? I know you mentioned that you'd heard it before."

"Yeah, there was some shooting. It's all quiet now, though. Are you up for going to the compound where I was rescued today instead of tomorrow? Some of the guys think it would be good for us to head back to the hotel tomorrow instead of Thursday."

"Oh really? Why is that?" Now Karen was studying Nate's face.

"Oh, just to stay on the safe side. You know, Abuja is a lot more secure than this place. And the hotel is probably the safest place in town."

"That's strange."

"Why is it strange?"

"Because you'd think it would be a target. There were a lot of Westerners there. Nate is there something wrong? Something you aren't telling me?"

Nate looked outside for a moment, and then back at her. How much should he say? Just as he started to answer, Billy Jones strode into the room with his usual easygoing style. He didn't seem particularly bothered. "Hey, Karen." He smiled.

"Hi, Billy, what's going on?"

"Not much. I just wanted to tell you that David Levine wants you to turn on your cell phone."

"What? Why?"

"Because he's been trying to call you. Anyway, give him a call when you get a chance. And then leave your phone on. Did he give you a re-charger?"

"I...think so. I'll check."

"If not, let me know. I've probably got something that will work. So, Nate, what time are we leaving for the rescue site?"

"I think we should go as soon as possible."

"Okay, that's fine. Just give me an hour. I'm going to head over there first and see what's going. Make sure there aren't any bad guys in the area."

Karen wasn't sure how to read Billy Jones—for the most part he kept his feelings to himself. But there was something in his eyes that caused her to feel another surge of alarm. She looked at Nate, consciously keeping her face expressionless. "You guys seem a little edgy today. What's going on?"

"Like I said, there was some shooting last night. We don't know much about it, but it went on for awhile and, since this is Nigeria, it's better to be safe than sorry."

An hour later, Karen, Nate, Billy, and their African driver rolled out of the gate in yet another well worn vehicle of dubious origins. They headed back to the main road, turned left, drove a few hundred yards, then made a right turn between two vacant, roofless structures. Half a mile later, they came to a stop outside a rundown, bullet-pocked cluster of mud-colored buildings. A couple of ragged banana trees rustled nearby. Karen glanced at Nate, and she could see that his jaw was set. He kept his own counsel while the four of them got out of the truck and started walking.

"Nate is this hard for you?" Karen quietly asked as Billy and the driver walked on ahead.

"I'm not enjoying it much," he told her. "But I want you to see where it all happened. I need you to know that it *did* happen, Karen. I didn't make this up."

She walked alongside him in silence, wondering if he resented being brought back to the location of his nightmare. It hadn't been her idea, of course, but right at the moment, she was fairly sure that he thought he had to go through this ugly flashback to get his book published. And that annoyed her.

The two of them walked along in silence, each of them lost

in thoughts—rather unpleasant thoughts

Billy turned around, suddenly remembering their earlier conversation. "Karen, did you call David Levine yet?"

"No, I'll do it later. I left the phone back at the compound."

"He's counting on me to tell you," Billy said firmly. "It's important to him. So don't forget about it."

Karen walked away from everyone else. She'd had enough of them for the moment. She turned toward an open area to the left and started to go inside one of the beat-up structures. "Hold it, Karen," Billy said sharply. "Let me go in first."

She sighed, getting an uneasy feeling about her place in the world and whether she was actually in it. She was about to follow Billy when Nate moved beside her and took her upper arm in his hand. "The helicopter was right over there in that direction," he pointed. "We came out of that doorway, next to where Billy went in." Nate's voice was calm; he had mastered his emotions again. "They dragged me off that way somewhere."

Karen stood still and looked in both directions, trying to envision the violent scene that had taken place so many months before. There were still burned areas on the trunks of small trees and on the side of the building. And of course there were bullet holes everywhere.

"Let's go inside," Nate said, still holding her arm.

They took two steps when gunfire shattered the quiet. The blast was sudden and earsplitting. They froze for a moment, then Nate pulled Karen behind a small wall, "Get down," he ordered quietly, as they both crouched, out of sight.

They could hear a scuffling sound inside the compound area, and in a few moments Billy Jones' voice clearly said, "Put your gun down. Lay it down right there, right now. That's good. Very good. Now you get the hell out of here! Get out. And stay out!"

Both Nate and Karen dropped to their knees, ducking down a few inches further, not sure where the person in question was supposed to "get out." Within seconds, they heard him rush past them, breathing heavily, his feet pounding the dirt as he ran at full speed away from them.

They waited, listening and hoping the crisis was over. They

could faintly hear Billy Jones moving around nearby, and after a minute or two, he came outside. "Where are you guys?"

"We're right here," Nate said quietly. "What happened?"

"Some local lowlife had come in here since I checked the place out a couple of hours ago. I don't know what he was after. He may have been waiting for somebody, or he may have been hiding out. But unless you two have a real good reason to stay here, I think we'd better get back. You have all the information you need, Karen?"

"Oh God, yes," she muttered. "Way more than I need."

"Let's go." Billy grabbed her by the arm with his left hand, much as Nate had done, but with a far firmer grip. His gun was in his right hand, and his eyes were scanning their surroundings like a searchlight on a dark night.

They rode back to the other compound in complete silence. Only after they were inside the gates, and one of the building supervisors had padlocked them inside, did anyone speak. "I'm going to phone David Levine," Karen said meekly. "I'll be back in a few minutes."

* * *

Nate had felt uneasy enough before. Now he was more anxious than he'd been since his first bout of nervous tension upon returning to Nigeria the week before. He paced around the dirt like a caged animal, unable to walk away from the gnawing apprehension inside him. He was afraid for himself, afraid for Karen, afraid of the unknown. Most of all he was afraid of the encroaching hostility that seemed to be moving toward him, as if he were a magnet for violence.

"God, help me," he murmured over and over. He had struggled with his faith at times after his abduction, wrestling with the predictable doubts about why "a God of love" would allow such a thing to happen. Most of that had resolved, however, as he came to see how many Christian communities in Nigeria were intensely suffering—and without much hope of rescue. He knew he had been lucky or fortunate or blessed, depending on the language he chose to use. Now he found himself muttering repetitious prayers, hoping they weren't bouncing off the heavenly gates like hailstones off a windshield. His anxiety felt like a physical affliction, and he wished he could swallow a pill and make it stop.

He sat down on an outside bench and put his head between his hands, trying to calm himself. He breathed deeply, exhaled thoroughly, and attempted to focus his mind on a peaceful scene that certainly wasn't anywhere near here. Just then Karen walked up to him, and her troubled voice broke into his reverie.

"Oh God, Nate. David Levine wants us both out of here. He says all hell is going to break lose in Northern Nigeria, and he wants us to get back into Abuja as soon as we can."

"I think he's right," Nate told her. "Billy Jones and I talked about that this morning, after all the shooting last night. He is making plans to leave here in the morning."

"Are you okay after today? I don't know about you, but I could use a drink about now."

Nate laughed in spite of himself. His eyes met Karen's in a look of unexpected camaraderie. "Yeah, I know. I'd like a stiff one myself. Don't expect to find one in this place. We'll have something in Abuja tomorrow night."

"So what's up with the no alcohol? Don't these guys at least get a beer or two after working in the sun all day?"

Nate shook his head. "Good question, Karen. It makes no sense to me either. Just some taboo they've cooked up, I guess."

"Who cooked it up?"

"Who knows?"

Karen sat down next to Nate, and as if it were the most natural thing in the world, he put his arm around her shoulders and pulled her next to him for a few moments. "We'll get through this, you know," he whispered. It occurred to him that he was suddenly feeling a bit better.

She turned her eyes toward him, and their large, grey depths reflected back to him some new feeling, something between amazement and relief. There was no particular reason to feel safe with Nate—Billy Jones was the man with the guns. But there was a kind of security in Nate's embrace, and it was exactly what she needed in that moment.

They talked quietly for a few minutes until the sound of

The Levine Affair: Angel's Flight

African voices from outside the gate interrupted their conversation. "Hello? Hello, brothers!" Someone was rattling the gate loudly. "Can we come inside? Hello?"

Nate and Karen braced themselves. Billy Jones suddenly appeared, along with the Nigerian guards, weathered, tough men who looked like they could take care of themselves. The three of them descended upon the gate, facing off with the strangers outside.

"What do you want?" Jones coldly demanded.

"We want to talk to the Christians here. We are from Ayuba."

"What the hell is Ayuba?"

"Ayuba is a Christian village an hour's walk away."

"You can't come inside." Jones said bluntly. "What do you want to talk about?"

By that time Nate and Karen had walked around behind Billy where they could see a group of six Nigerians standing outside the gate. Two of the men were wearing western suits, and the rest wore colorful local clothing.

"Three of our elders were shot last night," the group's spokesman explained, his voice calm and conciliatory. "Our village Ayuba is very close to Agalaba, the one that was burned to the ground not long ago. We are very much afraid. We need advice and help."

Billy Jones wasn't buying it. He shook his head, and was about to send them back the way they came—hour long walk in the heat or not—when Nate stepped in. "I think we should talk to them, Billy," he said mildly. "Just check them for weapons and let them in. Let's see what they have to say."

A couple of the older men from San Diego who were supervising the building project had been listening and nodded in agreement. "It won't cost us anything to hear them out," one of them said. "It's the least we can do for them."

Billy angrily shook his head. "Look," he said sharply, "I'm responsible for that lady over there," he motioned toward Karen, "and I'm not putting her in harm's way. You come with me." He directed her. "We'll wait inside. I can't force you to keep them outside," he shot back at Nate and the others, "but at least make sure they aren't carrying anything. And lock the gate behind them! We don't need anymore uninvited visitors!"

He wheeled around and ushered Karen across the courtyard into one of the bunk areas. "Just stay the hell away from the door," he snapped at her, standing just inside it with his arms crossed. At first they could hear the conversation going on outside while the two Nigerian guards patted down all the visitors, checking them carefully for arms. Then the group walked away from them across the dirt courtyard toward the office and dining area, and they disappeared inside. Their words were now incomprehensible.

Karen knew Billy was incensed, but she didn't want to miss out on the conversation. "Are they in the dining area?" she asked meekly. "Because if they are, maybe we could go into the office. We could hear them talking from there, but they wouldn't be able to see us."

A few minutes had passed without incident, and Billy mulled over the idea. Finally he shrugged and nodded. He glanced around outside. "Alright, I'll walk ahead of you," he told her. Within seconds they had made their way into the little office galley and were sitting on the floor, listening to the story the Nigerians had come to tell.

"My name is Efan Bada," one of the visitors began. "I am thirty years old. I am married and have three children. Our village Ayuba is small. We have less than a hundred people, including children. There are a few Muslim families, and the rest of us are Christians. We are all friends, and there has never been any trouble between us. In fact last night, when the jihad warriors arrived, it was one of the Muslim women who came to my home to warn us."

"What are the warriors after?" Nate asked. "Do they have a specific complaint against you?"

"We are Christians, sir, as I told you before. The jihad warriors have orders to destroy Christian villages. As you know, they destroyed this village's church a year ago, and I'm sure you've heard about the burning of the entire congregation in Agalaba. And you, sir," he gestured toward Nate, "aren't you the one who was held captive by them?"

"Yes, I am."

"Then you understand that jihad is against all 'infidels.' And even good Muslims who don't agree with the jihadist mullahs are also called infidels. Many of the warriors are not true Africans but Arabs—some of them are from Khartoum. They pay Africans to fight with them and have armed and trained some African militias."

"Do you have any kind of defenses for your village?" One of the workers asked. "Any armed guards or weapons?"

Efan shook his head. "We believe that God's word tells us to love our enemies," he said quietly. "So we have not armed ourselves. But when we see our grandparents, our wives, and our children murdered, some of us are willing to defend our village. The problem is we have no arms."

"I would gladly fight them," a younger Ayuban said angrily. "I am not a violent man, but I love my family, and before God, I will not stand by and see them murdered!"

Nate nodded. "We heard that three elders of your church were killed last night. Is that true?"

"Yes, but not only three men. Two of them had wives, and both the wives were killed. One of them was pregnant, ready to give birth, and one of the warriors cut her belly open and killed the baby, too. Cut him up in several pieces. A boy."

Karen caught her breath and fought off a wave of nausea. She looked at Billy Jones, who was still standing in the doorway. His jaw tightened. "Bastards," he muttered. "Filthy bastards."

The construction team from San Diego seemed incredulous, despite the briefings they'd received before making the trip, "All this happened because you are Christians? That's the only reason?"

"Yes, that is the reason. Our elders were captured, tied up, blindfolded and shot dead—a bullet through their heads. This happened because they had preached the Gospel on Sunday in another village. They are...they *were* evangelists," Efan explained. "We are believers in Jesus Christ, and so we try to obey his Great Commission to go into the world and preach the gospel to all people. He also told us to forgive our enemies, and we want to do that, too. But today forgiveness is very hard."

"How could you ever forgive them, when...?" One of the Americans seemed unable to complete his thought. "After all that?"

"Only with God's help can we obey the Lord," the soft-spoken Nigerian man answered. "Someday soon we will begin to forgive. But today we are here to ask for your help in another matter. All the Christian villages in our area are in danger. You know about Ogbu, and we are grateful for the work you are doing here. And you know about the young mother who is going to be stoned for adultery."

"But she's not a Christian, is she?" Nate asked, wondering if he had that story straight.

"No, she is a Muslim. But she has broken Shari'a law. She is being made an example to the world, demonstrating the purity of Islam. Under that same law, our elders were accused of proselytism. But of course they were never arrested or tried. The decision to kill them is just a matter of jihad. The jihadists are at war with us because we are not Muslims and we are not willing to convert."

"So in their view it's convert or die?"

"Yes, sir. Convert or die."

"What do you want us to do for you?"

"We know that the American media has taken up the cause of Jumoke, the young mother who is sentenced to death. We also know that you are Christians, and that you are here to help rebuild the church. We want you to ask Christians everywhere to pray for us. Will you do that?"

"Of course. But is that all you want?"

"Not only that. We are asking if you will please tell our story to your American media. Maybe if the West hears about our village, someone will help us."

Karen felt even sicker. She recalled her own reaction, just a few weeks before, to stories that she'd read about Nigeria. She didn't believe it then, and she knew she wouldn't believe this story, either, unless she'd heard it with her own ears.

Worse yet, she thought, *if I hadn't got involved in this because of my work, and if I didn't know Nate, I don't even know if I'd care.*

After promising the little delegation from Ayuba that they would do what they could to get the story out, they gave them sandwiches and soft drinks. A couple of the American men prayed for them before they left on foot, refusing offers to be driven back. "You may need your vehicles," one of them said. "And we will be safe now. The warriors will not bother us again today."

Later on, Karen tried to make sense of what she'd heard. "Why don't they just convert to Islam and save their families?" she asked Nate. "And why don't they stop sending preachers out into other villages? That's just crazy! Why is their religion more important than their family's lives?"

Nate was slow to answer, hoping he could find the right words. "Karen," he finally said, "for serious Christians, faith isn't a religion. Christians believe that Jesus is a real, living person. They talk to him when they pray. They will tell you that he answers their prayers. They think his words are just as important now as they were 2,000 years ago. For them to deny being Christians would be like denying that they know or love a family member. They think their relationship with Jesus is worth dying for."

"So would you call yourself a 'serious' Christian?"

Nate didn't hesitate, even though he had a feeling Karen would disapprove of his answer. "I would, and I hope I'd have the courage to die for my faith if I had to."

Karen started to say, "But that's ridiculous!" She somehow stopped the words from leaving her lips. She thought about the little group of desperate Nigerians and the story they had told. Maybe she couldn't relate to their dedication, but they weren't crazy fanatics. They were humble and honest and courageous. She wasn't able to see things the way they did, but she wasn't going to allow herself to mock them or trivialize them. Or Nate either, for that matter.

Something brought to mind her mother and her prayer group. She remembered Sean Murray's promise to light candles for her at his church. She recalled Nate telling her about praying during his captivity. Suddenly, for some reason, she thought again about her father, recalling how Patrick Burke had believed until he drew his last breath that some things in life were worth dying for. What would he say about those villagers and their tenacious faith? Would he suggest that they compromise for their enemies? Even though she couldn't talk it over with him, she knew exactly what he would say.

* * *

When Alexis Schofield's phone rang, she almost screamed at it. She was trying to focus her attention on the two dozen emails that had come into her mailbox over the past hour, and had already been interrupted five times by panicky human rights activists who were dithering over various questions, making last minute changes in their itineraries, or seeking reassurance about safety and security during their upcoming trip to Nigeria.

Their meetings would be held at the Abuja Sheraton. It was a full service hotel with air conditioned rooms, a beauty and barber shop, a lounge, and a concierge "...as you can see from your information sheet," she added as often as possible. Of course none of them had actually read it. So she typed and typed and typed.

Yes, a press release had been sent to international media outlets about the conference and there would be a press conference upon their return to Washington D.C.

No, there would be no sightseeing in Nigeria.

Yes, Cipro would provide some protection from food poisoning.

No, there was no way they could visit Jumoke Abubakar in her prison cell. Even the Red Cross and Red Crescent hadn't been able to do that.

Now she almost barked into the receiver, "Alexis Schofield. Can I help you?"

"Yes, you can," said a radio-announcer type of voice that oozed charm. "As a matter of fact, you're just the person I wanted to talk to. This is Pastor Ken Wilson." He paused, as if Alexis should recognize his name. She didn't.

"I would like to be involved in your human rights delegation this weekend." He continued, "Nate Gregory is the young man from my church who was kidnapped, and as I'm sure you know, I was privileged—with God's help, of course—to play a strategic role in his release."

"Did you receive an invitation to the conference, Pastor...?"

"Pastor Ken. Ken Wilson. No, I didn't exactly receive an invitation per se. But I have some church members working down there nearby, rebuilding a sanctuary that the terrorists tore down. Nate's down there too. I plan to make a surprise visit there tomorrow, just to thank them, you know, for their hard work. Maybe we can get the local press involved—a little free publicity, you know. Anyway, the next day I thought maybe I'd drop in on the conference and see what's going on there."

Alexis sighed. The conference was supposed to be attended only by invitation. On the other hand, this man did have a connection with the situation. She vacillated. Emil Carlyle, her boss, was on a plane to London, so there was no way to check with him. "I'll call you back in an hour, Pastor, uh, Wilson," she said, checking the notes she was scribbling on a legal pad.

"What's the hold-up?" he asked, sounding a bit less charming.

"I have to check on accommodations."

"Oh, that's okay. I've already got a room in Abuja. Look, I'll just show up and see you there. Thank you for your time, Ms...uh, Scoville."

"Schofield," she corrected. She heard only a dial tone in response.

Alexis sighed and wondered if that particular call could be categorized as a red flag—trouble ahead, or a yellow flag—annoying but no big deal, or a false alarm.

She glanced at the computer screen, and two more emails had already popped up. With due respect to any other callers, she took the receiver off the hook so the voice mail system would pick up. And she finalized the arrangements. So far six media-savvy, highly motivated people had confirmed, including Nate Gregory. Two—one of them Emil—would arrive in Abuja tomorrow, and the other four would fly in on Thursday. As of now, the delegation was comprised of a Jewish immigration lawyer, a women's rights activist who taught at Dartmouth, a Senator from the Mid-West, an Anglican priest representing Lambeth Palace, a free-lance P.B.S. documentary producer, Emil, and Nate.

And now, "Pastor Ken." Alexis thought she remembered

hearing about his efforts to see Nate Gregory released by his abductors. Hadn't he taken credit for the young man's eventual freedom? Yes, she recalled, and she and Emil had shared their doubts about how the pastor of a Southern California megachurch could possibly put together a high risk, high tech hostage rescue.

"I don't suppose he'll by camera shy," she mumbled aloud. "But what the hell? If he generates any press coverage at all, he'll be doing us a favor."

Chapter Seven

The watchful eyes of two security guards scanned the long hallway from their positions at each end while David Levine unlocked the door of his Claridge's suite. Even at a distance he could see that the men's bodies were taut, braced defensively as if they expected an ambush. He couldn't help but notice that the closer the Nigerian operation grew, the edgier his protection personnel had become. When it came to living in harm's way, Levine always said he was either resigned or fearless, and he was never quite sure which.

But as the door swung open, and a gentle flow of warm air greeted him, as if on cue, his secure land line began to ring. The loud, jarring ringer startled Levine. He cursed under his breath, admitting to himself that maybe he was a little edgy, too. He picked up the receiver on the second ring. "8649," he said sharply, answering with the last four digits of his private phone number.

"*David, it's Sean Murray in D.C. I hope I'm not calling too late.*"

"Not at all, Sean. Just walked in the door. What can I do for you?"

"*Good. I'm glad I caught up with you. Actually, I thought you might be interested in some information I received this afternoon. I have a memo here from a source that I know personally and trust completely, although I can't reveal his name to you...*" Murray stopped momentarily, thumbing through some papers.

"I understand, of course. What have you heard?"

"Well, to summarize...it's seems that our esteemed former Secretary of State—the one with all the good friends in Riyadh..."

"Yes, I know very well who you mean."

"He has been in touch with the President today."

"Let me guess. About the plight of Phil Taylor?"

"Exactly. Apparently he was pleading for some sort of military intervention on behalf of his 'good friend and colleague' Mr. Taylor."

"Indeed. I'm sure they are *very* good friends. And maybe they should contact their other very good friends in Saudi to do whatever intervening needs to be done." Levine smiled grimly. "So what did the President have to say about Mr. Taylor?"

"He said, and I quote, 'Hell, no! We're not risking one American soldier's life for Phillip Taylor! He knows the rules. And he's on his own.' That's word for word, David."

Levine chuckled and shook his head. "Poor bastard. I'm glad the President has a handle on this, Sean. I have no interest in seeing Taylor dead, but he's dug his own grave. You know his buddy Ed Friedman called me up last week, begging me to rescue him."

"I can guess what you told him."

"In all honesty, I had no choice. Not that I'd do it anyway. But my men are stretched thin as it is—and there are always surprises in any operation. We don't need any more complications, especially in the south. We've got plenty to do in the north."

"That's right." Sean paused thoughtfully. *"There is plenty to do. And I'll tell you one thing—I sure as hell wish Karen Burke was out of there. Her mother has called me every day this week, worried sick about her daughter. And I can't say that I blame her."*

Levine exhaled heavily. "She's a nice girl, Sean. And we'll take good care of her. But the sooner she's back here in England, or better yet in Los Angeles, the happier we'll all be."

* * *

A cloud of dust billowed behind a battered Isuzu Trooper, as it rattled its way toward the compound. Nate watched as it neared the gate and was relieved to see a familiar face in the passenger seat—another volunteer from the San Diego church whose name he had momentarily forgotten.

"Who's that?" Karen asked suspiciously, walking quickly toward him with a cup of coffee in her hand.

"It's another construction guy from our church. I think somebody told me he was coming to replace me, since I have to leave with you for that conference in Abuja. Can't think of his name, though."

Karen watched as the vehicle maneuvered its way through the gate and sputtered a few times after the engine was turned off. "Another finely tuned African motor," Nate muttered. Karen shrugged and headed for her room, planning to pack everything up so she would be ready to leave whenever Billy and Nate decided it was time to go. She was zipping up the interior compartment of her largest bag when Nate pounded on the door outside.

"Karen, you need to come and see this."

"See what?"

"Curt—that's the guy who just got here—brought a mini-satellite dish with him and a small television. We just got BBC World News tuned in, and not a minute too soon. It looks like all hell is breaking loose around here."

Walking quickly toward the small office area with Karen alongside, Nate continued, "That incident this morning was just one of many. Apparently during Friday prayers last week, several fanatical mullahs in Northern Nigeria were preaching hate in their mosques, spewing out all sorts of violent threats against Christians and Jews. And they were talking about women, and how much trouble they can cause in the world." He gave Karen a look, waiting for her reaction.

Karen's face reflected her bewilderment. "Women? Why women? I don't get it. Why would they suddenly be talking about the evils of women?"

Nate had already heard the question asked and answered in the few minutes he'd watched the BBC broadcast. "They think maybe it's to prepare the way for Jumoke's execution. It's crazy, but who knows what they're really thinking?"

They crossed the outdoor courtyard, and were suddenly

able to hear some sort of automatic weapon pop-pop-popping in the distance. Billy Jones walked outside quickly to make a call on his cell phone. Once they went into the little office, they saw that Curt's newly connected TV was surrounded by silent, troubled workman. Karen watched for a few minutes, and then decided to download some of the reports from the Internet. She found two or three that were interesting, but when she tried to make copies, she realized that the printer was jammed. Frustrated, she tried to rip a handful of black-streaked paper out of the machine. In her impatience, she tore it in half.

"Damn it!" she spat out, trying to grab hold of the torn edges, and getting ink under her nails instead.

"Watch your language!" one of the men responded, and to Karen he didn't sound like he was kidding.

"What are you, the Taliban?" she snapped back. "No drinking, no swearing. You want me to cover my head, too? Maybe you belong in a mosque instead of a church. Maybe . . ."

"Karen, it's okay," Nate interrupted, sending a warning look toward the others. "Here's the story I wanted you to see."

Just then, another angle to the BBC's "Death in Nigeria" story began to unfold. Several women, two Westerners and, three Africans had been assaulted in various Northern villages. Two were dead, the rest were critically injured. According to the locals that had been interviewed, all of the victims were Christians.

Karen stared at the little television in disbelief. She knew by now that the stories she had first heard about the persecution of Nigerian Christians were all too true. But it still seemed strange to hear it coming out of a news broadcast.

"You'd better watch yourself, young lady," one of the men said, trying to lighten up the atmosphere. "Better show us some respect."

By then she was sorry she'd lost her temper. Meanwhile, although this man was clearly teasing her, she knew that the ones causing the trouble in Nigeria weren't kidding. And no matter what she thought about showing respect for men in general, at that moment she was clearly a woman in a hostile corner of a man's world. To make matters worse, she was fair, red-haired, and dressed in a Day-Glo green shirt.

Finally, after wrestling with the printer for several more minutes while avoiding eye contact with anybody in the room, Karen managed to print out two news reports, including excerpts from one mullah's Friday sermon. It had been read in a mosque not far from there which, she knew from her earlier research, had been built by Saudi Arabian Wahabists. She read and reread the text:

"The enemies of Islam," the cleric had said just days before, "have decided to distance the Muslims from their religion. Therefore, they have made the woman the most important weapon in this destruction. Ostensibly, they are showing her mercy and defending her rights. Many Muslim women have been misled by this, because of their ignorance about their religion, which sees the woman as the man's partner and as possessing rights and obligations appropriate to her nature and character.

"The Western woman leaves the home whenever she feels like it, goes where she wants, and wears what she wants, without her husband's permission. Furthermore, in some homes the situation has reached the point where the woman gives the orders, and that is that... It is no wonder, then, that Western women have become masculine. But what is far more amazing is that some of the men have become feminine. You can see some husbands with nothing in common with men except external appearance, while the woman calls the shots and controls the children's fate without asking her husband's opinion, even without consulting him or informing him of her intentions.

"Permitting women to leave the home, so that they rub up against men in the marketplaces and talk with people other than their chaperones with some even exposing parts of their bodies prohibited from exposure - are forbidden acts, a disgrace, and such things lead to destruction."

Karen was contemplating the implications of the mullah's inflammatory sermon when she heard shouting outside. Billy, who had returned to the room a few minutes before, was on his way back out the door before she could react.

"Stay put!" he told her as he rushed toward the gate.

Less than a minute later, he returned accompanied by a

Nigerian teenager who was seriously out of breath and perspiring heavily.

"He ran over here from one of the local villages with a message for us," Billy told the group.

"One of the women in our village," the boy said between breaths, "is married to a Muslim man. He told her that there is a plan to destroy this place because you are rebuilding a church."

"When?" Nate asked, speaking for them all.

"I do not know when because there are many other plans, too." The boy paused, drinking nearly an entire bottle of water before continuing. "There will be much killing in the days to come. This man told his wife, and she warned our elders. And they sent me to you."

Having completed his mission, the young man rested while someone brought him two more bottles of water.

Billy was outside talking on his cell phone again when a burst of gunfire exploded not so far away. It was answered by other shots. Nate was watching Billy carefully, and Karen moved just outside the door to stand next to him.

"Are you scared?" he asked quietly.

Karen's face was pale but calm. "I'm not that scared right now," she said. "But I am convinced that we need to get out of here and back to Abuja. When do you think we're going to leave?"

"I'm ready now," Nate said. "It's up to Billy."

"I'm ready, too," she nodded. Both of them watched Billy pace across the dirt courtyard, back and forth, as he carried on a long conversation with somebody, somewhere—an anonymous person that apparently knew more about their plans than they did.

"What about the others?" Karen asked. "Will they leave, too?"

"Right now they're saying they'll tough it out. But they haven't had much time to think about it, and I'm not sure that's a good idea, anyway. If those warriors arrive, they'll be nearly defenseless, except for the two Nigerian guards."

When Billy returned to the room, Nate asked, "So what's the plan? Are we ready to roll?"

"Not yet." Billy shook his head. "I'm waiting for a call back. One of my guys is checking out the road to Abuja. We need to put together all the information we can before we start out."

"Are you worried about roadblocks or ambushes or bombs or what?"

"Yeah. All of the above." Billy smiled. "I'll let you know as soon as I hear something."

"We're ready to go now," Karen said. "David Levine told us to get out, remember? So we rushed around and packed everything as fast as we could."

"Welcome to my world." Billy nodded. "Hurry up and wait. I'll keep you posted, okay?"

They silently turned back toward the television just in time to see Phillip Taylor's face on the screen, with a banner that read "American Hostage in Nigeria."

Nate caught his breath. It was the first he'd heard about Phil Taylor's kidnapping, and it hit him like a clenched fist pounding into his stomach. "Oh my God," he murmured, staring at the slightly blurry face of a blue-eyed man wearing a Dallas Cowboys cap. "When did this happen?"

As if to answer his question, the reporter described the oilman's abduction and the surrounding events. Another picture of Taylor filled the screen. This one was taken from an Al-Jazeera video, which World News had refused to air "for humanitarian reasons." Taylor was clearly bleeding from a head wound. One eye was swollen shut, and he looked dazed and terrified.

Nate glanced around the room at the others. "Did you know about this?" he asked Billy.

"Yeah, I knew. I figured you saw the story online when it broke."

"I haven't been online for a day or two," Nate said bleakly, staring at the TV, his insides roiling. "And nobody told me."

"Nobody wanted to," one of the men said quietly.

It was quiet in the room as the workmen avoided each other's eyes. Karen stared at Billy, who glanced outside. "I guess none of us wanted to think much about it," Karen explained. "But anyway, it's an oilman, not a missionary, and it happened in the South not in the North. He was clearly where he shouldn't have been."

"I think we're all where we shouldn't be," Nate commented. "Things are falling apart here. I should never have asked you to come to Nigeria, Karen. Maybe I shouldn't have come myself."

Nate sat down cross-legged on the floor in front of the little TV. No one said another word. And when Billy Jones' phone rang again, nobody moved. "Yeah, so what'd you find out?" They all heard him say as he walked outside and started pacing again.

All the rebuilding work that had been moving forward so efficiently had come to a standstill. Nearly everyone at the compound was crammed in the little office, transfixed by the BBC coverage, which was punctuated by occasional bursts of gunfire outside. The two Nigerians, who had been serving as guards along with Billy, were both on high alert. One was crouched on the roof of an outbuilding, looking across the area from north to south, east to west. One hand was carefully positioned on his AK47, and the other held a pair of binoculars against his eyes. The other guard was stationed at the gate. He, too, had his gun at the ready. Those two warriors knew better than anyone else just how unpredictable the situation really was.

For a few moments, a global news summary turned viewers' attention to an earthquake that had just taken a dozen lives in China, followed by a breaking news brief about a ferry that had just disappeared in some foggy Philippine waterway. But before long the blood-red "Nigeria Uprising" banner was back at the top of the screen, and yet another report from a mosque was being broadcast live from Abuja.

"A sermon by a radical mullah in a Northern Nigerian mosque has called for jihad among the local population. It has drawn criticism from human rights groups, one of which—Humanity.com—is about to begin a conference at a nearby hotel. In this exclusive report, we have captured on video a portion of the mullah's message to his followers. You will hear it translated into English."

The anchorwoman's pretty faced was replaced by shaky, shadowy footage of a wild-eyed Arabic looking cleric, his fist clenched in the air. His words, spoken just miles away from the compound where Nate, Karen, Billy and the others were watching, were chilling. To Karen, who was by now caught somewhere between curiosity and craven fear, the "sermon" was almost unbelievable. "Surreal," she said to herself. "He's like a caricature."

"The true meaning of the word 'terror' as used by the media," the mullah shouted, "is jihad for the sake of Allah! Jihad is the peak of Islam! Moreover, some of our wisest clerics see jihad as the sixth pillar of Islam. Jihad—whether jihad of defense of Muslims and of Islamic lands, or jihad aimed at spreading the religion—is the pinnacle of terror, as far as the enemies of Allah are concerned.

"The Mujaheed who goes out to attain a martyr's death or victory and returns with booty is a 'terrorist' as far as the enemies of Allah are concerned. But for us, he is a valiant jihad warrior! That is why the true believer must not use this word 'terrorist.' Speak only of jihad, oh believers! And take your part in the battle! The kind of 'terror' that Islamic religious law permits is terrifying the cowards, the hypocrites, the secularists, and the rebels by imposing punishments—according to the religious law of Allah!"

* * *

In her damp, dark prison cell, Jumoke held her infant daughter against her breast and wept silently. Little Abeo seemed smaller than ever, and her feverish body was trembling again. For more than a day, she had not drawn any milk from Jumoke's breasts, and had been unable to swallow the smashed bananas that Jumoke had frantically tried to feed her.

"Abeo, Abeo, Abeo..." Jumoke repeated in a sing-song voice. "Please try to eat. Try, try, try." The child did not respond to her mother's voice, although after a few minutes, her trembling stopped.

Jumoke rocked the child, her tears dripping against the tiny, nearly bald head. She watched the baby closely, hoping for a sign of hope—a glimpse of recognition, a cry of hunger, maybe even a smile.

Deep inside, where she usually kept the truth hidden from even herself, Jumoke knew that Abeo was dying. She could feel the shallowness of the child's breathing. The weaker her daughter became, the more she felt as if she, too, were dying. And in reality, she soon would be. Once Abeo was gone, Jumoke's life would be finished.

"Mama, please come!" Jumoke cried out suddenly, yearning for her mother's embrace, and feeling like a child herself. Sweat poured down her face, mingling with her tears. She, too, was shaking all over, not from illness but from despair. Just as life was slowly draining out of Abeo, the last traces of hope were slipping away from Jumoke's spirit.

"Mama!" she wailed. "Mama!"

"Shut up in there!" a man's voice barked. He pounded his fist on wood somewhere.

Jumoke caught her breath. Sobs racked her body. She felt utterly abandoned in her fear and grief, forgotten by everyone. The nineteen years that lay behind her seemed as insubstantial as a mirage on a scorching Nigerian highway. All that lay before her was death. And it would not be the silent, numbing death that Abeo would surely pass into, but a violent explosion of pain, an unimaginable assault.

Abeo began to tremble again, and Jumoke turned her attention back to the ailing infant. "Abeo, Abeo..." she began the chant once more, vaguely aware that the afternoon light outside was gradually fading into another sleepless night.

* * *

Karen sat on the floor next to Nate, watching him as closely as she could without being obvious. He was lost in thought. She wanted to reach out to him somehow, but she felt inhibited by the men around her. It wasn't clear to her, anyway, that she could venture into the unknown territory where his mind had carried him. His thoughts were suspended somewhere between his own hostage cell and the nightmare that was unfolding for Phil Taylor in the Niger Delta.

A phone rang and everyone jumped. One of the men answered and handed it to Karen. "It's for you," he said.

"Hello? Karen Burke speaking."

"*Hi, Ms. Burke. This is Alexis Schofield in Washington. I'm the organizer of the Humanity.com conference.*"

"Yes, I know," Karen said. "I remember your name. They were just talking about your conference on BBC World News."

"*You're kidding,*" Alexis said, sounding worried. "*Why?*"

"Because of all the problems in Northern Nigeria right now."

"*I haven't heard anything, but I've been rushing around trying to get myself on a plane. Still, there hasn't been anything on CNN that I've seen.*"

"BBC usually gets there first," Karen pointed out. "In any case, Nate and I hope to get back to Abuja later today."

"*That's good. I wanted to let you know that two of our other participants have already arrived at the Sheraton. Let me give you their names and room numbers. Feel free to contact them when you arrive. I should be there tomorrow afternoon.*"

Karen wrote down the names and thanked Alexis for the call. She clicked the end button thoughtfully, a little surprised that there was no news about Nigeria in the U.S. She could hear gunfire outside. Not many hours before, she'd been dangerously close to a gunman herself. She glanced at Nate, who was by then standing in the doorway with his arms folded, staring blankly at the sky.

"Nate?"

He focused his eyes on her, trying to bring his mind back into real time.

"Any idea when we're leaving? I just got a call from Humanity.com. A couple more participants in the seminar are already at the Sheraton. Maybe we should ask Billy."

Billy was, meanwhile, sitting on a bench with his cell phone in his hand. He looked like he was waiting for something.

"Any idea when we are going to head out?" Nate asked.

Billy shook his head and motioned toward the phone. "Soon as I get the green light," he answered.

"What's the hold up?"

"Double-checking the road," he said. "There's some activity close to Abuja, and we're trying to find out if we should find an alternate route or take our chances with it."

"What kind of activity?" Karen interjected.

Billy stared at her with a look on his face that might have meant, "What kind of activity do you think?" Instead, he smiled, "I'll explain everything once I have all the information I need."

Karen and Nate exchanged glances. "Do you have voice mail on that world phone?" Nate suddenly asked.

Karen reacted with alarm. "Yes, and I should have checked it an hour ago! I ought to be carrying it around, just in case."

She hurried into her room, then reappeared, punching the keypad frantically. There were two messages, one from a restricted number, and the other from her mother.

She listened to the first message, which was from Sean Murray. *"Karen, I just want you to know that I'm keeping tabs on your situation there, and have just spoken to our friend in London. His people are well aware of your situation, and he has promised to make sure you're safe—you and Nate. I'm in touch with your mother, too. The main thing is that I don't want you to worry. We all agree, however, that you should get back to Abuja as quickly as possible. I'll be in touch."*

She looked thoughtfully at Nate. "Things must be falling apart pretty quickly. That was Sean Murray. I think he was trying to calm me down. Trouble is, he sounded even more uptight than we are."

Billy's phone rang. He flipped it open, sprang to his feet, and started pacing again. He said very little. Most of his conversation consisted of "Uh-huh," "I see," and "Right." After several minutes, he closed the phone and gestured toward the Land Rover Karen had arrived in. "Let's load up," he said.

Then, after an appraising look at Karen he added, "Do you have a scarf you could put over your head?"

She stared at him blankly. "A scarf?"

"Yeah. A scarf. In fact, there are a couple of things. First, today you'll want to put on something a little less colorful than what you're wearing. Do you own any black shirts? And you'd better cover your hair, too. We don't want to take any chances."

It was, as usual, a hot day. And now, besides having to put on a long sleeved black turtleneck, to add insult to injury, she would have to tie a pashmina around her hair—wrapping wool and silk around her head in 100 degree heat was not her idea of a good time. By now, however, she was no longer annoyed. She meekly went to her room, changed clothes, unfolded the shawl she'd brought for dinners out, and wrapped it around her long, curly hair. When she reappeared, Nate looked apprehensive. Billy nodded his approval. The Nigerian driver, who had a pistol sticking out of his pants, gave her the thumbs up and tossed their bags into the back of the vehicle.

"See you at home," Nate said quietly to Ryan and the others, shaking hands with two or three of the workmen. "You guys need to get out of here, too, you know."

"You'll be in our prayers," Ryan told Nate, who was buckling his seat belt. "Keep us in yours, too."

"Don't take foolish chances," Nate said. "Take it from me. I learned the hard way."

By then the vehicle was already backing up. The gate swung open, and the Rover rocked back and forth as it made its way across the ruts in the road and headed for the highway.

Billy, in the front passenger seat, had his AK47 resting diagonally across his chest and a small Russian Makarov pistol tucked into his waistband. He punched redial on his phone and waited only a couple of seconds. "We're on our way," he said. "I'll get back to you after the first check point."

Karen looked at Nate, who was buckled in behind the driver, staring out the side window. His jaw was set, his face tense. He couldn't have been more distant. His mind was still on Phil Taylor, and his intuition told him that the Texan was enduring agonies far beyond anything he had experienced or even imagined.

Partly for his sake and partly for her own, Karen reached over and touched Nate's hand, then slipped her own around it. As he turned toward her, the look of near anguish on his face melted into a faint smile. He took a deep breath, then exhaled it forcefully. "This could be a wild ride," he told her, pressing his hand against hers.

She noticed Billy Jones' reflection in the passenger side mirror and saw that he was wearing a dangerously determined expression on his face—a look she'd never seen before. *He is one battle-hardened man,* she told herself. *And thank God for that.* She tightened the pashmina around her neck with her free hand, and smiled back at Nate. "Looks like you may have to add another chapter to your book before this is over."

"As long as it has a happy ending," he said, with only the trace of a smile remaining on his lips.

* * *

When her telephone rang, Mischa glanced at the clock. 10:00 PM, Tel Aviv time. She laid aside the book she had been re-reading—a murder mystery by Batya Gur—and took a sip of white Bordeaux. She had been comfortably propped up on a half a dozen down pillows, wrapped in a silk dressing gown, enjoying a second glass of her favorite wine. Now she squinted at the caller ID on her secure phone—the special line her colleagues had installed for her. It was fairly late, and she wasn't expecting to hear from anyone.

The single word "unknown" appeared on the id window after the second ring. She momentarily debated about answering, then gave in to her curiosity. Intuition—or wishful thinking—told her it would be an interesting call. And it was.

She answered with a crisp, "Good Evening."

"Mischa. It's David. How are you?"

"My God! David! It's been so long. How are you?" Feeling suddenly worried, she added, "Are you all right?"

David Levine chuckled. *"I've never been better. But, far more importantly, how are you? How is my favorite Sabra?"*

She laughed softly. "I think you must have a number of favorite Sabras, David. But as for me, I am well. It has been so long since we've spoken I was sure that you'd forgotten my phone number. But then you've always been able to find me when you wanted to, haven't you?"

"Yes, Mischa, I always know where you are. And I hope you know how to reach me if you need to."

"If I need to, of course," Mischa said carefully. "But there must be more than friendly feelings behind this call. Otherwise, I'm sure we would have been in touch long before."

There was a brief hesitation. *"As much as I still delight in hearing your voice again, Mischa, yes. There is more. This is a secure line, as always?"*

"As always," she said with a slight smile. "Nothing has changed."

"I have something for you to do, Mischa, something that will prove to be well worth your time. And even if you are unable to complete the task, I will make sure that your efforts are well compensated. But I must ask you something rather delicate."

Now Mischa laughed out loud, and her laugh was hearty and infectious. "David, my friend, when did you ever worry about asking delicate questions? If I recall, the more delicate the question, the more effective your questioning techniques."

Levine laughed too. *"All right, all right. Touché. But this is exceptionally delicate, especially these days. Are you ready?"*

Mischa was still laughing. David had always made her laugh in spite of everything. "Yes, I am ready. What is your delicate question?"

"Are you willing to do your best work with...a black Muslim?"

Mischa was silent for a moment. "I suppose that depends on who it is you're talking about. An American Black Muslim? Do you mean someone who is part of Farrakhan's organization?"

"No, no. Not an American. This man is an African. He is the governor of a Nigerian state, Mischa. Abuja State to be exact. And he is posing certain problems in that area."

"Oh yes. I know about him and I've heard about some of those problems. He replaced a good man, didn't he? Less than a year ago?"

"That's right. The last governor was a trustworthy and sensible politician who worked overtime to keep Abuja free from radicalism. And he did well—Abuja was once a stable state—an oasis among all the other bastions of Shari'a law in the north. But just to prove that no good deed goes unpunished, the Nigerian President appointed the governor to serve in his cabinet. Now the man is not only sidelined and virtually powerless to influence anything, but to make matters worse, he's been replaced by this criminal."

"I see," Mischa said thoughtfully. "So how soon do you need me to go to work?" Knowing Levine well, she glanced at the clock and not the calendar.

They both spoke the word at the same time: "Yesterday." And again they laughed.

"Now let me ask you a delicate question, David. How much are you willing to pay me?"

"More than ever before," Levine immediately replied. *"It is an urgent situation, and I have just learned that he has a taste for, shall we say, foreign women. If my information is correct—and I know you will verify everything yourself—it will be easier than anything you've ever done. And, as I said, far more lucrative."*

Mischa thought for a moment. "Shall I leave tomorrow?"

"What about tonight?"

"Impossible. I will check some things and call you back. Give me his name and address. I'll let you know within the hour."

"Good. That's good news, Mischa. Let me give you the number for my direct line. That way you can reach me immediately. Anytime, Mischa. As always."

Chapter Eight

Inside the Land Rover not a word had been spoken for more than half an hour as the big vehicle roared toward Abuja. Everyone knew that each passing minute brought them closer to the first roadblock, and no one was looking forward to that unavoidable obstacle, or the two others that came after it. Billy Jones was tense, but not because of that. He knew that the stationary Federal Republic of Nigeria roadblocks were the least of his worries. It was the non-stationary ones—the haphazard ones thrown across the road illegally by local thugs or, worse, jihadists—that were the most dangerous.

Penetrating the silence like a scream in a dark room, Karen's world phone suddenly rang. She gasped involuntarily. Nate muttered something under his breath. Billy Jones' face hardened even more.

"Karen Burke," she answered, trying to keep her voice even.

"Karen, it's Sean Murray. Are you on your way to Abjua?"

"Yes, we've been driving for about 45 minutes," she told him, checking her watch. "So far, so good," she added.

"I'm glad to hear that," Murray said evenly. *"I do have a little information for Nate. Would you mind handing the phone to him?"*

"Hold on."

"Wait a second, Karen, one more thing first. Your mom has talked to me several times..."

"Oh God, I hope she's not a basket case." Karen started to apologize. "I'm sorry if she's being a pest."

"No, no, she's not at all. I told her to keep in touch with me.

She just wanted me to tell you that she and Dr. Martin are praying for you."

Karen paused, trying to process the still-strange information that her mother and her doctor were, well, friends. "Thanks, Sean," she said after a moment. "Give them my love. Anything else? Okay, here's Nate."

Nate looked at her quizzically when she handed him the phone. "Sean Murray," she explained.

"Hello?"

"Hello, Nate," Sean said. "We haven't met, but of course we know each other anyway. I have a little news about someone you know—Ken Wilson, who I understand to be the pastor of the church you attend, right?"

"Yes, that's right." Nate said, frowning slightly. "Is he all right?"

"Well, he's in good health as far as I know," Murray began, *"but he may be trying to contact you. And if he does, based on what I know from the people I work with, I would advise you not to arrange any contact with him."*

"Not to arrange contact?"

"Right. No contact."

"Okay. That's fine. But why would he be trying to get in touch with me anyway?"

Sean tried to keep the cynicism out of his voice as he explained, *"You're aware of Phillip Taylor's kidnapping and the circumstances surrounding it?"*

"Yes, I heard today that he's an oilman from Texas, and he was trying to reopen a refinery in the Nile Delta when some militants abducted him."

"That's correct, Nate. But it seems that Ken Wilson has it in his mind that he can negotiate with Phillip Taylor's kidnappers."

"Why? That's absurd!"

"Well, yes, those of us that work in these areas are clearly concerned, not only about his safety, but about the complications he might inadvertently cause."

"That's interesting," Nate said, "because he has been saying that he was responsible for my release from captivity. I've never been sure that his claims are entirely true, although I have no proof either way."

Sean didn't hesitate. *"It's not true, Nate. He had very little to do with your release other than bringing your captivity to the attention of those who were able to assist you."*

"So why would he want to contact me now?" Nate asked.

"He's trying to get to the human rights conference in Abuja, and we hear that once he's announces his intentions to the press, he will go to Port Harcourt to meet with a radical Islamist mullah at a mosque down there. In any case, Nate, I advise you to steer clear. If he gets as far as Abuja, which I hope to God he doesn't, don't let him drag you into the Taylor situation."

Nate was speechless. "What's his point?" he finally said.

"I can't give you an answer about motives," Sean replied evenly, *"but I can tell you that he's out of his league. With any luck, he'll get turned back when he tries to get into the country. We've alerted their immigration officials about the situation, but we can't be sure as to how they will handle our request. In any case, the last thing we need is another American hostage in Nigeria."*

* * *

Joe Brac was making his way from the shooting range he and his men had set up at the Feeding the Hungry compound. Leaving the others behind to finish up a practice session and heading to their Quonset hut, he glanced up at a Cessna that was droning in the distance. Whose was it and why was it there? His sense of danger had increased dramatically in the last 48 hours, thanks to repeated conversations with David Levine, Sean Murray, and his other contacts in the region. He reminded himself that 99% of small aircraft are harmless, but he kept his eye on it anyway.

He unlocked the door and walked into the office, glancing at the board where someone had scribbled a to-do list. Irritation rippled through him. Why hadn't the notes been erased? He tried to remember who had made the list in the first place, looking around to see if there was evidence of anyone having been in the office.

Secrecy is safety, he thought, *and safety means survival. Somebody should have...*

Just then his cell phone rang, interrupting his thoughts. "Feeding the Hungry," he answered.

"David Levine calling," a woman's voice announced. *"One moment please."*

"Hello, Joe," Levine said after a short delay. *"I have some new information for you. I've added a new team member to your group."*

"I see," Brac said, not especially pleased. It was true that they had lost a valuable team member when Rambo had been killed in the Phillip Taylor ambush. But at this late date, Brac hadn't really planned on replacing him.

"This is unorthodox," Levine began, *"but the person I've chosen is well prepared to deal with one specific issue—that is, the matter of the Governor."*

"Great. Who is he?"

"Actually, I'm talking about a woman. A beautiful woman, I might add."

"A woman. Okay..."

"Like me, she is an Israeli. She has worked for me several times before, and she is not only effective but almost completely untraceable."

"I see," Brac murmured numbly. "And she will be dealing only with that one specific matter?"

"That's correct, although she is very capable in every other way, too."

"Will she work alone?"

"Yes, she works best alone."

As if a dimmer switch had been gradually turned on, a face began to reveal itself, brightening in Joe's memory. *Surely not,* he told himself. *Impossible.*

"Her name, at least for our purposes, is Mischa."

"Mischa," Brac repeated quietly, with a growing sense of disbelief. "Does she have a last name?"

"Yes, but we won't be using it. She is on her way to you now and should be there around 21:00. Please brief her and make her aware of our timetable. Provide any help you can. She'll call you when she reaches Lagos. I've given her both of your contact numbers."

"I look forward to meeting her," Brac said quietly. "Sounds

like she'll make our job a lot easier. Thank you."

"Give her my regards," Levine said before ending the conversation.

Afterward, Joe looked absently around the cluttered room, which was littered with empty water bottles, rucksacks, a computer, a roll of duct tape, and an assortment of headphones, cords, and a digital camera. He tried to envision Mischa walking through the door, glamorous as a diva and deadly as a hidden dagger. He could hardly imagine such a thing.

Years before Kate, there had been Mischa. The sultry, silken nights in Jerusalem hadn't been many. Their intense interludes could never have lasted forever, but to those days, it still seemed as if it had been far too short. Her face, her touch, her body still haunted him. She, too, had been a warrior. And the highly combustible mixture of drive and energy they brought together had exploded into heat, light, and shock waves of deep pleasure that he would never forget.

Joe caught his breath involuntarily, just thinking about it.

With some difficulty, he brought his mind back to Mischa's professional tactics—the ones he knew about, anyway. They bore a striking resemblance to the style of "special assignments" Levine had just described. Could there be two women with the same nationality and *nom de geurre?*

If so, Brac promised himself, *Levine will never know we've met before. And as for Kate,* he thought, resisting a surge of anxiety and reaching for his cell phone, *she'll never know we've met at all. Come to think of it, I'd better call her right about now. If I don't, I'll have the devil to pay when I get home.*

* * *

The Land Rover increased its speed immediately after passing through the second of three government checkpoints. For such a big vehicle, it accelerated with a surprising surge of power, and before long the landscape outside the windows was little more than a blur of green and brown. To the relief of everyone in the car, their passage through the checkpoints had been uneventful. The next one was just about six miles outside

Abuja, and once they had passed it, the rest of the trip would be, or at least should be, trouble free. Forty-five minutes, give or take, and the worst was over.

For now, Billy Jones was on high alert, and nothing escaped his eyes. They systematically scanned the horizon and its periphery, back and forth, like a machine. He was almost quivering with tension. And the more the others relaxed, thanks to the ease with which they'd progressed, the more vigilant—and silent—Jones became.

All at once he broke his silence with two staccato words: "Holy Shit!"

Everyone in the truck's eyes fixed on the road and became instantly aware of unusual movement ahead of them. Clouds of dust rolled upward as two trucks pulled diagonally across the highway, and a handful of men scrambled around the trucks, moving barricades into position. They were a ragtag bunch with filthy looking clothes and unshaved faces. They carried a mixed bag of weapons, and ammo belts hung loosely across some of their bodies. This was no regular military squad, but most likely a group of renegades or criminals setting up to prey on the innocent.

Billy pushed some coordinates into his cell phone, sent them in a text message, then flipped the phone shut and ordered Nate and Karen, "Get down on the floor. Now! Move!"

"Oh my God!" Karen screamed as she and Nate unfastened their seatbelts and slid into an awkward crouch position behind the front seats. Karen put her hands over her head and closed her eyes. So tightly was she wedged into the seat behind Billy that she could hardly get her breath. Her body was rigid, frozen with fear.

"Keep your heads down!" Billy barked. "Stay out of sight."

Karen could feel her heart pounding in her ears. She was conscious of every breath she took. The problem was that the more she thought about breathing the more difficult it became. She thought she was suffocating and was desperate to move, to stretch out her torso so her lungs could expand.

"I can't breathe," she whispered to Nate. "I can't breathe!"

Nate put his right hand on the back of Karen's neck. For some reason he felt calmer than he would have expected himself to be. "Lord, help us," he said quietly. Strangely comforted, it occurred to him that after his months of captivity, he was grateful not to be alone in the dark. Whatever was happening here was definitely bad, but he intuitively sensed that he'd been through worse.

Seconds later the Land Rover braked abruptly, and the passengers were violently rocked forward and back. Nate pressed his fingers more firmly against the nape of Karen's neck, hoping to console her. They rolled to a stop.

"Get out of the truck," the leader shouted in heavily accented English. Billy focused on the imposing threat that faced them on the road. This group reminded him of the *technicals* he had come in contact with in Somalia—lawless groups that had roamed the country and raped or pillaged everything that crossed their path. Billy knew he had no time to ponder or second guess. He had to act quickly and decisively.

He crisply ordered the driver, "When I say 'go,' get out of the car and stand behind the door with your body and weapon hidden. Wait for my move. You got it?"

"Yes. Got it," answered the driver. Billy opened his door and stepped out. The driver did the same. Billy kept his weapon hidden behind the door and stared intently at the leader of the group. The man had the kind of cold, lifeless eyes that reflect too many years of merciless killings. Billy had seen that look before. He knew in his gut that there could only be one ending to this standoff. He also noticed that the other troublemakers were standing around a little too nonchalantly, probably under the influence of ganja, waiting for their leader's next move.

Billy returned his look to the leader and watched him closely. Briefly, almost indecipherably, he saw a flicker of change in those dead eyes.

Time to boogie, Billy thought. "Take 'em down!" he shouted.

Immediately he and the driver opened fire. On both sides of the truck, the command was answered by a burst of gunfire, and by a symphony of abrupt grunts, screams, and moans as the leader and several bad guys were propelled to the ground.

As he and the driver both jumped back into the Rover, Billy shouted, "Turn around. Back the way we came."

The driver shifted into reverse, then made a U-turn, fishtailing wildly as he floored the accelerator. Another burst of gunfire from Billy's gun exploded, accompanied by the pinging crash of metal shredding metal as a poorly aimed hail of bullets pounded into the front of the truck.

Karen was feeling faint and nauseous, still unable to breathe. Panicked, she raised herself back up into the seat, gasping for air. She opened her eyes and looked back. Five or six men lay on the road behind them, and she saw a row of bullets from Billy's automatic weapon cut an angry swath out of a barricade and tear the face off another crouching African. Only one man was left standing.

"Get the hell down, God damn it!" Billy roared at her. She stretched herself across the back seat just as the rear window shattered. Glass rained down on Nate and Karen and a blast of outside air rushed around them.

"Slow down," Billy told the driver. "I need to take out one more. We don't need any witnesses whining about this."

Two more bursts of deafening gunfire, and the last man fell, his midsection torn apart. With that, the driver hit the gas and they were all but airborne. Karen shook with fear, barely aware that the deafening sound of Billy's gun had stopped. By now the Rover was hurtling along the road at breakneck speed on its way back the compound.

"There's nobody left to follow us," Billy told the driver as he scanned his side mirror. "But keep it floored anyway."

"I don't think there's anybody left alive," the driver said, searching the scene behind them in the rear-view mirror. All the shooting had stopped. The assailants lay dead behind them, each in a pool of blood.

As the driver raced toward the last government checkpoint they had passed through before the ambush, he waved frantically at the guards there, who remembered him and motioned the car through without stopping it. With that official blockade between them and any surviving terrorists, the driver slowed down a little.

"We may need the petrol later," he explained to Billy.

"You're right." Billy nodded, turning toward the back seat. "All right, you can get up. But, Karen, why didn't you stay down? You're damned lucky to be alive!"

She tried to explain, but her voice was too shaky for words. "I'm sorry," was all she could muster as she sat up and looked around. "I'm so sorry."

Nate stretched himself back into an upright position. There was glass everywhere, and they both moved in slow motion. Nate was stiff and shaken, but still relatively calm. Almost by instinct, he reached for Karen. "Close your eyes," he told her. He carefully brushed some fragments of glass out of her hair and off her shoulders. Then he pulled her over next to him and enfolded her in his arms.

They examined their wounds as best they could. All of them were minor—some nicks in the back of Nate's neck were bleeding, and Karen had a few cuts on her fingers. He could feel her body quaking in his arms.

"Are you okay?" he whispered.

Seconds passed before she answered him, "Not really."

"We'll be fine now," he reassured her, holding her as tightly as he could, willing her to be calm. She took a long, shaky breath and shook her head. She wasn't sure that she'd ever be fine again. She noticed that the sun had dipped between two hills in the west, leaving a faint peach tint in the sky. The long day was nearly over, and they had somehow survived it. But they were far from safe.

"So what was that all about?" Nate asked Billy.

"That was all about us trying to get to Abuja, and some bastards thinking they could stop us."

"But why?"

"Why the hell not?" Billy said bitterly. "You're Americans. You've been living on a Christian compound, rebuilding a church they burned down. Didn't you hear what that boy told us? They wanted to shed blood today. Your blood. My blood. Stay or go, they had us in their crosshairs. Kill a car full of Americans and they've made a statement about their superiority."

"And what happens now?" Nate asked. "Do we stay there tonight? Do we try to leave tomorrow? What are our options?"

"Soon as we get back inside the gate, we're going to hunker down for the night. I'll talk to my people and see what our options are tomorrow."

"Like what?"

"Like no more questions till tomorrow."

Billy Jones had killed several men in the brief course of their journey. It wasn't the first killing he'd ever done, nor by any stretch of the imagination would it be the last. Still he didn't take it lightly, and had more than enough reasons for feeling agitated and annoyed. He'd seen ten different ways they all could have been killed. They were damned lucky, as far as he could tell. And he was deeply disturbed, not only by the action they'd seen, but by the impossibility of thinking not only for himself but for a couple of clueless, helpless civilians.

Yeah it's my job, he silently reminded himself. *And yeah, it pays well. Very well. But for God's sake...*

* * *

As the light dimmed in her fetid cell, Jumoke found herself staring at Abeo's bare feet and legs. Her mind seemed to be playing tricks on her. Were those tiny legs changing color? She looked carefully, aware that the sunlight was quickly dimming outside the small, barred window. Still, where the infant's skin had once been deep brown, there was now an ashen tone. Or was there? The light was dim, she wasn't sure, but it seemed to begin at Abeo's feet, and was moving upward toward her knees. One thing she was sure about: despite the heat, the baby's feet were cold to the touch.

Jumoke shivered, feeling chilled herself, wondering if some strange spirit had overtaken her baby's body. What could it be? The child's breathing had been labored for days. She was used to that by now and it no longer troubled her. It was only, she told herself, because Abeo was working so hard to get well.

Once more the little body began to tremble, and once again Jumoke held her daughter tightly against her breast, silently pleading with Allah, the merciful, the compassionate, to strengthen Abeo's body, to allow her to live. Maybe then Jumoke, too, might live, and be a good mother.

Abeo's breathing seemed to be slowing, and in an odd way it seemed less urgent. She inhaled, exhaled then rested;

breathed then rested. Something about the change in rhythm calmed the young mother. The child's trembling stopped and her breathing slowed even more. Jumoke waited expectantly for each new breath. Inhale. Exhale. Breaths came and went, came and went.

Then, finally, there was nothing. Abeo didn't breathe again. Jumoke watched and waited, but there was no movement. The tiny body seemed suddenly lighter, as if it could float away— out of her arms, out the tiny window, upward on the breeze, weightless as a chick's down.

As Abeo's spirit drifted away, Jumoke's best dreams died, too. In the harsh reality of the prison cell, Jumoke was at last completely alone. There was no longer another soul to share her sorrow, to buoy her wild hopes. She was abandoned by the child to whom she had once given life. And her own existence, which her little daughter had protected, would soon drift away, too. Just as Abeo had flown away, soon Jumoke would be gone, too.

Survival instincts told her, however, that she should tell no one of the death. So Jumoke clung to the lifeless baby, holding her close as ever, knowing that for every moment the guards believed Abeo to be alive, that she—Jumoke—would live that much longer. She pretended to nurse. She sang a lullaby. She talked baby talk. She even laughed aloud as her imagination animated Abeo's empty face with a responsive smile.

From months to weeks to days, by now Jumoke's survival had narrowed itself to hours and minutes. It was just a matter of time until the guards discovered the truth. Until they called the judge on the telephone. Until he said the words—"In the name of Allah, Most Gracious, Most Merciful. All praise and thanks are due to Allah, and peace and blessings be upon his messenger—today the sentence of death by stoning against Jumoke Abubakar, who has committed the sin of adultery, will be enforced."

* * *

As they approached the compound, all four of the passengers in the Land Rover stiffened a little, expecting, as they say, the unexpected. Karen, who was becoming more and more miserable about her poor performance, was still firmly encircled by Nate's arm. She was ashamed of her weakness, embarrassed by the panic that had gripped her.

Billy Jones was still staring out the window, his jaw clenched and his blue eyes cold as a winter sky. The driver, calm and controlled, made the left turn that would lead them to the end of the journey, either into an ambush or into the safe haven that waited behind the gates.

It was nearly dark as they pulled up to the chain link fence. One of the two Nigerians, who had taken over for the guards that had accompanied them, quickly released the padlock and waved at them, his face devoid of expression. Meanwhile, no one else appeared. The compound looked strangely deserted. Nate and Karen pulled away from one another and looked around. No one came out to greet them. They had been gone less than three hours, and the group of more than a dozen volunteer workers seemed to have vanished into thin air.

Neither Nate nor Karen dared say another word to Billy— he'd made it clear that he wasn't interested in making conversation or answering any more of their questions. They meekly opened the doors and got out. As soon as the driver unlocked the back compartment, they tugged their luggage out.

"I'll walk to your room with you," Nate told Karen, "and make sure it's okay."

Billy Jones, of course, was ten steps ahead of them. By the time they got to Karen's sleeping quarters, he had already looked it over fronm top to bottom and shined a flashlight into every corner. "It's fine," he told her.

Karen put her stuff on a bed and sat down shakily, watching with a growing sense of uneasiness, as the others left. The room was shadowy, and she didn't want to be there by herself. She was exhausted from the ordeal they'd been through and, still fully dressed, she stretched out on the bed and closed her eyes. She yearned for sleep, but every time she started to doze off, her body jolted as if electricity were surging through and she awoke in alarm. Everything was getting darker by the minute, and for some reason she began to stare at a hole in the ceiling. She had noticed it before—it looked like a construction mistake, like a gap had somehow been left between the thin insulation and a cross beam.

But now the hole seemed to grow larger. Irrational fear gripped Karen. What was inside there? Her heart was pounding rapidly in her ears, and her breath came faster and faster. She sat bolt upright on the bed. All at once, like some nightmare come to life, there was movement near the ceiling hole. Karen cried out as an enormous roach emerged. It crawled along the ceiling, then tumbled to the floor and scuttled toward her end of the room. In the quietness, she could hear its legs, its every movement against the bare cement.

On a better day, Karen might have laughed at herself. She'd seen the roaches before and knew they were comparably harmless. But there was nothing funny about the dizziness that was spinning through her mind. She closed her eyes and tried to breathe more slowly. She impulsively grabbed the dogtag around her neck. Her self-confidence was shattered, and she had no place to turn except toward the unseen—her father's memory, her mother and Sean Murray's prayers, and the invisible world those things implied.

Karen Burke, the promising young editor of New Spirit Press, the Henry Weiss Book Company's "faith" imprint, was looking her own personal lack of faith full in the face. In that terrible moment, she longed to discover some kind of Spirit greater than her own. Did such a thing exist? She had always thought of herself as a self-made woman. Now, independent though she was, she recognized a chilling reality: in that moment, when she needed most to reach out for help, unless there was some Other she could turn to, she was utterly alone.

"Help me..." she murmured, shivering in fear. "Please help me!"

There was no answer. But as seconds ticked by her fear seemed to recede like an ebbing tide. A faint tingling awakened in her hands and feet, and warmth flushed her face. She inhaled deeply. Then, impulsively, she got up. Everything spun around. She steadied herself, placing both hands on the bed, lowering her head for a moment and again inhaling deeply. Her mind gradually cleared. She rushed to the door. "Billy!" she called out.

Jones was within shouting distance, talking to one of the Nigerian guards. He immediately walked over to her.

"I...I'm not sure I want to stay here alone," she confided, almost whispering. "I guess I'm pretty scared."

"It's fine," he told her with what, to her, seemed like a surprising amount of compassion. "The Nigerians have been telling me that everyone else here made a break for it while we were gone. I think it would be better anyway if you'd just take your stuff over to the men's dorm and bunk there tonight. That way the three of us will all be under one roof. Tomorrow we'll decide about how to get to Abuja. We may go straight back to Lagos instead. I'll let you know."

"So Nate and I don't get to vote?" Karen asked, trying to be light-hearted and sounding more assertive than she felt.

"You can vote all you want," Billy said coolly. "But the final decision won't be made by you or by me. David Levine signs the check. And David Levine gives the orders."

Subdued by Billy's tone, she grabbed her bags and went with him to the men's "dorm" in silence.

"Nate, Karen's going to spend the night here," Billy explained as they walked through the door. "I think everyone else has left."

Karen sat down on one of the beds while Billy filled Nate in. There was no sense of danger in his tone. He simply reported that the rest of the construction crew had departed by choice for some unknown destination and were under the protection and direction of the local community. In the meantime, neither friend nor foe had showed up at the compound.

"So how come they left?" Nate asked. He was concerned about his co-workers, and especially Ryan, whom he had come to respect during his time here.

"They went with those local villagers that were over here earlier. They all drove away together in two vehicles. They took all their baggage, but left a letter in the office in case anybody was looking for them. They'll come back in a few days, once everything settles down."

With that, Billy went out to make a phone call, and Nate retrieved the letter from the office. He brought it back and read it aloud. "We decided to take our friends' advice and evacuate the compound until the threat of danger has passed," Ryan had written hastily on a piece of printer paper. "We expect to return in a few days. Please keep us in your prayers."

"Are you worried about them?" Karen asked when he finished. "Do you think they've walked into a trap of some kind?"

"Not really," Nate told her. "Anything can happen, but the villagers that came here are good people. Like you heard, they're Christians, but they're getting most of their information from local Muslims who have no ax to grind in this situation. They are all united in their dislike of the jihadists. I think our guys will be fine."

"To be honest," Karen told him, "I'm more worried about us. I wish we had some idea about what we're doing tomorrow, don't you?"

Nate nodded, pulling her next to him and kissing her on the forehead. "I know what you mean. I want to say I have complete faith that everything will turn out all right, but there are no guarantees in this life. All we can do is hope and pray."

"I thought God always answered prayers," Karen ventured.

"Yeah, he does." Nate smiled. "Sometimes he says 'Yes,' sometimes he says, 'No.' But most of the time he says, 'Yeah, I hear you. Wait awhile and I'll get back to you with my answer.' Sometimes it takes years before you know what he's going to do."

"Sounds like he works in publishing." Karen frowned.

After Billy Jones came back, they followed him into the sanctuary the volunteers had been reconstructing. It was dark inside, but his flashlight illuminated most of the small room. And for a few moments the light rested on the carved crossbeam that read "Beauty for Ashes."

Karen stared at it, searching her memory to summon its source. Shakespeare, perhaps? "Remind me who said that," she asked Nate. "I can't place the quote."

"Oh, it's part of an old Hebrew saying."

"You mean from the Bible? Like a Psalm or something?"

"We'll it's poetry, but not from a Psalm. One of the prophets said it, and then I think Jesus quoted it later. It's something like this: 'I'll give them beauty for ashes, the oil of joy for mourning..."'

"That's nice, but what does it mean? I don't understand who is saying it."

Nate picked up a Bible that had been left in the room by somebody. "Billy, can I use your flashlight for a minute?"

"You can have it. I'm through looking around."

"Good, thanks." Nate thumbed his way through a few chapters and then found the passage he was looking for. Somebody had marked it with red ink. "Here's the part Jesus quoted," he said.

"'The Spirit of the Lord God is upon me; because the Lord has anointed me to preach good tidings to the meek; he has sent me to bind up the brokenhearted, to proclaim liberty to the captives, and the opening of the prison to them that are bound...to comfort all that mourn... to give unto them beauty for ashes, the oil of joy for mourning, the garment of praise for the spirit of heaviness...'"

Karen looked at him blankly. "I don't get it. It's beautiful poetry, but what does it have to do with this place?"

Nate looked back at the text, "Well, I think they chose it because of the work they were doing here. 'And they shall build the old wastes,'" it goes on to say. "They shall raise up the former desolations, and they shall repair the wasted cities...'"

"That makes more sense." She nodded. "Beauty for ashes is a lovely phrase. Especially here, when you think about them burning down churches."

Nate looked at her thoughtfully. "Not to mention our own lives, and the dreams that have been torched. Maybe it's about that, too. Who knows?"

And as Nate remembered Suzanne, and as Karen unexpectedly recalled her unhappy past, they walked quietly out of the nearly-completed room sanctuary. They made their way into the dining area, where Billy was sitting alone.

"You guys want a drink?" he asked unexpectedly.

"I'd love a drink if I could only figure out where to get one," Karen told him.

"I'll be right back," Billy said. Momentarily he reappeared, clutching three little airplane bottles of Johnny Walker Black

Label. He handed them out solemnly. "A shot each will do us good," he said with the hint of a smile, "and it won't be enough to do us any harm if the bad guys decide to show up in the middle of the night."

Later, the three of them headed back to the dormitory-style room, which contained eight single beds and two bunks. Billy went out to talk to the Nigerian guards and to make a few more phone calls. Karen and Nate took turns, brushing their teeth with bottled water, using the toilet, and pulling on the t-shirts and boxers they both slept in. More exhausted then they realized, each of them stretched out—Nate in the bed he'd been using all along, and Karen on an adjacent one that was still unused, its clean bedding carefully tucked beneath the mattress.

"Are you scared?" Nate asked Karen again.

"I'm too tired to feel anything," she answered.

"Well, you know where I am if you need me."

Karen dozed off at last, waking up briefly when Billy returned to the room and bedded himself down. Trying to remember the beauty for ashes quotations, she fell asleep again, awakened hours later by the sounds of distant gunfire. She turned on the little Maglite she carried with her, squinted at her watch, and thought it said 3:18. More awake than before, she focused on the sounds outside, wondering how close the shooting really was. As she listened, she could hear Billy Jones snoring lightly in a nearby bed. She began to worry. Was he drunk? Had he downed so much Johnny Walker that he was useless to her and Nate?

Another volley of gunfire pop-pop-popped, this time closer than before. She stiffened. What if the jihadists decided to come into the compound right now? What would she do? Who would protect them all? She shivered, wishing she had the kind of faith Nate did. He would be praying by now.

"God," she said under her breath, "if you're out there at all, help us."

She listened for a few more seconds. Shooting. Billy's rhythmic snoring. Silence.

Just then she heard Nate whisper, "Karen? Are you awake?"

"Yes."

"Are you okay?"

"No."

"Come over here."

A kaleidoscope of emotions spun around in her mind. She was angry at herself for being needy. She was uncertain about her feelings for Nate. She was relieved to know that she would be in his arms and afraid of what that might mean. She was frightened by the gunfire. She was uncomfortable about Billy Jones' presence in the room. The colorful fragments of ideas fell into place like shapes in a kaleidoscope, seemed to settle, then moved into new, even more disturbing patterns.

Setting it all aside, she got up and tiptoed the three or four steps to Nate's bed. He lifted the sheet and blankets and she climbed inside. For the second time that day she was consoled by his warm embrace and quieted by his nearness. It was not the time for sex, although Nate's hand soon found its way to the bare skin near her waist, and as she curled against him, she could feel his pleasure in her closeness. They both rested, silently, in the darkness, warmed by one another's presence. Before five minutes had passed, they were sound asleep.

* * *

Joe Brac and six of his seven Special Operators—Billy Jones would join them soon enough—gathered in the small office at the Feeding the Hungry compound. Since their first meeting in Alabama a few weeks before, they had been refining their plans and rehearsing, as best they could, every movement of their mission. Situation, Mission, and Execution, Brac pounded away at them. Preparation Phase. Decision Phase. Act Phase. Over and over and over the details they went. And the to-do list on the board had expanded exponentially as new Intel emerged. Sketches of Jumoke's cell and the surrounding village were taped to the walls, and they had discussed their strategies redundantly.

They knew that the two key priorities of their mission were Jumoke's rescue and the assassination of the Governor of Abuja. They also knew that other urgent circumstances could quickly arise. With that in mind, they had reviewed the floor plan of the Abuja Sheraton, and the layout of the compound where Karen had been staying and where Nate had worked on the church reconstruction project.

Brac and his men were professionals, more than aware of the uncertainties of their mission, more than confident in their skills at improvisation. Years of military experience had exposed them to every sort of exigency, and between them all there were few scenarios they couldn't envision. Given the right weapons, the proper communications gear, and halfway decent intelligence, they knew they could rise to nearly any occasion.

Were they nervous? Afraid? Apprehensive? Brac would never know for sure. They weren't about to let him know. He looked across the room at them, remembering some very challenging scenarios he had faced with various members of the group at different times. He hadn't yet told them that Mischa would be involved in this mission—he knew they wouldn't like it at all. She was not only an outsider, she was also a woman. And respect her though they might, their machismo would probably still recoil at her "intrusion" on their mission. He could guess that at least one or two of them would complain bitterly.

He had rehearsed his speech already. Now it was time.

"Guys," he began, "we've added a new wrinkle to our plans. And it's going to save us both energy and manpower. Since we lost Rambo down in the oil country, David Levine has brought an extra operator into our group, specifically to deal with the neutralization of the Governor."

"Who's the operator? Do we know him?"

"I doubt it. For one thing, the new operator is not an American. For another, she is a woman."

Watch the eyes, Brac had always told himself, and you'll find out all you need to know. His men's eyes were looking at each other, then at him. A couple of pairs were rolling heavenward. "A woman?" one of them said. "What in the hell is Levine thinking?"

"Well, I know something about this particular woman," Joe explained. "I've heard about her. She is one of the most skilled assassins in the world. She knows how to get close to powerful men, and once she gets into the bedroom, the story's over. All we have to do is provide some coverage for her as she comes and goes. She'll take care of the rest."

"You know this woman?"

"I know a lot about her," Brac half lied. "As they say, her reputation precedes her."

"So if she's not an American, what is she? The African queen?"

"No, she's not African, either. She has been very well trained by a loyal American ally—perhaps the most loyal of all..."

"Oh God. Not a Brit!" one of the guys said, baiting their former SAS team member.

"No." Joe was smiling by now. "Any of you ever have any dealings with Mossad?"

The room fell silent. There wasn't a man there who, somewhere along the way, hadn't been involved in training exercises in Israel. They all knew about the I.D.F.—the Israeli Defense Forces. And at their level of expertise, there wasn't a time when their work with the I.D.F. hadn't included certain special tactics developed by Mossad, particularly their unique proficiency in intelligence. Not to mention the removal of unsavory characters from leadership roles.

"I'll assume your answer is Yes. In any case, our new teammate has raised assassination to a fine art—every job she does is a masterpiece, although she never leaves a signature."

"So she needs a couple of snipers to cover her ass? Is that it?"

"She'll be here later on tonight," Joe answered with a wry look. "We'll let her speak for herself about how she'd like to have her ass covered."

Chapter Nine

The well-dressed American was just a little too cocky as he slapped his blue passport down on the immigration counter at Murtala Muhammad International Airport in Lagos, Nigeria. He waited expectantly as the uniformed passport control officer leafed through the pages, studying it carefully.

"You're Mr. Wilson?" The officer's dark brown eyes looked at the passenger coolly, taking note of his blue chambray shirt and Tommy Bahama khaki slacks.

"Right. I am Pastor Ken Wilson."

"And where is your Nigerian visa, Mr. Wilson?" the African asked, flipping through the pages yet again.

"I was told I wouldn't need one by the people who arranged my trip for me," he said, sounding haughtier than he felt. "If necessary, of course, I'll be happy to purchase one."

"And what is the purpose of your trip?"

"I'm attending a human rights conference. I'm an invited guest."

"Invited by whom? The Nigerian government?"

"No, no. I'm the guest of a group called Humanity.com. They're meeting in Abuja, and I need to get there as quickly as possible."

"And what is the meeting about?" the officer persisted.

"It is a meeting to..." he paused, searching for just the right explanation, "to create a support system for the Nigerian people who have practical needs for medicine, financial, aid and...and of course food."

"I see." The African studied Wilson's passport again, then

double-checked a printed list on the side of his workspace. Without comment, he picked up the receiver on his phone and dialed. To Ken Wilson, who in the best of times was not a patient man, the Nigerian's every move seemed to be done in slow motion. *Apparently he doesn't know the meaning of the word efficiency,* Wilson thought angrily. *Or maybe he just doesn't like his job. Whatever. The truth is, he's probably just lazy and stupid.*

A few words were exchanged on the phone, and the officer hung up and placed Wilson's passport on the left side of his desk.

"You'll need to stand aside and wait," he said calmly.

"For what? For a visa officer?" Wilson asked, his eye narrowing.

"No, sir. We have to check with our supervisor. Your name is on a restricted list."

"*My* name? Restricted? Why?" Ken Wilson was not accustomed to having his plans thwarted. "Do you know who I am?" he demanded, remembering that his church had once donated a few cases of one of his not-so-successful books to a Nigerian ministry. Surely someone would recognize his name.

"Yes, sir," the agent said without rancor. "You are Mr. Kenneth Wilson. I will be with you in a few minutes. Stand aside please, so I can assist the people in line behind you."

"Why can't you just stamp my passport and let me through?" Wilson complained. "I'm going to a human rights conference, for heaven's sake. Don't you realize how important that is?"

Wilson was tired, frustrated and more than a little irritable. He'd flown from LAX, with a five hour layover in Amsterdam. He had been on the move for almost 24 hours, and hadn't slept a wink. He was eager to get to the conference and then to find his way to Port Harcourt. He had convinced himself that he could talk Phillip Taylor's captors into letting their hostage go. Ken Wilson knew that he could talk his way around most anything and was capable of being uncannily compelling when he had to be. That's why this unexpected detour was puzzling. It had to be some kind of a mix-up. Probably some other Kenneth Taylor was a trouble maker, and the State

Department's wires were crossed. Why else would his name appear on a watch list?

Wilson waited for forty-five minutes, growing more outraged with each tick of his watch. He was seething. Every few minutes he tried to reason with the officer, tried to charm him, tried to intimidate him. Nothing made any difference whatsoever. He went to the men's room, came back, and waited another half an hour. Finally a heavy-set African man in a rumpled grey suit approached him.

"Mr. Wilson?" he said in a booming voice.

"Yes, I'm Ken Wilson. What seems to be the problem here?"

"Please come with me."

The two walked without speaking, eventually finding their way into an empty office in the airport's administrative area. It was a dark, cramped space that smelled of stale smoke. The African flipped on a light and sat down heavily. He motioned to a plastic chair across from his desk. "Sit down, please," he rumbled, lighting a cigarette.

Wilson glanced around, noticing a faded 1980s era photograph of Yassar Arafat pinned to the wall. "What is your name?" he asked, trying to keep his voice calm and pleasant.

"I am Mr. Ismael Oshodi," the man said officiously.

"And are you the visa officer here in Lagos, Mr. Oshodi?"

"No, I am not. I am a representative of the government of Nigeria. I have brought you here because there are some irregularities with your case."

Wilson coughed and frowned. "I see. Um, forgive me, Mr. Oshodi, but would you mind not smoking? I'm very allergic to smoke," he explained, fanning the air with his hand.

Mr.Oshodi stared dispassionately at Wilson, took a long drag from his cigarette, then exhaled with a contented expression on his face. He repeated, "As I was saying, there are some irregularities with your case, Mr. Wilson."

"What case? I'm an American visiting your country. There is no case! What is the problem, here? I need to talk to your supervisor!"

"I am in charge of this matter," Oshodi said, puffing a column of smoke toward Wilson. "And I am informing you at this time that you must return to Amsterdam on the next KLM flight."

"What?" Wilson exploded. "That's disgraceful! It's inexcusable! It's is stupid and unjust. I will do no such thing! I need to speak to someone at the American Embassy immediately!" Wilson fumbled with his cell phone.

"You will not find them helpful," Oshodi said with a slight smile. "This is not only the decision of our Nigerian government. The United States of America's Department of State," the words rolled out with grave authority, "has requested that the Republic of Nigeria block your entry into our country."

The two willful men stared at each other. Determined as Wilson was, the African clearly had control over the situation. To make matters worse, he was enjoying it thoroughly.

"Why on earth would they do that?" Ken Wilson burst out, breaking the silence and jumping to his feet. "I demand a phone call to the U.S. Embassy! I demand an attorney—an *American* attorney!" He took a step toward the desk. A heavily armed Nigerian soldier instantly appeared at the door, and roughly gripped Wilson's left arm in his powerful right hand.

Mr. Oshodi smiled slightly and nodded at the guard. "You are very welcome to talk to the U.S. Embassy, Mr. Wilson. In *Amsterdam*. I'm sure you will find an American attorney there, too. For now," he said, glancing at his watch and lighting another cigarette, "you'll be pleased to know that your flight leaves in less than two hours. You will be required to wait in a secure area until boarding."

"But why?" Ken Wilson cried out plaintively. "Do you know why? Can you explain this?"

Oshodi stared at Wilson for another long moment, then rummaged through one of the scattered piles on his desk. He located a dog-eared document and pulled a pair of broken glasses out of his pocket. After surveying the stapled sheets, he handed them over to Wilson without further explanation.

The pages comprised a thread of email messages between embassies—an exchange between two middle-level bureaucrats who were reiterating the will of their superiors. It was not "policy" they were expressing, but something far more inflexible—a decision by someone, somewhere that could not be fully explained, and most certainly would not be reversed.

Wilson, who was more shaken and exhausted than he realized, could not focus his attention on the three pages of single-spaced type. He did, however, read and reread one paragraph, which both humiliated and infuriated him.

"We are well aware of the crisis you face in the Nile Delta," the document read, "and of the abduction of Mr. Phillip Taylor, an American citizen. We are reluctant to complicate that situation by permitting another American, who appears to be a televangelist, to come into contact with Taylor's captors. Mr. Wilson has publicly stated that he seeks to negotiate Mr. Taylor's release. As you know, the U.S. Government does not negotiate with terrorists, nor do we support the intervention of others, American citizens or not, who pursue such negotiations. We bear in mind the unfortunate case of Terry Waite, who, in his 1987 efforts to seek the release of American hostages in Beirut Lebanon, was taken captive himself, and remained a hostage until 1991—1,760 days later."

Wilson pulled his eyes away from the page he had read several times and turned to Mr. Oshodi. The African smiled almost imperceptivity as he pulled a boarding pass out of his pocket and handed it to the soldier.

"Mr. Wilson, you are in seat 24D. My friend here will make sure that you— and your bags—are on the flight to Amsterdam. Have a safe journey."

* * *

While the six men reiterated and rehearsed and revisited their plans for what seemed to them like the thousandth time, a woman appeared in the doorway of the warehouse. The chatter died out all at once, as twelve eyes fixed themselves upon her. She was about 5'7" and slim, with muscles as firm as a leopard's. Her olive complexion was framed by a bob of gleaming black hair. Her dark eyes were large and intelligent. The woman's lips curved into an ironic smile as she folded her arms, and looked the ragged group of men over like a queen assessing her ill-kempt court.

"You must be Mischa." Brac lied with professional ease,

pretending he'd never seen her before. "I'm Joe Brac. It's a pleasure to meet you." He extended his hand. Hers was warm and soft.

"Likewise." She smiled into his eyes. He immediately knew that she remembered. But of course she did. How could either of them forget? Nevertheless, they shook hands like strangers. Joe then introduced each of his team members to her, one after the other. It crossed his mind that perhaps one of them had also met her before. If so, like Joe Brac, he wouldn't dare reveal it either.

Once the formalities were over, Mischa turned her attention to Brac, "So what is our timetable?"

"We're waiting for word from Mr. Levine," he answered. "In the meantime, we need to know what we can do to help you with your specific task. We thought that perhaps The Judge, our very talented sniper, and Angel, who specializes in Intel and communications, might be of some help to you."

Mischa looked the soldiers over and laughed softly. Some were offended; the rest were curious and intrigued.

Joe Brac had seated himself on the edge of the desk, crossed his arms, and was watching the scene unfold with some pleasure. For a moment or two, as he appreciatively watched Mischa's cat-like movements and the subtly of her body's athletic form, he pondered the fact that he hadn't made housing arrangements for her. He briefly envisioned her spending the night in his room, then recalled—with an instant of disappointment—that Levine had taken care of her accommodations.

"Your watchfulness will provide an extra measure of safety for me, I am sure," she smiled, glancing at Brac. "As long as you don't become overprotective and, as they say, blow my cover."

"We know how to keep a low profile, too, ma'am," The Judge said quietly. "This isn't our first mission, you know."

She laughed outright, flattering him a little with her flashing eyes. "Of course it isn't," she said. "It isn't my first mission, either. Together, I'm sure we'll make it very successful indeed."

With that, the warriors settled into an uneasy truce. With their usual precision, they began to reconfigure the plans they had developed to secure the area around the Governor's mansion. They had previously intended to penetrate his security parameter with their best marksman: one man, one rifle, one bullet. Now that marksman would keep vigil while the governor attempted to penetrate a very different and very desirable objective of his own. In the process, with Mischa's help, the African politician would find himself engaged in an unforeseen scenario. And if all went well, his life story would reach its climax with a gruesome finale that, even in his most perverted or paranoid fantasies, he could never have envisioned.

* * *

"Holy Shit!" Billy Jones muttered. He was staring at the TV when Nate and Karen walked into the compound's small office at around 8 the next morning. They found him in possession of a half-empty pot of coffee. He had gulped down more than four cups of the wickedly strong brew while watching their circumstances go from bad to worse on BBC World News. Billy didn't have to say another word. Both of them quickly saw that the dangers around them had intensified, and that they had blissfully slept through intensifying riots and encroaching gunfire.

As such reports often do, the news stories concentrated on the worst case scenarios in Northern Nigeria. Still, even if the reporting was a little heavy-handed, the situation was far from good. It was too hot for ski masks or *balaclavas*, but in scattered Nigerian cities and town throngs of Africans, along with a scattering of insurgents representing several other nationalities, people had taken to the streets. Many of them wore white headbands that bore crude, hand-written Arabic markings declaring their commitment to jihad. Their numbers had boiled through neighborhoods surrounding militant mosques in towns and villages as well as in Kano, Abuja, and Port Harcourt.

Five car bombs had exploded within three hours, leaving more than a dozen dead, and more than thirty injured. An attempt to blow up the American Embassy in Abuja had been foiled, but there were numerous reports of blasts in local villages, rumors of massacres, stories of shootings of civilians, and interviews with tearful Christians who lamented the recent loss of their homes, mindless slaughter of their herds, and the devastation of their hope.

During a break between reports, Karen realized that she had left her world phone somewhere. She rushed around looking for it, and once she located it, she discovered that she had a voice mail message from Sean Murray. He had received word that their group's attempted return to Abuja had been aborted. He was clearly worried, although he did his best to lift her spirits. *"Don't think for even a moment that we've lost track of you,"* he said mildly. *"We know precisely where you are, and we are keeping a weather eye on what's going on around you. Karen, I want you to be brave, and to think of yourself as a warrior. You, Nate, and Billy will make it through this, and we'll all have a drink together when you get back to civilization!"*

Billy, meanwhile, had been on the phone almost constantly since their return to the compound. He had talked to Joe Brac, to two members of the team, and to David Levine himself.

"Angel's Flight is getting closer," Levine told him, his voice warm with excitement. *"I know you've missed some of the latest plans for take-off and landing, but you'll be up to speed in no time. We are close to another great accomplishment! Can you get yourself back to the Rally Point we used the last time, during Mr. G's rescue?"*

Although the insurgents in Northern Nigeria weren't the most high-tech group in the world, the organizations that supported them knew all about cell phones and eavesdropping. Levine was well aware of that, and that's why his terminology wasn't exactly discreet. However he was also cognizant that by the time that group in question recorded the call, transcribed it, analyzed it, and acted on it, the mission would be over. Anyway, he knew in his gut that no one would conceive of rescuing Jumoke. She was, in the eyes of her captors, utterly worthless. Why would anyone care about her?

"I can get myself wherever you want me to go," Billy said. "It's about a 45 minute jog."

"Do you trust the two local boys who are staying with you there?"

"To be honest, at first I wasn't so sure about them. But I've been watching pretty carefully. They really are good guys, and they do what they're told."

"I'm glad to hear that, because as much as I hate to do it, we're going to have to leave our friends in their care for a day or so. And during that time, if the way clears, they're going to have to make the same trip to Abuja again. What I want to hear is that they've checked into the hotel and are having a drink on me."

"I understand, sir."

"And Angel, make sure everybody knows how to deal with the unexpected. As for you, get set to go jogging and I'll make sure you get where you need to go!"

"Thanks, sir. The sooner the better."

Billy Jones had walked outside, as was his habit, while David Levine briefed him on the plans for the mission. When he went back into the little office where the TV was on, he stopped to watch for a few moments, well aware that both Karen and Nate were staring at him.

Karen's face was pale. "Billy, how are we ever going to get out of here? The whole country is ready to explode!"

Billy nodded, gesturing toward the television. "I'm sure you know that journalists make everything sound twice as bad as it really is."

"Billy, are you kidding me? It *is* bad."

"You're right, it's bad enough. And it's not going to improve any time soon."

"So what are you going to...?"

The compound phone rang, interrupting Karen's unnecessary question. It was Alexis Schofield calling for Nate, apologetically reporting to him that the human rights conference at the Abuja Sheraton had, for all practical purposes, fallen apart. Of the five people who had made it into Nigeria, two had already flown out of Abuja and were on their way to Lagos and out of the country. Two were still at the hotel, uneasily awaiting word from their bosses.

"And one," she told Nate, *"got turned back at the border!"*

"Who got turned back?" he asked, glancing at Karen. His eyes widened as he heard the name Ken Wilson.

"Why on earth did he get refused entry?" Nate vaguely recalled that Sean Murray had warned of just such an action.

"No one knows—sounds like a bureaucratic snafu to me. The poor man was exhausted. I guess he gave a sermon last week that God might lead him to talk to the kidnappers of that Texas oilman. He wanted to convince them to let the poor guy go. Maybe that got him in trouble with the powers that be. Who knows?"

Nate glanced at his watch. He was already feeling waves of anxiety and it wasn't even 8:30 in the morning. He knew that the only thing holding him together was his sense of responsibility for Karen. He looked at her face, and the newly-communicated affection he felt for her made him feel even more distressed. What had started out as an interesting adventure was quickly transforming into a web of bad news, danger, and frustration. Everything seemed to be disintegrating around them. As he stared at the TV, Nate felt a wave of panic pressing against him. He breathed a prayer for help, but with it came a surge of bitterness.

My God! he thought. *How could you allow such good intentions to turn out so badly?*

At the same time, Karen was strangely at peace. Despite her panic attack the night before, their unexpected sleeping arrangements had comforted her, and even now there was something flickering within her that felt like hope. She recalled her night terrors with a measure of embarrassment. Sure, things were bad, but what a great story! She touched the chain that held her father's dogtags, recalling Sean Murray's admonition to "think of yourself as a warrior." For no particular reason, she remembered that Sean had been lighting candles in his church half way around the world, beseeching heaven to get her home safely. And in spite of herself, she had a hunch that heaven might do just that.

* * *

Jumoke's mother squatted next to her daughter on the filthy floor and put her arms around the shivering girl. Jumoke still clutched her dead baby in her arms, pressing Abeo's face against her breast. The two women rocked softy, rhythmically, with tears of mute lamentation streaming down their swollen faces. They could not cry out or wail; only the kindness of a friendly guard had made the mother aware of the daughter's loss. They soundlessly wept as one, and not only over the loss of Abeo. They both knew that they might never meet again.

"Mama, go," Jumoke finally whispered. "They'll kill you, too."

They held each other all the tighter, as if anticipating the moment when a less friendly guard would appear, would seize the infant's stiffening body, and would announce to all the world that Jumoke was no longer nursing her child.

"I have to go to Chad for a few days," the older woman whispered, hating the words even as they left her mouth. "My brother says I should get away before it's too late. But my darling, how can I leave you?"

"Mama, go! Please go! Go *now*." The girl's croaked whisper was interrupted by shaky breaths. She was so weak, so shattered, that she could not offer another argument. All she could do was repeat the words, "Go to Chad! Go to Chad! Go to Chad!"

Mother and daughter's final goodbye was cut short when the guard appeared—the friendly guard—who whisked the mother away, saying, "They know about the baby. They are coming."

Less than a minute later, a member of the local Shari'a council swept into the squalid cell and coldly pulled Abeo's body away from Jumoke. "Your sentence will now be enforced," he said to her, holding his immaculate robe away from the floor. "Your disgraceful life is over."

As he left, holding Abeo's pitiful remains like a sack of rotten vegetables, he turned and gave Jumoke a fierce look. "You filthy whore!" he muttered in a low, angry voice. He spat twice in her direction as he turned away.

* * *

Karen was rummaging around in the compound's small pantry, looking for something to eat. There wasn't a lot of food left for them, and she felt a moment of alarm wondering how they would restock the shelves if the violence continued for more than a couple of days. They had heard no gunfire that morning, but the news reports continued to worsen. Even CNN had finally started airing a few reports under the banner "Crisis in Nigeria."

"Billy, are you going grocery shopping for us today?" she asked.

"I'm going out all right," he said with an odd look, "and I may not be coming back for awhile."

Karen's eyes widened. "What do you mean, 'I'm going out'? Are you really leaving? What are you talking about?"

"Once I get the word from Mr. Levine, I'm going to join Joe Brac and the others for a little while. We've got some work to do."

"My God! What about us?" Nate asked in disbelief. "Are you just going to abandon us?"

"Hell, no. You've got two perfectly capable Nigerians here that know more about this part of the world than I do. They're in touch with the same people I've been talking to, and they'll make sure you get back to Abuja." Billy tried to sound as convincing as possible, well aware that his two charges were shocked and frightened about his impending departure. They had assumed he would be with them until they were safely on their way home.

"You've got work to do?" Nate frowned. "What kind of work? What are you talking about?"

Billy smiled. "You'll hear all about it soon enough."

Just then the television flashed with a breaking news story. A reporter's photograph appeared alongside a map of Nigeria, and a live telephone call crackled, "It is being reported that Jumoke Abubakar, the nineteen-year-old Nigerian woman who has been sentenced to death by stoning for adultery, will be put to death within the next 72 hours. Because she was nursing her infant daughter, her death sentence had been temporarily suspended until the child was weaned. But it is now being reported that the child has died."

"Do we know the cause of the child's death?" the anchorwoman inquired, absently adjusting her blonde hair.

The reporter's voice responded, "We have no further information at this time. We are, of course, closely monitoring the situation."

Billy Jones stiffened as he stared at the screen. He knew that his cell phone would ring momentarily. He coolly walked outside and called the two Nigerian guards into an area where Nate and Karen could not overhear his instructions. "I'm going to head out of here pretty soon," he told them. "You have two things to do. Number one, make sure those two are protected 24 hours a day. Number two, get them back to the Abuja Sheraton as soon as you're told the road is clear. I'm leaving you a cell phone and a radio. My team will contact you by radio if there's anything you need to know, so leave it on at all times. And keep the cell phone with you, too, and leave it on while it's recharging."

The two soldiers, who had been commandos in the Nigerian Army, had also been trained by British SAS specialists. They asked a few questions, nodded in assent, and shook Billy's extended hand. "Thanks for your help," he said. "I need to brief them, now," he said, heading back into the office area.

Karen and Nate stared at him when he strolled back inside, looking more disinterested than he felt. They had noticed his abrupt departure and his conversation with the two men. "What the hell is going on?" Karen demanded in a low, hard voice. "Don't we have the right to know what you're doing? It just so happens that our lives are every bit as important as your damned job!"

Billy held his hands up in mock fear. "Now just hold everything," he told Karen. "Take it easy! Just because I'm not telling you every detail of my plans doesn't mean I'm not taking care of you."

The vaguely amused look on Billy's face made Karen think that he was making light of the situation. She was infuriated by his seemingly cavalier attitude. "Billy, do you have a wife? I hope to God you don't, because if you do, she must hate your guts! You are the most condescending, arrogant..."

"Karen, stop. Wait a minute," Nate interrupted. "Let Billy finish." He reached for Karen's hand. She pulled it away, still fuming. But she fell silent.

Billy shot Nate a grateful man-to-man look. "My personal life really isn't any of your business," he said quietly. "But yeah, I do have a wife. And yes, at times she hates me. I haven't been home for awhile, but as far as I know, we're still married." He stopped briefly, until both Karen and Nate made eye contact with him again.

"Now as for you two—I am going to participate in a short-term mission, and once it is complete, I'll be back. In the meantime, you stay put unless those two gentlemen outside tell you otherwise. They are well armed, well trained, and perfectly capable of providing round the clock protection for you until I get back. Once they are assured that the road is safe, they will get you to Abuja. If that doesn't happen before I finish my work, I'll come back for you myself. So I'll either see you in Abuja, or I'll see you back here."

"It's pretty much what I would have expected," Karen remarked, her voice icy.

"What's that supposed to mean?" Billy shot back.

"Men always leave me, and they do it just when I need them most," she informed him. "I guess it's just the nature of the beast."

Billy glanced at Nate, who said, "Karen, why would you say that? I'm not leaving you. Doesn't that mean anything?"

Karen looked away. "We can talk about it later," she concluded. "We haven't had that conversation, at least not yet, but believe me…"

"I'm not leaving you, Karen," Nate said emphatically, taking her hand in his and holding it firmly.

Karen remembered the terrible sense of loneliness she had felt the night before. She had cried out for help. Was Nate somehow part of the answer? Again a faint, almost unrecognizable, ripple of hope stirred within her.

Just then Phil Taylor's kidnapping and captivity was recapped on the television. "You're not going to rescue that guy, are you?" Nate asked Billy, his eyes widening.

"Hell no, I most certainly am not." Billy shook his head sadly. "And I don't think anybody else is, either. His days are numbered. That reminds me, Nate. Do you know how to use a handgun?"

"Of course I do," Nate frowned, not liking the way the conversation was going. "Why do you ask?"

"Would you come with me for a minute? I want to give you something."

* * *

The cheerful photograph of Phil Taylor that had circulated around the media bore little resemblance to the battered, blindfolded visage that the handheld camera was videotaping. The man's upper lip was blackened, and his mouth was barely able to move as he pleaded for mercy. "Oh, God, help me. Help me, help me. Please don't let them do this... don't let them..." His voice dwindled, then regained some energy. "Mr. President, I beg you to intervene on my behalf. Please make peace with our Arabic brothers. Please..."

Taylor was surrounded by five men. The room they were in looked like a prison cell, whitewashed and nondescript. There was a green banner in Arabic attached to the wall behind them. Their faces were hidden behind black scarves, with only their dark eyes glittering into the camera.

"Tell the truth," one of the captors, who seemed to be the leader of the group, demanded in heavily accented English. "Tell them you are C.I.A. spy."

"I...am a...I'm sorry."

A captor on Taylor's right slapped the hostage sharply. "He told you what words to speak. Speak it now!"

"I am a C.I.A. spy. I confess that I am..."

"Tell them you have dishonored Allah," the interrogator interrupted. "Tell them you are infidel! Christian infidel!"

"I grew up a Christian," Taylor mouthed, trying to sound as ambiguous as possible. He was so frightened that he could not think clearly. He wanted to pray, to plead with his mother's God. But he had no hope of an answer—he had been away from his childhood faith too long.

"My mother was a Christian...but I'm...I believe in all religions...one God..."

Another slap across the face stunned Taylor. Blood began to dribble from his nose.

"You see what we have?" the interrogator said to the video camera. "We have infidel. Infidels like this defile our religion and steal riches from our poor people. We now show the world what happens to filthy American spies! Allahu akhbar!"

"I didn't steal from you," Taylor cried out. "I..."

Taylor was silenced by another sharp blow to the face. As the pain shocked him, despair rushed through his body. The last vestiges of hope fled, and he could only hope for a quick end. Even that desire eluded him as his imagination envisioned the terrible pain that lay between him and oblivion. He tried to scream, to cry out in terror, but not a sound came through his lips.

One of the other men in black slowly read a statement in Arabic. Taylor was visibly trembling, incomprehensibly mouthing words from time to time. He seemed to be rocking back and forth, perhaps in a feeble attempt to free his hands, which were bound behind him.

Suddenly the five men moved forward as one, repeating in unison, "Allahu Akhbar." They roughly threw the shrieking American to the ground with a thud. The camera moved awkwardly to focus on his face-down form. Four of the captors held his arms and hands firmly behind his back and immobilized his flailing legs and feet. He grunted in pain as one of them stamped his foot in the middle of his back and held it there.

Phil Taylor groaned in a ghastly voice, his wretched appeals for help nearly drowned out by the men's loud, rhythmic chanting. "Allahu Akhbar! Allahu Akhbar!" they repeated.

Then the fifth man yanked Taylor's head up by the hair, pulling it backward, and began to saw at the back of the American's neck, grinding into his upper spinal column with a large knife. Taylor's cries weakened, and a gurgling sound bubbled up from his throat. His body twitched, fighting futilely for life. Blood spurted from his neck with each movement of the blade, pulsing with the beat of his heart.

The camera unsteadily followed the action as Taylor's dripping head, at last completely severed from the motionless body, was lifted triumphantly by the executioner. He handed the bloodied knife to one of the others. He ripped Taylor's blindfold off and revealed the Texan's wide, terrified eyes staring blankly into the distance.

"Allahu Akhbar!" he shouted. "Behold the fate of the infidel!"

Chapter Ten

Susan Burke, Karen's mother and God-fearing woman that she was, had pounded on heaven's gates constantly since her daughter's arrival in Nigeria. Prayers in private. Prayers with friends. Prayer candles. Prayer meetings. And as far as she could see, prayer or no prayer, the situation was going straight to hell with every passing hour.

On a more earthly plane, she had telephoned Sean Murray daily, sometimes two or three times a day. He was invariably calm, concerned, and in her view anyway, a little condescending with his reassuring platitudes. She realized after the third or fourth call to him that she didn't know any more about Karen's situation than she'd known in the first place.

But Sean was a lot more helpful than Frank Goldberg, Vice President at Henry Weiss Book Company. Karen's boss was no longer taking Susan's calls.

Susan Burke had tried to get a phone number for David Levine, but to no avail. Claridge's Hotel, where she knew the billionaire resided at least part of the time, claimed to have no knowledge of him.

Finally, for the last two days when she'd called Karen's world phone, she'd heard a voice mail recording and had left increasingly urgent messages, all amounting to some variation of "Call Home!" She had received no response.

Susan had poured out her worries to Dr. Ray Martin, who persistently reminded her that "God is in control, his timing is perfect, and God never makes mistakes." Much as she appreciated his relentless spirituality, she was becoming increasingly irritated with him. Blind faith wasn't what she thought she needed at the moment. She was far more grateful for the sedatives he had prescribed, which at least allowed her to sleep.

Now Susan Burke sat alone, trying to track developments on the BBC's website. Her computer was out of date and therefore extremely slow, and her five-year-old modem sometimes failed to connect. She was aware that the situation in Nigeria was worsening, and she knew Karen was still at the village compound in Ogbu. But now she saw the report of Phil Taylor's beheading. The news story had been carefully edited for Western sensibilities, but the photograph of the man's body, with the severed head next to it, was enough to sicken her. Her anxiety was quickly turning into panic, and she felt utterly alone.

She had her hand on the phone, trying to think of someone else to call, when its ring startled her. Breathless with fear, she answered.

"Is this Mrs. Burke?" The man's voice had a distinctly foreign accent.

"Who's calling please?" she asked suspiciously.

"This is David Levine, calling from London."

Her stomach knotted. She immediately envisioned the worst. "Oh God, is it about Karen?"

Levine recognized the terror in her voice. *"Mrs. Burke, please don't be alarmed. Karen is fine. She is well. I am calling simply because I heard from Sean Murray that you were deeply concerned, and I want to assure you myself that your daughter is just fine. I spoke to one of my men moments ago who has been in her company constantly. He informs me that she and Nate Gregory are inside locked gates with 24-hour guards on duty. And the two of them are prepared to leave for Abuja, and then to travel on to London. They'll be on their way as soon as we are certain that the road to the airport is secure."*

"What do you mean by 'secure'?" Susan snapped. "Why wouldn't it be secure?"

Levine's thoughts moved from the reality of Nigeria's jihadists and the bloody trail they were leaving behind, and instead he focused on this woman's personal concerns. Thankfully she seemed to know very little about the accelerating violence in Abuja State. *"I simply mean that we are taking every precaution to assure Nate and Karen of a safe journey. We have friends on the ground throughout the area and elsewhere in the country, monitoring everything for us. The only reason you haven't heard from Karen is because we've asked her not use her phone."*

"Why on earth can't she use her phone? Why would you cut them off from their families?" Susan wanted to trust this man, but her daughter's silence had become intolerable.

"Because of security issues, Mrs. Burke," Levine said evenly, trying to keep impatience out of his voice. *"She is in good hands, and we are in touch with our people constantly. I called to give you her love,"* he said, stretching the truth rather generously, *"and to pass on a message: she said, 'Tell my mom not to worry.'"*

Susan's eyes filled with tears. "She knows how much I worry about her," she admitted, her voice breaking. "So you are confident that she'll be back in touch soon?"

"Within the next 24 to 36 hours," he vowed, hoping he was right. *"Meanwhile, just be assured that all is well."*

"Could I have your phone number?"

"It would be better if you gave me your contact numbers," Levine sounded faintly apologetic. *"I am notoriously hard to reach. But I will most certainly call you as soon as your daughter leaves Nigeria."*

There was nothing more to say. After thanking him and hanging up, Susan stared lovingly at a framed photograph of their family that sat in a place of honor next to her telephone. Her beloved husband Patrick was gone. The thought of losing Karen was unbearable. She wiped her eyes, and tried to pray again.

Just then it suddenly occurred to her, looking back at the photograph, that Patrick Burke would have something very specific to tell her if he were nearby. "Just settle down, Susan," she could almost hear him say. "Let the girl spread her wings a little, for God's sake. She'll never forget this escapade—she's having the time of her life!"

Susan sighed, shook her head, and laughed nervously in

spite of herself. She knew Patrick very well—certainly well enough to recognize his point of view when she heard it. And whether she agreed with him or not, she somehow sensed that she wasn't really alone after all. Taking a shaky breath, she turned off the computer and thoughtfully walked into the kitchen to make herself a cup of tea.

* * *

Karen followed Nate and Billy outside, and watched as the two men talked at length about the Makarov pistol Billy was leaving with Nate.

"Are you sure you won't need this?" Nate asked, holding the compact weapon awkwardly as if it might fire spontaneously.

"Hell no, there's plenty more where that came from. We use these old guns in the field so they don't attract too much attention. My guys have got a whole bunch of new stuff with my name on it at their base camp. And anyway, let's face it, you may be glad you have it," he told Nate, glancing at Karen to see if she was listening.

Of course she was. She looked away.

"I hope I don't have to use it," Nate said, "but I will if I need to."

"Good. You don't ever want to be afraid to defend yourself. Just focus your mind on what needs to be done, and don't worry too much about your feelings. Like they say, your mind is the most powerful weapon you own. Anyway, let's make sure you know what to do in an emergency." He took the gun from Nate, looked it over carefully, and polished it with the front of his shirt.

They walked into a clearing near the back of the compound, where Bill gave Nate a brief shooting lesson. "The trick to good pistol shooting versus fair pistol shooting," explained Billy, "is rear site, front site, and target alignment. Once you've got everything lined up, the emphasis shifts from focusing on the target to focusing on the front site. Remember: front site focus. Front site focus. Just keep it in mind every time you pull the trigger—immediately re-focus on the front site and you'll hit what you're aiming at every time. Got it?"

Nate nodded uncertainly.

"Okay. Now let's pop a few caps."

Nate knew the basics about using a handgun, and although he was nowhere near as accurate as Billy, after putting the new technique to work, he managed to hit a soda can at a reasonable distance, and he didn't miss it by much when he moved back ten or twelve paces.

"You'll be okay." Billy smiled.

"I sure hope you're right."

"I'm going to be leaving you more ammo than you'll think you need." Billy grinned when they were finished. "Better safe than sorry. I've got some other things for you, too. I'll leave the ammo with your baggage, and get the rest of it now. Whatever you don't use, you can just leave it with one of us once we get you to the airport."

Billy returned a couple of minutes later and gave Nate and Karen a global positioning unit. He hurriedly demonstrated how to utilize the waypoints and directions that were programmed into it. He also left them with several infrared Chem-Lights and colored smoke grenades. "I seriously doubt you're going to need any of this," he explained, "but it doesn't hurt to be prepared for an emergency."

Karen glanced at Nate, who was studying the GPS in fascination. *God, I hope we don't get so lost we need a GPS,* she thought, feeling more uneasy by the minute.

It was late morning when Billy's phone rang again. After a quick conversation with someone, he clicked off, walked to his sleeping area, and returned with his rucksack bulging on his back. "I'm going to head out now," Billy told them. "You need to be ready to leave at a moment's notice. I think Levine will move you out of here in a few hours. Meanwhile, do what those two gentlemen tell you to do." He motioned toward the big Nigerian who was standing at the gate, his finger firmly in place next to his AK-47's trigger.

"So you completely trust them?" Karen asked in a low voice.

"I trust them with my life, and you can trust them with yours. Come with me while I brief them once more, so you'll all be on the same page. Then do what they tell you. Everything's gonna be all right."

Billy glanced at Nate. "Did you find that extra ammo I left with your gear?"

Nate laughed. "You left enough for a world war!"

"Yeah." Billy nodded with a grim look on his face. "Well, let's just hope we don't find ourselves in the middle of one."

* * *

As late afternoon shadows deepened into night, Mischa studied herself in the guest house mirror one last time, adjusting her blond wig slightly and applying just a little extra lip gloss. She wasn't dressed in her characteristically elegant style. Instead she was wearing a black polyester suit with elbow-length sleeves and a dangerously short skirt, an ivory lace camisole that revealed more décolleté than she normally exposed, and patent leather sandals with stiletto heels. On her left wrist she wore a trendy, two-inch wide stretchable bracelet richly covered in glittering semi-precious stones. It matched her drop earrings beautifully, but would serve an even better purpose later on. Even though her attire was purposefully seductive, Mischa managed to retain a look of sophistication—just enough, she knew, to catch the governor's ever-wandering eye.

Her target would be attending a reception that afternoon at a local restaurant. She had, through her many international contacts, managed to wangle an invitation. She was well aware of the man's taste in women. She had read multiple reports about his areas of personal vanity. She had even been briefed about his various sexual preferences.

Keeping all that in mind, Mischa had planned the coming rendezvous—and its denouement—with great care. In her small, leather handbag she carried a tiny applicator, less than an inch and a half long, containing a meticulously-crafted suppository of the world's most virulent virus. It was designed to be melted and fully absorbed into the human body within 30 seconds of insertion.

Although it was the first time she had used this particular formulation, the general technique had proved tried and true in the past. She knew that until the time she put the application to good use, she would engage her prey in flirtation, flattery, and foreplay. She would tell him what he wanted to hear about his importance, his influence, and his future. She would touch him and tease him, and by putting all her skills to work, and with a little luck, he would attempt to add her to his long list of sexual conquests.

Once he succeeded, she could get down to serious business.

The car she had hired dropped her in front of the restaurant. She reminded the driver about their arrangements for a quick pick-up later that evening and made sure she had his correct cell phone number. She smiled at the security people at the restaurant door, who were flirting with two pretty young hostesses and paying little attention to her or the name she gave them.

The reception was a glitzy affair, lavish by African standards. The celebration marked Worker's Day, a Nigerian holiday that coincided with whatever Marxist May Day revelries still took place around the world. In recent years, because of the country's unhappy economic realities, Worker's Day was no longer a joyous occasion for Nigeria's unemployed masses or for the working poor who made scandalously meager wages for their efforts. The governor, however, was more than happy to celebrate heartily with his elite cronies and to make sure the festive occasion was well reported in the *Abuja Mirror* the following morning. At the very least, it was a great photo op, and he loved seeing his picture in the paper.

There were about 100 people in the restaurant, spilling into its outside courtyard, where a fountain splashed lazily in the heat. Mischa noticed that a dozen or so Muslim women were in attendance, their heads and bodies modestly covered. But there were also, as she expected, a group of worldly looking Africans, Westerners, and Middle Eastern types, both men and women, who all seemed to be congregated in one room, noisily enjoying themselves. It didn't take long to see that they were well into a large bowl of punch that apparently contained something more exhilarating than the usual Islamic fruit juice. And, predictably, in the midst of that happy group, there stood His Honor, the Governor of Abuja.

Mischa's tall, lithe frame and blonde hair soon caught the

big man's eye. He was about 6'3", a little overweight, but handsome. He wore an expensive Italian suit, and his cuff-links and tie clip were large and flashy. Thanks to her three-inch heels, Mischa could look directly into his eyes, which she did, a smile playing around on her lips. Her enticing expression wasn't wasted.

"Oh, if you'll excuse me, I must say hello to another guest," the governor quickly told a frumpy looking German dowager who, until Mischa appeared, had been extolling the virtues of the European Union.

Mischa smiled broadly at him as he walked toward her. "I think we must have met before," he grinned, amazing her by using the oldest line in the world. "Am I right?"

"You mean you don't remember?" she teased.

He laughed loudly, revealing several gold teeth. "I remember well enough to welcome you back to Abuja," he improvised, hoping his charm would cover up the fact that he'd been with so many women that he could possibly remember them all. "Remind me of your name," he said softly, his liquid brown eyes moving frankly from her face to her breasts and back again.

"My name? But you must try to remember, darling." She kissed her fingers and then touched his right cheek with them. "And I will help you."

The party had hardly begun, and the gregarious host was already longing to leave. He was notoriously easy to seduce—far too easy, his staff and bodyguards had noted on many an occasion. Keeping an eye on him was impossible. A couple of his henchmen watched his glowing face as he moved in on Mischa. They quickly turned away, half jealous, half disgusted. Even they could see that this woman was in a class of her own, well beyond the local girls who came and went from the governor's private apartment, sometimes alone, sometimes in twos or threes, at all hours of the day and night. He had even been known to entertain boys, but his first choice had always been beautiful white women.

As for Mischa, her carefully calculated plan needed to take place close to the governor's bedtime, which she knew to be around 9:30 PM. That way, no one would check on him until morning. A reliable international intelligence group with whom she had excellent connections had exhaustively interviewed one of the governor's former mistresses, and she had offered up a wealth of personal information about him. Sordid as it all was, there was little about the man's life that had to be left to Mischa's imagination.

Because of the time, Mischa knew she would have to string him along for another hour or so, but that wasn't so difficult. She had known men like him before. A little cat and mouse game would only serve to excite him. And by the time she was ready to accomplish her mission, she wanted him to be very excited indeed—too excited to pay close attention to anything but his own overwhelming sexual intentions.

A few moments of small talk later, a young Nigerian girl with carefully braided hair and an innocent face sidled up to the governor and touched his arm. "Sir?" she said. "I was hoping we could talk for a few minutes." She looked infatuated and a little sad. For Mischa, the timing was wonderful. She smiled at the girl and winked at the governor. "Lovely to see you," she said. "I hope we meet again."

"But wait," he whispered urgently, "I must talk to you more."

"Of course, I will be here," Mischa said as she walked away. She made her way to the punch bowl, which had been refilled. She tasted the fruity liquid, and almost laughed aloud at its potency. It wasn't just spiked—it was about 90 percent alcohol. She carried the plastic glass around but did not sip from it. The last thing she wanted was to be even slightly drunk. She needed her mind to be perfectly clear, and her reflexes instantaneous.

She struck up a conversation with a couple of African men in cheap suits, happily discussing the weather, the latest local news that she had gleaned from the morning paper, and the wonderful celebration of Worker's Day—the best she had ever attended. Mischa was soon made aware of the governor's presence again, as he briefly and brashly cupped her left hip in his large hand before interrupting the conversation.

"Hello again." He smiled.

Mischa's face animated with delight. Her mind, however,

was elsewhere. She reminded herself of the other women, beginning with the young mother who was awaiting execution by stoning for committing adultery. Jumoke wasn't the first to suffer that brutal fate. Mischa recalled several who had been viciously lashed, sometimes more than a hundred times, for "fornication." Some were Christians—they made especially appealing victims. Some, like the governor himself, had been Muslim—but not good enough Muslims to impress his Saudi benefactors. Expressing his devout adherence to the strictest form of Wahbist Shari'a law, he had publicly and violently abused dozens of women. In the meantime, on a daily basis, he was carrying out his own outrageous sexual exploits.

What a filthy swine, she thought.

"Well, hello there," she said, with a lilt in her voice. "And have you remembered my name yet?"

The governor's relentless advances intensified as the minutes passed. She excused herself, stepped away to the ladies' room, and took the opportunity to carefully slip the small insertion device beneath her sparkling bracelet's elastic band. When she came out, she began talking and laughing with a group of women. Pouting like a spoiled child, the governor reappeared, boldly took her by the arm, and led her away from the crowd, which was by now beginning to diminish as guests headed for dinners elsewhere.

"I need to talk to you privately," he said, his eyes roaming hungrily over her body. "Could you spare a little time with me? I'd like to share a drink with you in my home. It is so difficult to have a conversation in a place like this."

"How kind of you," Mischa responded. She glanced at her watch and brushed a strand of blonde hair out of her eyes. It was 8:45 PM. Perfect timing.

The ride back to the governor's modern-looking residence was an exercise in minor sexual assault. While the two of them made their way down a hallway to his suite of rooms, he was already pulling off his tie, unbuttoning his shirt, unfastening his belt. Once the door was closed, he literally ripped Mischa's camisole off.

The man's obsessive lust, his frantic disrobing, and his desperate yearning for an explosive orgasm actually served to make Mischa's job easier. He was so crazed that she could respond to him with complete calculation. She cooperated with him fully, keeping one eye on the time and the other on her sparkling bracelet.

Before twenty minutes had passed, as he writhed and moaned and groped in all his sweaty, naked glory, she made her move. As if teasing him with yet another titillating thrill, while biting him playfully on the neck, she painlessly slipped the suppository into his rectum. She continued to toy with him for another half a minute or so, and then whispered, "I need to go to the washroom. I'm so sorry. I'll be right back."

Once she had locked herself inside the marble bathroom, she flushed the little applicator down the toilet. Then she waited. Her watch ticked off one minute, then another. She had been assured that the strain of Ebola virus she'd used was so lethal that it would start manifesting symptoms such as escalating fever and severe stomach pain within five minutes of entering the body; diarrhea and vomiting would begin just moments later. Full hemorrhagic meltdown would be complete within five hours. By the time someone found His Honor, thanks to his demands for privacy, his internal organs would have dissolved into liquid. He would be a sorry sight to whoever found him—and long dead.

Mischa listened, holding her breath. When she heard a slight groaning sound she smiled slightly. *Right on time,* she thought, congratulating the research team in South Africa, where the deadly viral formulation had been developed. She cautiously opened the bathroom door. "So sorry to keep you waiting..." she began.

"I'm feeling a little strange," the governor explained worriedly. "Must have been the food."

"Oh, my darling, how terrible for you! And we were just getting started."

He stared at her slender, nude body and instinctively reached his hand toward her. Then a terrified expression crossed his face. A deep surge of pain seized him and he cried out loudly. He was sweating profusely.

"You're very sick," she said sympathetically. "I'll go get some help. By the way, my name is Jael. Now do you remember me?"

"No, don't go, Jael," he murmured. But he was very ill indeed. Mischa hurriedly tugged on her clothes, buttoned her suit jacket over her torn camisole, ran her fingers through her disheveled blonde wig, and rushed out of the room. She could hear the governor retching as she quietly closed the door behind her.

A lone sniper atop an outbuilding adjacent to the governor's residence had seen the amorous couple arrive less than twenty minutes before. Now, Judge was amazed to see Mischa reappear. He couldn't get his head around the short period of time she had stayed inside. He stared in disbelief as she strode out a side door and made her way toward the street. She said goodnight to the gatekeeper, who had seen many a woman come and go, and moved with a steady gait from the driveway into the street outside. He watched as she calmly took out a cell phone and summoned her driver.

"Judge to Coyote One," he spoke quietly into his radio, "Cinderella is clear. Repeat, Cinderella is clear. My God, Coyote, that woman is way too fast for me! I'm getting the hell out, too."

* * *

D-Day minus one, Joe Brac told himself for the umpteenth time, checking his watch as he paced around the WWII-era hangar on the Feed the Hungry Compound. The air was filled with the plaintive sounds of Willie Nelson singing *Seven Spanish Angels*, mingling with acrid clouds of cigar smoke. As he examined every nook and cranny of his new toys of destruction, he puffed and chewed on a Cuban cigar until the stogie looked like it had been stomped on one end and blown up on the other. The hangar floor was covered in ashes as Brac strode, crawled over and under, touched and poked every moving part of the truck and helicopter. If kicking the tires would have told him anything worthwhile, he would have done that, too.

He didn't have to remind himself that he and his team were about to embark on an extremely complex mission. Every moving part of their equipment, every split- second of their timing would be essential. There was no room for error. For weeks, all aspects of their assignment had been methodically planned and coordinated. He and his Special Operators had been preparing for the raid to rescue Jumoke since the initial planning phase and training at L Farm in Alabama. And now, since deploying to Africa, they had been tasked with two more operations.

To make things more complicated, the liquidation of a terrorist cell had to happen almost simultaneously with the rescue of the Nigerian female prisoner, Jumoke Abubakar.

The other operation, no less worrisome for Brac, had been the assassination of Abuja's brutal Governor. *At least that bastard is history,* Brac smiled, still awed by another of Mischa's devastating success stories.

Each aspect of the dual mission had to be planned separately with regards to both equipment and strategy. The terrorist stronghold was in a compound located just a couple of miles from the village where Jumoke was being held. The plan was to attack the terrorist camp with a heavily armed Russian HIP helicopter. This airborne assault would not only provide a diversion while Jumoke's rescue took place, but would also draw defenders away from her location while Brac's "secret weapon" rolled into place.

Brac looked admiringly at what he called the Trojan Horse. In light of the double mission and the limitation of having only one helicopter, he had adapted a plan that he had used successfully in Afghanistan to surprise unsuspecting Taliban and Al Qaeda. The technique had surreptitiously delivered US-led Counter Terrorist Pursuit Teams (CTPTs) into villages, surprising the enemy on their home turf.

During the Russian occupation of Afghanistan, the Taliban had become particularly sensitized to the sound of approaching helicopters which signaled an early warning of threats. Because of this unavoidable noise factor, in many instances raiding parties had come up empty handed or, worse, had been met with a hail of gunfire and RPGs from an impromptu ambush.

The CTPTs had taken those lessons to heart and had applied an ancient solution to a new situation: the Trojan

Horse. Brac proudly recalled his Horse's triumphs in Afghanistan knowing that the same sensitivities to raids and the same messaging systems that had existed in Afghanistan were prevalent in West Africa. Hell, it had worked in the battle of Troy, not to mention other subterfuges throughout military history. Why not in Nigeria?

Brac's Trojan Horse consisted of a 1994 vintage heavy duty flatbed Mercedes truck, equipped with a 435 hp V8 engine, 4 x 4 wheel drive, and a beefed-up suspension system. On the surface, it looked the same as hundreds of other utility trucks traveling the roads of Afghanistan or Nigeria or most anywhere else in developing countries. The surprise lay in what rested atop the flatbed of the truck: a huge empty container that, from the outside, had been artfully constructed to look like a load of timber. The ruse was accomplished by piling logs lengthwise across the top of the hidden compartment.

At the back of the truck, where two large doors swung open, additional timbers had been cut off at various lengths and stacked against the false wall to create the illusion of a top-to-bottom load of wood. The sides appeared to be typical slats, secured by sidings to the bed. However, skillfully concealed in those slatted sides were two sets of roll-up doors on each side. With the slightest upward pressure, the doors would glide effortlessly up and the Trojan Horse would deposit its cargo of heavily armed warriors on its unsuspecting target.

Down the center of the back compartment were two rows of bucket seats, securely bolted to the flatbed floor, with each row facing the opposite roll-up door. The rows consisted of six seats, its occupants firmly secured by a quick-release harness system during movement. In arms racks around the interior walls an array of weaponry was ready for action, and shooting portals were strategically concealed throughout. It was a benign-looking but formidable war wagon. Brac was confident that it would give them the edge they needed to accomplish their hostage rescue.

Thanks to Levine and his excellent contacts, Plasan Sasa Composite Materials, an Israeli company, had equipped both the helicopter and the Trojan Horse with state-of-the art ballistic protection. The helicopter, the truck cab, and the truck's hidden compartment were all retrofitted with Plasan SASA-Armour Protection Kits (APKs). Plasan's flexible ceramic armour (FCA) and SMART armour represented the next generation of ceramic add-on technologies, and the PL2000 was the lightest armouring material capable of defeating AK-47PS and 7.62mm NATO ball ammunition. To protect a range of threats from 7.62mm up to 12.7mm APM2 threats, the helicopter and truck were also equipped with armoured seats for pilots and aircrew. The floor, seats, wall, and doors had all been fitted with a modular, portable, or fixed protection kit, or a combination of them all.

As for the helicopter, it looked like an armed variant of the Russian MI-17HIP, the MI-8TV—the same bird they had used to rescue Nate Gregory. It was fitted with 7.62mm machine guns and six external weapons racks containing S-5 rockets. The helicopter also carried AT-2 Swatter 9M 17P Skorpion anti-tank missiles, which could readily cope with any armored or reinforced obstacle that might be encountered along the way. To carry the extra payload and improve the hovering ceiling, the HIP had also been fitted with a powerful TV3-117VMA engine.

Meanwhile, to dot the eyes and cross the tees on any selected targets of opportunity, one of the two aircrewmen had been trained as a medium-range sniper. His weapon was an M20—which amounted to an M14 7.62mm semi-auto rifle with Harris bi-pod and Bushnell Elite 4200 Mil-dot 6-24x40 scope. From a moving platform, a sniper with that weapon could take a man down comfortably at ranges up to 500 yards.

Brac now diverted his attention to the individual team equipment. Since no cross-country travel was anticipated, they would go in heavy. Each man would wear a Level IV NIJ STD Tactical Assault Vest, equipped with ballistic plates. This would defeat a direct hit from an AK47 and, he hoped, keep fatalities to a minimum. The remainder of the equipment was the same they had used in Nate's rescue: SIG Sauer 229 pistols, Colt 5.56mm M4A1s with EOTech sites, M249 SAW light machine gun, and the Stoner Rifle fitted with a Leupold 3-12x50 scope. Located in their combat vest, each team member, except the sniper, would carry a basic load of 400 rounds of 5.56, an assortment of smoke, fragmentation, and stun grenades, night vision optics, communications equipment, a Garmin GPS device, medical kit, and two quarts of water.

Brac checked and rechecked the To Do List and then went over the acetate-covered equipment list yet again, this time marking off each item with a grease pencil. He played and replayed both aspects of the mission in his mind and assured himself that there was redundancy built into every phase of the operation. If Murphy's Law—that old diehard enemy Brac called "Murphy" for short—entered the picture, he wanted a backup plan to take care of it. Phase Lines had been entered into the GPSs as waypoints and it was at these various Phase Lines—Alpha, Bravo, Charlie, and Delta—that certain actions would be initiated.

For example, the helicopter pilot, code-named Bumblebee, knew that when Brac radioed that he and the guys had reached Phase Line Charlie, that meant that the Trojan Horse was approximately one mile from Jumoke's village and had pulled off the side of the road feigning a flat tire. On receiving that cue, the helicopter would take a zigzag route to the terrorist stronghold, enact several mock landings to simulate the delivery of ground forces, and then take the rats' nest under fire with both rockets and machine guns. This action would not only provide a diversion, drawing security forces away from Brac's primary objective—Jumoke's rescue—but would kill a whole bunch of bad guys that had been terrorizing that part of the country.

The sniper team and light machine gunner would also be deployed at Charlie. They would work their way to the objective, move into good concealed positions, and provide covering fire when the remainder of the team came rolling into the village within the bowels of the Trojan Horse. Yes, Joe Brac reassured himself, the plan seemed sound. But as always, before any mission, he was edgy. He wanted nothing more than to get on with it.

Brac called everyone together that afternoon for one final brief back. This was the third time they had been through it, up one side and down the other, and he knew that at least a couple of pairs of eyes rolled heavenward when he got them together yet again. Everybody knew that Brac was a stickler for even the minutest details and would not rest until he was totally satisfied with every aspect of the operation. They also knew that his attention to detail added up to better odds on their survival. Each of the men carefully briefed his portion of the mission and was then questioned specifically by Brac; not only about his responsibilities but about the tasks of every one else on the team.

At long last Brac was satisfied. Even Angel, who had spent considerable time away from the training process with Karen and Nate, hadn't missed a beat. He hadn't had as much time to train and prepare as the others, yet he'd given a flawless brief back.

So they were ready. They knew it themselves, and as they left the final briefing, Brac nodded his approval. Once they were gone, he took a Cohiba out of his desk, snipped the end, lit it, and took several satisfying puffs.

I love it when a plan comes together, he mused. *This is great shit. Nous Defions.*

Chapter Eleven

With Billy Jones gone, Karen and Nate were restless and uneasy, each of them lost in an anxious fog. They didn't say much to each other for more than an hour, unwilling, at least for the time being, to talk about their fears and frustrations. Eventually Nate plopped down in front of the television and stared blankly at BBC World News. Karen stood behind him, her arms crossed, gazing at the screen. Their spirits weren't exactly lifted by what they saw—yet another terrible report from Nigeria.

As if the news about increasing violence weren't bad enough, now there was another morbid twist: the Governor of Abuja had been found dead, and by all accounts had succumbed to the Ebola virus—the horrific hemorrhagic fever that had appeared in Sudan, Congo and Côte d'Ivoire a few years before. More recently it had recurred, in a different form called Marburg, in Angola. Whatever name it bore, it was a catastrophic disease, very easily transmitted, a modern-day horror most people had been too happy to forget about.

Along with more than 100 other guests, the governor had attended a Worker's Day celebration the night before. He had probably shaken hands with every person there, as well as having shared the food buffet and the punch bowl with one and all. Now it was feared that anyone who had been in contact with him might become infected. Medical experts with long, grave faces spoke of a possible epidemic—perhaps even a pandemic—as they raised key questions: Where had he contracted the disease? How had it found its way into Nigeria?

Who would be stricken next?

"My God! Ebola!" Nate murmured. "I think I'd rather be shot than die from Ebola!"

"What about beheading?" Karen was fighting off feelings of nausea. "Which is worse, having your internal organs melt down or having your head sawed off?"

"That's a tough call." Nate shook his head mournfully. He turned to look at Karen, and the sight of her pale face filled him with remorse. "Look, Karen, I am so sorry I dragged you into all this. Honestly—it is the stupidest thing I've ever done. I don't know why you're even talking to me!"

Karen studied him, not sure whether to be irritated or touched. "Nate, I think we're both grown-ups. I made a decision to come here. You didn't decide for me."

"But I told you it would be safe..."

"It was my responsibility to find out for myself whether it was safe or not," she said quietly, but with a determined look on her face. "My boss pretty well said I had to come. My father's old friend Sean Murray encouraged me to come. David Levine wanted me to see for myself what was going on here and paid for everything. So how can you take all the blame?"

He looked away from her. Tired and distressed, he felt like crying, but he didn't want her to know he was that soft. Men like Billy Jones made him feel like a stereotypical 21st Century "sensitive male" and he hated it. He wanted to be tough and strong, but his emotional makeup always got in the way, especially when he was stressed. And right at the moment, the word "stress" fell far short of describing his turbulent state of mind.

"Nate? Are you okay?" Karen sank in the chair next to him and took his hand. He came close to pulling it away—her gesture felt a little like pity to him—but he didn't. Instead he leaned over and kissed her cheek.

"I'm fine." He smiled. "Just a little tense."

As if in response, a burst of automatic gunfire rattled in the distance. It wasn't close enough to be seriously dangerous, and in spite of themselves they both chuckled. "Yeah, I guess you could say things are a little tense." Karen nodded.

They sat quietly, hand in hand. "I'm glad we're together,"

Nate finally said. "But this is a ridiculous way to try to get to know each other."

Karen squeezed his hand, instantly distracted by another burst of gunfire, closer than before. "How scared are you?" she asked him. "I mean, do you honestly think we'll ever get out of here alive?"

Nate thought for a moment before he answered. "After what I went through before, when I was in captivity, I guess this really doesn't seem so bad. I'm more anxious than scared. You know, nervous. Stressed. But like I said, I'm glad we're together. I'm glad Levine's men know where we are. I'm thankful we're not in a hole somewhere, thinking we've been forgotten."

"Nate, you may be anxious, but there's something calm about you, too, and I really like that. How can you be anxious and calm at the same time?"

Nate chuckled. "Maybe I'm just a good actor. But I've got a pretty deep peace inside that we'll be okay, that we'll be taken care of. I have a pretty strong faith. Still, that doesn't mean I'm not apprehensive when..."

Nate fell silent as a single shot rang out, reverberating in the still air. They heard a shout from one of the Nigerian guards, but they couldn't understand what he was saying. They both jumped to their feet.

"No, get down!" Nate said, pulling Karen down next to him. They both ducked onto the floor, away from a small window that opened to the courtyard. He put his arm around her. "Whatever is going on out there is getting closer by the minute."

They stared at the television in silence, as if it were some sort of an electronic clairvoyant, able to provide them with all the information, instructions, and insights they so desperately needed. Thirty seconds later, the picture vanished. The screen went blank. The light in the room dimmed. The power had shut down, leaving them with no TV, no computer, no lights. Nate picked up the phone. There was no tone. The generator outside had stopped, probably out of petrol.

"Billy told me to turn my cell phone back on," Karen remembered suddenly. "I think it's completely recharged—it should be okay for a few hours."

"Where is it?"

"It's in the sleeping area. Maybe we should go over there anyway, before it gets too dark." She looked toward the window apprehensively. "It's more sheltered there."

"We'll have to cross the courtyard. Are you up for that?"

"Let's go while we can," she answered. "I want to get that phone turned on. I should have done it before Billy left."

They listened for more shooting, but momentarily everything was still. To their knowledge, not one bullet had invaded the compound, but the sounds of distant guns were enough to make them feel exposed and vulnerable. As they made their way across 15 yards of open courtyard, hearts pounding, they scrambled like a pair of crabs, trying awkwardly to stay close to the ground. They heard another shout and two loud shots rang out, the bullets ricocheting.

"My God!" Karen whispered. "That was so close."

Nate had Billy's pistol in hand, looking in all directions as they scuttled through the door on the other side. The dormitory-style room was framed with two windows facing the courtyard. They went to the far side of the room and yanked mattresses off a couple of beds so they could stay on the floor, away from the windows.

Another volley of gunfire exploded, and the Nigerian soldier who had been guarding the compound gate unexpectedly burst into the room. Nate was so startled that he shakily pointed Billy's gun toward him.

"No!" the Nigerian demanded. "Put the gun away! I am sorry to alarm you. But I have something important to tell you!"

Nate tossed the gun down, his hands trembling, and jumped to his feet. "What is it?" he asked. "What's happening?"

"Mr. Nate, we have received a message from those Christian villagers who came here the other day. The message is that jihad warriors are coming this way. They have burned one village to the ground. Two more villages lie between them and us."

"What do you mean when you say the villagers sent a message?" Karen was puzzled. "How did they send a message?"

"They sent one of their young boys. He ran to tell us. He is on his way back to them now."

"Why would they do that?" She was horrified. "Why would they take a chance with a child's life?"

"Because they want to make sure you are safe." His simple answer hung in the air.

"So what are we going to do?" Nate asked the soldier. He was beginning to wonder if they would make it out of here, after all.

Karen studied the Nigerian closely. It occurred to her that, until that moment, she had not even seen him as a person—he was like an extra in a movie. Now he had become her bodyguard. "I'm sorry—I can't remember your name," she said weakly.

"My name is Chioke," he told her with a warm smile, taking no offense at her oversight.

By then Karen had pulled the cell phone out of the recharger and turned it on. There was one message, left just about an hour before. She listened to it carefully, and then saved it. "There's a message from Joe Brac, that military guy who's in charge of Levine's men. He says we need to stay where we are, keep the lights out—as if that were a problem— and wait for further instructions. He says he and his 'boys' have to take care of a couple of things, and then they'll send Billy Jones back to get us out of here. Here, you listen to it, too."

Chioke stood in the doorway, his legs planted firmly apart, his shoulders tense. All at once his eyes narrowed. He turned away, stepped outside, and closed the door. They could hear him speaking quietly into his microphone, listening to someone's instructions coming through his earpiece.

Both of them were abuzz with adrenaline and fear. Despite the heat, Karen's hands were cold as ice. Nate took her in his arms and held her close for a few moments. "Karen, I don't want anything to happen to you," he told her, trying to keep his voice calm and steady. "I...really care about you. I mean that."

She choked back a sob and pulled away from him. "You're a good man, Nate. I think maybe..." she was struggling to control her emotions. Her face was wet with tears, but she somehow managed to avoid the hysteria that was beginning to swell inside her once again. For several minutes it was quiet—both in the room and outside.

The two of them tried to calm themselves, breathing deeply, summoning their inner resources. "Karen," Nate finally said, "I need to tell you something."

"Okay. What?"

"Even if I could leave right now, I wouldn't do it—I wouldn't leave you. Why did you say the other day that men always leave you? What happened to you that made you say that?"

"Oh God...not now. I'll tell you some other time. Hasn't anybody ever left you?"

Nate waited a long time to answer, so long that Karen thought he wasn't going to. At last he said, in such a quiet voice that she had to bend her head to hear him, "My wife died."

"Your *wife*?"

"My wife died," he repeated. "She died about three years ago. She had cancer, and she didn't make it. So yeah, I guess you could say she left me. She left both me and our little girl."

"You have a little girl? You never told me that before, either!"

"I guess the subject never really came up. Suzanne died when Chelsea was two."

Karen was silenced. Her agitation had turned into a weird numbness, and she felt as if she were having a bizarre dream. Nothing seemed real to her except Nate's physical presence, and now he seemed to have changed, too, into a stranger—a married man, a husband, a father.

"I'm so sorry," she whispered. "I really had no idea."

"We've had plenty of other things to talk about, Karen. Don't worry about it."

Another exchange of gunfire exploded somewhere. "God help us," Nate murmured. "Save us and keep us..."

"Nate, maybe we should find the keys to that SUV we were in before, and just make a break for it."

"What about Billy?"

"What about him? Who knows if we'll ever see him again anyway? I think we're pretty much on our own."

"No, Karen. I think we need to wait. Joe Brac said Billy

would be back."

"I don't trust Joe Brac," she said crisply. "He's...the kind of man I don't trust?"

"Why?"

Karen had no answer for Nate's question. "I don't really know," she finally replied, "just a gut feeling I guess."

Nate looked at her closely, trying to see past the set expression on her face. All he could discern was fear—like the outside sky, growing darker with every passing minute. "Karen, I think you've got to set that feeling aside for now," he declared, sounding more convinced than he felt. "Brac is Levine's man. And if you can't trust anybody else, at least try and put some faith in David Levine. Because *my* gut feeling tells me that he and Brac know what they're doing. And—let's be honest—you and I really don't have a clue."

* * *

At last Joe Brac's "D Day" had arrived, and so far he wasn't especially impressed with it. For him, the day's activity had begun hours before the first light of morning, and his old nemesis Murphy was seriously on the prowl. Mechanical problems and avionic glitches with the helicopter had already delayed the team's departure time twice. Meanwhile, Angel had somehow managed to contract a case of dysentery, and had stayed up most of the evening, as Playboy had wryly reported, "making love to the porcelain goddess."

What else could go wrong? As always, Brac dealt with it, literally putting to use 100 miles of tape and bailing wire and, in poor Billy Jones' case a heavy dose of Esdifan and an IV bag of fluid. Once again the Time On Target (TOT) was rescheduled—this time for late afternoon, just before dusk.

Once the entire team assembled at the airfield, the sun was sinking toward the west. After the brief backs the night before, Brac had given everyone some time off to relax, unwind, and take care of personal business. Except for Billy, they were all somewhat rested and had eaten a hearty breakfast and lunch. After getting a green light from the helicopter pilots, they had fallen in on their equipment. For one final time Brac inspected each man and his equipment and asked a few more last minute questions. Finally, he was satisfied.

Before Brac could think of something else to double-check, Angel, pale but alert, announced, "Chief, let's get it on!"

Following Angel's lead, they all boarded the Trojan Horse. Brac glanced around, gave the high sign to the heli pilot and his crew and boarded the truck. The two Nigerian drivers Angel had hired weeks before jumped into the vehicle's cab and cranked the engine. It roared to life and they were off. Every one of them knew that a young woman's life lay in their hands and there would be no turning back until they had successfully completed their mission.

The Mercedes Benz truck rolled eastward down the road, cruising lazily through several villages, past women gracefully carrying baskets on their heads, men ambling along in pairs, kids riding bikes, and battered vehicles of all shapes and sizes. A fine dust drifted into the back as the team sat silently in their harnesses. One of the guys played with a GameBoy, a couple of others read pocket books, and the rest just sat there cat napping or staring into space while the truck moved steadily toward its destination.

Brac radioed in Phase Line Alpha, then Bravo, and settled back into his seat. Back at the airstrip, the pilot and his crew began their final flight check and started their engines.

Approximately one mile from the village where Jumoke was being held, the truck pulled off to the side of the road. One of the Nigerian drivers jumped from the cab, ran to the front right tire, glanced around, and quickly jabbed an ice pick into the sidewall. It went immediately flat. At the same time the sniper team and machine gunner rolled out of the truck, hit the dirt, and disappeared down an embankment. The two shooters would quickly work their way up the brushy banks of a nearby wadi and get into position to cover the snatch.

Brac pulled his radio from his tactical vest and radioed in.

"Bumble Bee, Bumble Bee, this is Coyote One. Over. Come in, Bumble Bee."

"Coyote One, this is Bumble Bee. Go ahead."

" Bumble Bee, we've reached Phase Line Charlie. Proceed immediately to Tango village and fire 'em up."

"Roger, Coyote One. See you at the club. Keep the beer cold!"

Immediately Brac motioned for silence throughout the back. There was no doubt in his mind that they would know when Bumble Bee reached the terrorist compound—all hell was about to break loose. They would be able to hear the rocket and machine gun fire, even though they were a couple of miles away.

The two Nigerians moved about with deliberate slowness as they went through the motions of removing the flat tire and struggling to get a spare tire back on. There were numerous breaks, more than a few cigarettes, and a lot of laughter and back slapping as the twosome acted like inefficient idiots, stalled for time, and waited impatiently for Bumble Bee to initiate the final phase.

All at once everyone heard the telltale sounds: crump, crump....rat-a-tat-tat, rat-a-tat-tat. The explosion of rockets, the firing of machineguns had begun in the distance. By then the warriors were twitching with energy. *Wait, wait, wait,* they warned themselves. *Be patient. Give the Tangos around Jumoke plenty of time to rush to the rescue.* They listened closely, anxiously as Bumble Bee roared in straight out of the setting sun, rockets and machineguns blazing.

Seconds later the terrorists in the compound—the same Tangos who had torched a local village and burned it to the ground—had just settled into a relaxing dinner of goat and rice. They were caught completely by surprise. Those that were not blown to bits by rocket explosions or riddled with bullets as the HIP made its first pass, scrambled for their weapons and the nearest cover.

Bumble Bee banked sharply and came in for another attack. More Tangos fell, but now a few began to return fire. An RPG was launched in the general direction of Bumble Bee but missed badly. The helicopter fired another rocket. Baroom! A secondary explosion rumbled. Bumble Bee's rocket had apparently hit an ammo stockpile. Maybe it wasn't such a small terrorists' nest after all.

Brac and his team were reading the battle's progress by ear, interpreting every sound. Now the countdown for the

Trojan Horse's part of the two-prong mission was ticking. In less than a minute, they would be on their way. Brac was just about to give the driver the go ahead when his satellite phone unexpectedly rang.

This can't be good, Brac thought as he clicked it on. "Brac here."

"Brac, this is Levine. We have a problem." Brac stared at the phone in disbelief.

"This is not a good time for trouble, Levine. What kind of a problem?"

"I've just received word from one of the guards who was left with Karen Burke and Nate Gregory. He says the surrounding villages are being overrun. We've got to get the two of them out of there."

Brac listened intently. "Hold it a minute, Boss." He turned to Billy Jones. "Angel, did you discuss a Go-To-Hell plan with Nate and Karen before you left?"

Billy Jones nodded his head in the affirmative. "I left them a GPS with waypoints and directions programmed in, and some emergency signaling equipment, plus a pistol and ammo."

"Hey Boss," Brac said to Levine, "I'm told that a general plan is in place. I'll think on it some more and get back to you."

"I'm afraid we don't have much time to play with," Levine countered nervously.

"Dammit!" shouted Brac. "I can only do one thing at a time! You quit worrying. I'll get them out. If we don't move right now, we may as well not move at all. Goodbye!"

Brac clicked off, shaking off his frustration, resolutely refocusing his mind on the task at hand. "Let's go!" Brac shouted to the two Nigerians in the cab as he tucked the SAT phone back into his vest.

The Trojan Horse lurched forward and headed down the road toward the village. The team members could still hear the battle going on in the distance and Brac could only hope that some of the guards assigned to Jamoke's cell and the surrounding area had taken the bait and had hustled off to help their comrades in the besieged village nearby. *I'd rather be lucky than good,* he thought. In actuality, he was both, but overconfidence would not serve him well right then and he knew it. Brac looked into the eyes of each of his men one last time. He encouraged them, repeating a phrase some of them had heard him say more times than they could count.

"Stay low....move slow," he said.

The dust covered truck lumbered into the center of the village and rolled slowly to a stop. Abruptly the doors slammed up. Five men in jungle camis piled out, three on one side, two on the other. They fired as they ran, the guns blazing, moving purposefully, headed in specific directions. The diversionary attack on the nearby terrorist compound had apparently done its trick. The remaining local Tangos, by and large, were caught completely off guard. Brac and his men overlooked no "targets of opportunity" along the way. Less than half of Jumoke's original protectors—several Africans and a few Arabs—were felled, one after another, into bullet-riddled remains. Without delay, the Trojan Horse's team blasted its way into the building where they knew Jumoke was imprisoned.

Brac charged through one side of the mud brick structure, firing as he went, with Angel covering his backside. Except for Jamoke, they knew there were no friendlies on the scene. Anything and everything that moved was stitched with 5.56mm. Just as they rounded a corner and caught sight of Jumoke, cornered and desperate, both Brac and Billy saw a Tango about to unload his AK47 into her.

Angel's reaction time and marksmanship had always been impressive; that day it was nearly miraculous. Before the African could so much as curl his fingers around his trigger, Angel had fired three times and never missed a vital organ—two shots hit the unwary Nigerian in the chest and one caught him in the right temple. With a pained grunt, the would-be killer crumpled to the floor like a sack of feed, and his weapon clattered harmlessly onto the ground. Brac stepped over him, shot the lock off the tiny, filthy cell where Jamoke had been imprisoned for weeks, and grinned.

So far, so good.

Jumoke was wide-eyed with terror. Her mouth was open, but she could not make a sound. Minutes before, she had been suddenly awakened by the sound of gunfire. She had caught her breath and sat up unsteadily on the mat that served as a bed, clutching the dirty sheet with both hands. She had tried to scream, but to no avail.

Now she squatted, trembling in the corner of her cell, anticipating what she assumed to be her final end. She had repeatedly envisioned in her mind a heroic rescue, but it had always been silent and secretive. She had never conceived of anything so explosive and violent and bloody as this. She watched as two strangers entered her cell. Both were obviously white. They had painted their faces with camo stick and one of them still had a silly smile on his face.

"Jumoke," he said, "we've come to help. We're gonna get you out of here."

Hearing her own name, Jumoke murmured, "Thank you..." She tried to stand up and take a step toward them, but her knees buckled. She stumbled badly and fell into Angel's arms. He caught her, threw her over his shoulder, and headed back the way they had come. He and Brac rushed outside, and this time Brac was covering Billy's rear as they sprinted for the truck. Firing could still be heard sporadically but by now it was obviously one-sided—Levine's warriors had completely neutralized the village. Now it was time for them to get the hell out of Dodge. Brac blew a whistle and everyone began to rendezvous at the truck.

Angel eased Jamoke into the back while Brac took one last look around. He counted each man on, and once they were all boarded the doors were slammed shut.

The Judge, having had a satisfying outing as a sniper, now put on his medic's hat and carefully hooked Jamoke to a IV bag. Meanwhile, the Trojan Horse wheeled around and cantered back toward its barn at the Feeding the Hungry compound.

As for Brac, he allowed himself only a few moments to savor the operation's success before turning his attention toward the next challenge. *It ain't over till it's over. But still,* he smiled, *Ajax, the hero of Troy, would have been proud of that one.*

* * *

The silence surrounding Nate and Karen was almost as

disturbing as the gunfire had been. Momentarily they could hear nothing but the deceptively peaceful sound of crickets and their own unsteady breathing.

Talking to Nate somehow distracted Karen from the dark thoughts that continuously crept into her mind. She needed to talk, to hear her own voice. "You know what I don't understand?" she asked feebly.

"What's that?"

"Why such awful things happen to people. Why did your wife have to die?" She waited for Nate to answer, but he had nothing more to say on the subject. "Why have I been through my stuff? It wasn't as bad as yours, but still, why?" she continued. "And what about the people in this country? It's got to be the worst humanitarian disaster on the planet."

"It's bad," Nate agreed. "And they're wonderful people, all but a few of them."

"That's my point," Karen said. "Why do they have to live this way? And another thing, I don't understand them trying so hard to warn us. They always seem to be risking their lives. Is it because they're religious? To be honest, the Christians I know at home are pretty wrapped up in their own little church world. It's like some cool club they all joined, and nobody else is welcome. I can't imagine them being as unselfish as these people, can you?"

An image of Pastor Ken's well-appointed church appeared in Nate's mind, followed by the memory of the clergyman's self-serving attempts to take credit for Nate's rescue. "I don't think it's a very good idea to judge Christianity by the way some American Christians act," Nate told her.

"Like we shouldn't judge all Muslims by these crazed radicals?"

Nate paused. "Well, yeah. I guess it's the same, in a way, but..."

"So you do you think these Africans are trying to help us because they're super-religious?"

Nate was trying not to be exasperated by the conversation. He wanted to listen to what was going on outside, to reflect on their options, to figure out some kind of an escape plan. He knew, however, that Karen's chatter was her alternative to hysteria. "I don't know about that, Karen. Sometimes super-religious people murder other people in the name of their religion. But these Africans here aren't like that."

"What do you mean? Why are they different?" Gunfire crackled not far away.

Nate tried to focus his attention on Karen's pale face. "I think they're actually willing to risk their lives for other people."

"Yeah, but why?" she persisted.

"I think they do it for love, not religion. It's pretty simple, really. They believe God loves them and so they love him back. And they love other people, too. They have so little materially that relationships like that..."

Suddenly gunfire exploded all around them. They could hear the two Nigerians shouting at each other again, and firing their AK47s.

"Oh God!" Karen caught her breath, more terrified than she could possibly express. She felt a wave of light-headedness and wondered if she was going to faint. "Oh, God, get us out of here! If you can get us out of here, I'll believe. I swear it. I'll believe in you if you'll help us. Oh, my *God!*" She squeezed Nate's arm so tightly that her fingers hurt.

Suddenly they both heard a shot, a horrible scream, and a crashing sound. Without a word, they understood that one of the Nigerians outside had been shot. Seconds later Chioke rushed in. "We have to get out of here," he told them, shining a flashlight around the room. "Get whatever Billy Jones gave you and leave the rest," he ordered. "Follow me."

As they grabbed what they needed, rushed out the door, out the compound gate, and into the night, Karen suddenly panicked, thinking she had left the cell phone behind. Then she remembered that she had shoved it into her pocket. With shaking hands, while she tried to run and keep up with Chioke, Karen flipped it open. She pressed a number.

"Brac here."

"Joe, this is Karen Burke."

"Who?"

"Karen Burke! Can you hear me?"

She was already breathing hard. She was a runner, but this

was a far cry from the boardwalk in Santa Monica. They were racing at top speed in the dark, tripping over rocks, ripping their way through bushes. At that point Nate still had a tight trip on Karen's upper arm, trying to keep her alongside him, and the Nigerian was shouting back at them, "Hurry. You must run faster! They are close behind us. Run as fast as you can!"

"Karen?" Brac shouted. "Where the hell are you?"

"We're running away..." she stammered. "One of the Nigerian guards is dead. We are running for our lives."

"Which way are you running?" Brac shouted. "Do you know which way you're running?"

"Nate, where are we? Which way are we going?"

"West," Nate told her.

"West," she repeated between breaths. "We're running....west."

"Is the other guard with you?"

"Yes... Chioke is here. And he says we have to run for our lives."

"I'll call you back in a minute," Brac snapped. "Don't stop—do whatever Chioke tells you."

Bumble Bee was still raining hellfire on the terrorist compound when Brac radioed. "Bumble Bee, Bumble Bee, this is Coyote One, over. Come in, Bumble Bee."

After a brief delay, the response came through, "Coyote One, this is Bumble Bee."

Brac could hear shooting and explosions in the background. "We've recovered the package. Break off your attack and be prepared to provide pursuit coverage. Over."

"Roger, Coyote One."

"And Bumble Bee, standby for further instructions in reference to a developing situation."

"Roger that. Just tell me what I need to do," responded the pilot. "Standing by."

As Trojan One raced back toward its home base, Brac settled on a simple plan to rescue Karen and Nate. In impromptu situations like this the best strategy was one based on the KISS principal: Keep It Simple, Stupid. That was exactly what Brac had in mind.

"Angel, the pilot can read the homing signal from their GPS, correct?"

"Yes, I left the other unit with him."

"Bumble Bee, Coyote One here. This is what we're going to do..."

* * *

Karen was drenched in sweat. Her clothes were torn, and she was bleeding from several scratches. The damage continued to be inflicted as she, Nate, and Chioke thrashed their way through the bush in the dark. Nate had done his best to stay close to her side, despite the fact that he'd been trying to keep an eye on Billy's GPS unit. He hadn't really listened to what Billy had told him about the gadget, and now in the dark, straining to keep up with their athletic Nigerian guard, he wasn't at all sure they were heading in the right direction.

"Where are we going?" Karen asked for the third time.

"Not sure," Nate panted. "Billy had something in mind."

"There's nothing out here. Nothing! God, we're going to die!"

Karen would have been enraged if she hadn't been so frightened. Their desperate flight felt eerily unreal to her—she was pushing herself harder than she'd ever pushed before. She was oblivious to the stings of snagged skin and the stab of side cramps. Only two things were on her mind—the sounds of sporadic gunfire behind them and their agonizing forward movement.

Their pace was brutal, but they couldn't stop to rest. Chioke knew better than they did that their pursuers were excellent trackers and knew the countryside. If they so much as slowed to catch their breath, they would be caught in no time. Nate, who had been rescued out from under their pursuers' noses, was a prize trophy that they longed to bag and brag about. And although Chioke's urgency had provided them with a ten or fifteen minute head start, they knew they couldn't keep up their tempo for long.

All of a sudden, Karen was jolted by the sound of her phone. *Oh, God, please, God,* she silently prayed, *let it be help.*

Just as she was fumbling to answer, she stepped on a rock

The Levine Affair: Angel's Flight

and sharply turned her ankle. Losing her balance, she fell on her hands. The phone hit the dirt and the battery tumbled away into the dust. "Oh my God!" she screamed. Nate and Chioke stopped. Well trained guard that he was, Chioke immediately took his place behind them, putting himself between Nate and Karen and their pursuers, his AK47 at the ready.

Karen located the phone, grabbed it and the battery, and with shaking hands put it all back together again.

"Hello, Hello!" she shouted. With Nate's help, she got back on her feet, and panting for breath, they started running again. A piercing pain shot through her ankle, but she ignored it. "Oh my God! I lost the call!" she shrieked, her voice harsh with panic, hot tears mingling with the sweat that was already pouring down her face.

"He'll call back. Keep moving," Chioke ordered her as he ran past, moving out ahead of them again.

Seconds later, the phone rang. Karen heard a calm voice saying, *"Karen, this is Brac. Can you hear me?"*

"Yes, Yes!" she screamed into the phone. "I'm so sorry. I dropped the phone, and..."

"Okay, okay." Brac interrupted. *"Don't worry about it. Now listen carefully to me and we'll have you out of there in no time. Here's what I want you to do..."*

Brac explained that the helicopter was on its way.

"But how will it find us?" Karen wailed. "It's dark, and there's no road."

"There's a homing device in your GPS." Brac sounded almost surreally composed. *"We know exactly where you are. Just keep running and—now listen to me carefully—are you listening?"* Brac could hear Karen's heavy but uneven breathing. He knew she was crying, and hoped against hope that he had her full attention.

"I'm listening..." she said, collecting herself. "Yes, I can hear you. We're okay. What do you want us to do?"

"Okay, good. Now when you first hear the rotor blades, you need to drop to the ground and activate the two infrared Chem-Lights. You have them with you, right?"

"Nate," she said, "You have the lights, right?"

- 225 -

"There right here," he said, patting his backpack.

"Yes, we have the lights."

"Good. With Night Vision Goggles on, the pilot will see you clearly. The Chem-Lights will stand out like beacons for the helicopter crew, and the bad guys won't be able to see them at all. You're all set, right?"

"We're all set," she said, jogging alongside Nate and glancing at him. He gave her a hopeful thumbs up.

Brac radioed the helicopter again and quickly reconfirmed the plan with the pilot. After he clicked off the radio, he drew in a long, deep breath and wished to God that everything would work the way it was supposed to. There wasn't a whole lot of redundancy built into this particular plan, and that wasn't the way Brac liked to do things.

A few seconds later, the fleeing trio heard the thump, thump of a helicopter approaching from a distance. Nate and Karen hit the ground, and Chioke, who positioned himself standing over them, quickly pulled the two infrared Chem-Lights out of Nate's backpack, snapped them on, and waved them high overhead.

The helicopter, traveling due east at stall speed, was trying to pick up any sign of movement below. All at once the pilot saw a cluster of lights moving across the ground, heading in the same direction he was.

"Shit!" he said, looking the scene over carefully through his Night Vision Goggles.

"Coyote One, we've got approximately two dozen Tangos moving rapidly in pursuit of our principals."

"Bumble Bee, can you locate the Chem-Lights?"

Sure enough, looking toward the horizon, the pilot spotted the two infrared Chem-Lights.

"Damn!" he muttered. Nate and Karen were less than a quarter of a mile in front of their pursuers. And they were no longer moving.

Bumble Bee didn't really have to think very hard about what to do. He roared over the Tangos, made a sharp bank turn, and came directly at the flashlights and torches, machineguns blazing and rockets firing. *That should buy us a few minutes.* He smiled, heading back toward the Chem-Lights.

The three on the ground had been listening hopefully as the thump-thumping grew increasingly louder and closer, only to be nearly deafened by close-range explosions and cries of agony. Nate and Karen were speechless with fear. Had their Chem-Lights inadvertently called in an enemy helicopter? If so, they were three sitting ducks in the dead of hunting season.

Thump, thump, the rotor sound closed in on them again. It grew louder and faster, and all at once a huge downdraft of air threw dirt and rocks everywhere. With flying debris biting into their faces, they instinctively closed their eyes. Karen suddenly felt herself being pulled in the direction of the whirling sound and thrown unceremoniously onto the helicopter floor. She opened her eyes again—almost afraid to look—and saw Nate and Chioke next to her.

As the chopper lifted off into the sky and tilted forward, accelerating into the black of night, a pinging sound rang through the cabin. One of the surviving Tangos below them was angrily shooting upward with a handgun. His bullets bounced harmlessly off the hi-tech Israeli armor. Seconds later, his futile efforts at revenge were permanently ended when one of the Bumble Bee crew lowered a 7.62mm machine gun in his direction and opened fire. To the relief of everyone aboard, a deadly barrage of bullets flashed downward, blasting him and a couple of his cronies all the way to Paradise.

* * *

Feeding the Hungry's ancient airstrip had no rows of chasing blue lights, no painted numbers, and no tower. But it was smoothly surfaced, and by the time Karen and Nate arrived there, courtesy of the Bumble Bee team, it was bustling with activity. Two corporate jets, their lights off, were parked on the tarmac adjacent to the landing strip. A group of a dozen men or more was gathered nearby. One of the private jets had its engines running. And as Karen and Nate walked away from the helicopter, Karen was trying valiantly not to limp on her throbbing ankle. They stopped to watch a black woman, dressed in what appeared to be rags, being rushed past them. She was borne in the arms of two men, one of whom held a plastic IV flask above her, its needle in her left arm.

"I wonder..." Nate whispered thoughtfully, his face unexpectedly brightening with awareness. "I'll bet..."

"You wonder what?" Karen interrupted, looking puzzled. "What do you bet?"

"You remember when Billy Jones left us and said he was going on a mission? I wonder if the mission was to rescue that woman who was going to be stoned for adultery. You know, Jumoke something-or-other. Maybe that's her!"

Karen's brow wrinkled in concentration. Her brain wasn't exactly working at top capacity. "Nate, I'll bet you're right," she said emphatically. "I *know* you're right. That makes perfect sense. And when you think about it, her situation was a lot like yours." She stopped short of saying Levine had planned both missions. "That's the connection—rescuing innocent captives."

Nate stared at her, then glanced up to see Billy Jones heading over to greet them.

"Speaking of connections..." he began, his face alight with complete amazement. "Oh my *goodness*!"

"What connections? What do you mean?" Karen asked, but Nate ignored her.

"Billy Jones—*now* I know who you are!" Nate clasped Billy's hand in both of his.

"You know who I am?" Billy grinned. "Of course you do. I'm Billy Jones—but you just said that, didn't you?"

"No, I mean I know why you've always seemed like someone I should recognize. That's because you were part of the team of guys that rescued me, weren't you? I didn't place you before, because you had a beard and long hair. Am I right?"

Nate's face was flushed with excitement. Angel just smiled.

"Am I right?" Nate asked again. "Tell me if I'm wrong!"

"Yeah, I was there. Mr. Levine hired us to rescue you," Billy explained. "Some of us are part of his permanent team. And Joe Brac organized the whole thing for Levine. But I guess I thought you knew all that."

"I just can't believe I didn't figure it out before!" Nate said, half-embarrassed. "I guess I should have known. It's so obvious."

"Yeah, well it is and it isn't," Billy said with a laugh. "Joe and the rest of us don't make a big thing about who we are or what we do. And Levine isn't real excited about publicity, either."

Karen watched this exchange with increasing pleasure. "Nate, Mr. Levine told me himself that he was responsible for your rescue. That's why he wants you to fly to London with me. He wants to meet you."

"Did you tell me that before?"

"I may have told you that you're invited to come to London with me—I honestly don't remember. But I know I didn't tell you about Levine, because he asked me not to."

Just then Joe Brac walked up and extended his hand. "So you're both alive and well, I see. You two are tough customers!"

"We're alive and well thanks to you," Karen said quietly. "How can we thank you?"

"Hey, we're just doing our job," Brac chuckled. "Don't give it a second thought."

By that time the private jet with the African woman aboard was revving its engines, turning and taxiing for take-off. "So was that woman Jumoke?" Nate asked eagerly. "The one they were going to stone to death?"

"That's Jumoke," Brac nodded. "We paid her a visit tonight. We also gave our best regards to her captors." He and Angel exchanged a quick glance.

"So was that Levine's mission, too?" Karen asked.

"Oh, you can ask him about that when you all get to London. He'll be happy to answer your questions."

"But where are they taking her?" Nate watched the plane lift off and slowly disappear in the West African night sky.

"To be perfectly honest," Brac said, "I don't know. Levine sent a team to pick her up and take her to a secure site with a state-of-the-art hospital. I think I heard that her mother's already there. Jumoke is in pretty bad shape and she needs some TLC. She'll also need a new identity and a new address. And nobody's going to know about any of that except Levine, the jet's crew, Jumoke, and her mother."

"So is David Levine still worried about her life, even now?" Karen frowned. She couldn't grasp why Jumoke would be at risk after being rescued from her death sentence

"Jumoke will wake up tomorrow morning with several

fatwahs against her. And if she's located, someone will most certainly kill her."

"What's a *fatwah*?" Karen knew she had heard the term before, but couldn't remember what it meant.

"You know how Jumoke was sentenced to death by a Shari'a court?" Brac asked. "A *fatwah* is an authoritative legal statement by an Islamic power player. In Jumoke's case, it means that some mullah could say that Allah wants her dead because she was sentenced to capital punishment by stoning and then escaped. It's like that Salmon Rushdie case— remember that? The fatwah against him was imposed by the Ayatollah Khomeini in 1989 because he thought Rushdie's novel, Satanic Verses, was blasphemous to Allah. The same kind of thing will probably happen to Jumoke. She'll need a new start. And Levine will see that she gets it."

Nate nodded, still stunned by the revelation about Levine, Billy Jones, and his own rescue. Like Karen, he was beyond exhaustion. They were both filthy, scratched up, hungry, thirsty, and buzzed with adrenaline. "So where do we go from here?" he asked Brac and Angel.

"Jet number 2 over there is for you two," Jones replied, motioning to his right. "You'll be back in London by morning."

"And what about you?" Karen asked Brac. She was fighting tears and feeling an unexpected sense of gratitude to both him and Jones. "You saved our lives. You guys were like...like our guardian angels. Will we ever see you again?"

"We're not angels, Karen," Brac laughed, "but yeah, you'll see us in London once we get things cleaned up around here. I guess Levine's planning a celebration and wants to meet you, Nate. Trust me, Billy and I will join you before the booze is gone. But for now, you two ought to wash up, grab some bottled water, and board your plane."

"Is Chioke going to London, too?"

Joe shook his head, "Choite has plenty to do right here. I don't think we can afford to have him out partying right at the moment. He's pretty indispensable. Anyway, we'll see you two there. Why don't you go ahead and get ready for your trip."

"Where do we wash up?" Nate asked.

"I'll show you." Angel headed for the Quonset hut with

Karen and Nate following behind. As they walked inside, in the better light Angel looked them up and down and whistled softly. "You two are quite a sight. You can use the shower if you want to. How 'bout if I tell your pilot you'll be out there in 15 minutes?"

"Sounds good to me," Nate said.

Too tired for words, Karen simply nodded.

Chapter Twelve

Despite the panic that ensued when Nate and Karen fled the compound with Chioke, they had somehow managed to locate their wallets and passports, and had stuffed them, along with Billy Jones' Chem-Lites and ammo, into Nate's backpack. Everything else they owned had been left behind—clothes, toiletries, books, cosmetics. If the terrorists acted according to their usual modus operandi, they would torch the compound, burning it and everything in it to the ground.

Now, as Karen made her way into the Quonset hut's bathroom and shower area, she noticed a container of contact lens wetting solution. Her eyes had been burning and stinging for two hours, and she grabbed the plastic bottle greedily. *Don't ask permission, apologize later,* she told herself. *It's better than going blind.* Since she no longer had a contact case, she popped her contacts out one at a time, flooded her red eyes with the solution, cleaned the lenses as well as she could, and put them back into her eyes. She shook the bottle when she was finished, relieved that it still contained plenty of liquid.

Afterward she showered quickly, washing her hair with a tiny bottle of complimentary hotel shampoo that she found next to a battered bar of soap. It smelled like cheap perfume, but she didn't care. It occurred to her that all the intricate preparations she'd made for the trip, all the careful planning of toiletries and beauty products and wardrobe, hadn't really been that important anyway. She stared at the weary, damp face in the mirror. There she was—no makeup, no hair style, no lip gloss. A couple of scratches at her hairline were still oozing a little. *You look like a refugee,* she told herself. *But then that's pretty much what you are, isn't it? What you see is what you get.*

After she emerged from the bathroom, Mark Steele—"The Judge" who was once again in his compassionate medic mode—wrapped her sprained ankle tightly in an Ace bandage. By the time she and Nate were ready to make their way out to the airstrip, to her surprise she was able to put nearly all her weight on it. Steele also handed them both a couple of tablets, "to help you relax on the flight back."

Once they were buckled into their seats on the small jet, they ate the diagonally- cut turkey-cheese-and-whitebread sandwiches the crew provided for them, downed some bottled water and swallowed the mysterious pills without questioning what they were. They didn't say a word to each other. Nate simply took Karen's hand, tucked it under his arm, and closed his eyes. Within seconds he was asleep.

Karen glanced around the plane's cabin, randomly trying to remember the last thing she'd heard from her boss, Frank Goldberg, and worrying irrationally about whether she still had a job. Her anxiety didn't last long. Whatever Mark Steele's pills were, they were more than effective. The next thing Karen and Nate knew, they were landing at David Levine's airport of choice for his unique aviation needs—Stansted, located north of London.

Just over an hour after that, at about 8 am, Karen limped into Claridge's Hotel with Nate at her side. They bore little resemblance to the other elegant guests that were being served at the reception desk, but they were warmly welcomed anyway. Noting their swollen eyes, ragged clothes, and pallid countenances, hotel employees escorted them to the third floor, made sure they knew what rooms they were in, and discreetly left them alone. Inside their Junior Executive Suites, each of them found a gift basket which contained, along with a few gourmet food treats, a tooth brush, toothpaste, small bottle of mouthwash, a hairbrush, a comb, a small deodorant stick, and a pair of brand new Lacoste warm-ups. Accompanying it was a note:

"Welcome back to London! It is a great relief to have you here safe and sound. Please enjoy yourselves in any way you'd like to—sleep, bathe, use the hotel spa if you like, and order whatever you want from the room service menu or in the bar and restaurant. At around two, someone from my staff will contact you about purchasing whatever you may need for the rest of your time here. Our small get-together will take place tomorrow evening at 7 pm, beginning in the Lobby Bar and followed by dinner. In the meantime, enjoy yourselves. All the best, David Levine.

Before she slipped between the crisp white sheets on her big bed, Karen picked up the phone receiver and dialed her mother's number. There was no answer, and at the voice mail tone she said, "Mom, it's Karen. I'm safe in London. You don't need to worry about me any more. I'm at Claridge's. I need to get some sleep right now, but I'll call you later on. I love you. Bye."

She started to call Sean Murray, too, but realized that she didn't have her address book and couldn't remember his number. Another loss, her calendar and date book—it would take awhile to get life back on track. With a sinking feeling, she thought about her job and Frank Goldberg. She would have called him, too, but she was too weary to face whatever he might say.

Instead, she checked her home voice mail. There were six or seven calls from people who didn't know she'd left the country. When call number eight began, she just shook her head.

"Hey, baby," Sid's voice sounded a little confused. *"So where have you been? I think maybe you told me you were going somewhere, but I can't remember. Anyway, do you want to hang out? I'm home tonight..."*

"Oh my God!" she said aloud as she emphatically deleted Sid's message. *That's more than enough news from home for now,* she assured herself replacing the receiver in its cradle. Everybody else, including Frank Goldberg, would just have to wait.

* * *

Once Joe Brac had finished securing the base at the Feeding the Hungry compound, he watched his men head toward their various flights home. He confirmed with David Levine that he and Angel would be on their way to London in a few hours. And only then did he begin to think about going home. That, of course, brought Katy Slagle to mind.

He rummaged through his bag in search of his personal phone, turned it on, and waited to see is he had messages. Kate had never failed to keep in touch with him—sometimes to a fault. But today, nothing. He sighed and tried to remember: when was the last time he had been in touch with her? It must have been the night Mischa arrived. He'd talked to Kate briefly then, spurred by guilty feelings about his continuing fascination with the beautiful Israeli. One thing was sure, no matter whom he ended up with—if he ended up with anybody at all—Mischa would always own part of his past. If there was such a thing as a soul mate, that was Mischa. They were connected by some deep understanding of each other, not to mention the intense sensuality they had always shared.

On the other hand, Brac knew very well that Mischa wasn't the kind of woman who would ever want to settle down with one man. And even if she did, how would it feel knowing that when she went off to work, her job usually entailed seducing foreign troublemakers and then killing them? He shook his head. *That would be a stretch,* he thought, *even for me.*

In the meantime he tried to remember what he had last said to Kate. Had he somehow angered her? So much had happened since. He faintly recalled telling her that he expected to be at Claridge's Hotel in London when the mission was over, and that he'd call her from there. In the past, that wouldn't have stopped her from leaving text and voice messages just to say hello, just to keep in touch. But maybe she was busy.

Brac's concern was interrupted by Angel, who walked up with his bag and baggage. "Let's roll," he said.

"Give me another minute or two to make sure everything's secure in here," Brac told him. Angel nodded and sighed, knowing that Brac would always take an extra few minutes to double check himself. It was obsessive, but effective. Often as not, he found something that hadn't been done right the first time. Angel dropped his duffle bag, sat down on the edge of a bunk, slipped his rucksack onto the floor, and waited.

Brac, in the meantime, was asking himself why he was so detail-oriented in matters of war, and so unfocused when it came to keeping the peace with the women in his life. Minutes later he returned, nodded to Angel, and the two of them headed out. Chioke, the Nigerian soldier, was waiting for them in the Land Rover. Dressed in Polo shirts and Dockers, the two Americans looked like a couple of corporate bureaucrats, flying back to London on business.

Once they arrived at Heathrow they went their separate ways. Angel was picked up at the curb by a woman in a Jaguar. He had told Brac that he would be staying with friends—he never mentioned their names—in a South London suburb. "I'd have to say Operation Angel's Flight was another success story," he said as they clapped each other on the back. "Your Trojan Horse is still one for the books." He smiled. "See you tomorrow night." He waved as he climbed into the sleek convertible.

Brac located his driver and sat thoughtfully in the back of a black Mercedes while his baggage was stowed in the trunk. He pulled out his phone, stared at it for a moment, then put it away again. He wanted to talk to Kate, but he wasn't quite ready to do so. He decided to wait until he checked into the hotel, so he could call from his room in complete privacy.

By the time he arrived it was nearly 9:30 PM. He walked into the hotel and looked around at its art nouveau splendor. He had been there a few times before, but the quiet elegance still took him off guard. *Not quite as hospitable as the Quonset hut*, he thought with a sly smile, *but I guess I can make do.*

Joe checked in, telling the desk clerk that he didn't need an escort to his room. "I know my way," he explained, "and I'm familiar with the floor plan. Thanks, though. Have a good day."

He punched the button on the small elevator adjacent to the concierge's desk and stood waiting, nearly asleep on his feet. Until that moment, he hadn't realized how tired he was. *A good night's sleep will do me a world of good,* he told himself. *A good sleep, a big English breakfast...*

"Hey, Joe, welcome to London!" A familiar voice startled him back to reality. He turned around and found himself looking at Kate's smiling face. Her arms opened to him, and he dropped his bags and gave her a big hug.

"Well, this is a surprise!" he said, giving her his biggest smile.

"I couldn't wait to see you," she told him, "so I booked myself a flight. I figured you'd be glad to see me, too," she said flirtatiously, in her usual self-confident way.

Joe *was* glad to see her—no question about it. Whatever ambivalence he was experiencing was surely the result of his mental and physical exhaustion. He put his arm around her shoulders and took her to his room with him. He didn't get to sleep quite as quickly as he'd intended, but he was a happy man anyway. Everything he'd planned to do alone—undress, shower, eat and sleep—they did together. There was no serious talk, no worrisome quibbling over when he'd last called, nothing to rob them of their pleasure. *Coming back from a war zone and finding a beautiful woman waiting,* he told himself, *is not something a man should take lightly.*

Brac didn't take it lightly. He never really had. Yet somewhere, just beneath his consciousness, there was an unsettled feeling. When it came to his relationship with Kate, at the core of his being he was satisfied, but he was not contented. He believed that he really loved her, and yet somehow he couldn't quite imagine spending the rest of his life with her. What was it? Was something wrong with him? Maybe, because he couldn't really imagine spending the rest of his life with anyone. Something wasn't right—that much he knew. And no matter how many times he had tried to sort out the details with himself, he really could not understand what was wrong, or how to make it better.

* * *

Karen woke up at about noon. She tossed and turned for half an hour, and finally gave up on sleep and rolled out of bed. Under normal circumstances she would have enjoyed the famous Claridge's "waterfall" shower, the plush towels, and the fragrant spa products. She would have carefully put on her make-up, taken her time with her hair, and selected her clothing thoughtfully. She had, however, awakened to anything but normal circumstances.

Yes, the note said that Mr. Levine's representative would help her replace her clothes and other lost items. But she wasn't sure how something like that would work, and there were a few things she needed right away. So after she brushed her teeth and hair, she hurriedly pulled on the Lacoste warm-ups that David Levine had provided, tied the filthy cross trainers she'd already worn for far too many days, grabbed her room key and wallet, and headed for the lobby. Her ankle was sore, but not as bad as she would have expected. It was swollen and slightly bruised, but all things considered, not too bad.

"Is there a department store around here anywhere?" she asked the concierge.

"Yes, Miss, Fenwick's is a short walk from here. Just turn right when you leave the hotel and stay on this side of the street. It's a couple of blocks away, on the corner. You can't miss it."

"What about a drug store?"

The concierge hesitated only for a beat. "Oh yes, a chemist. After you leave Fenwick's, head straight toward Oxford Street. You'll find a Boots there."

Karen wasn't sure about all the details, but she could ask again along the way. At least she could replace her contact case and solution, lip gloss, and mascara. Maybe she would get lucky and find something decent to wear, too. Maybe she'd buy a purse. Maybe even shoes. Right then, she couldn't even remember what she'd packed in the first place. A wave of fatigue swept over her just thinking about it.

But the moment she stepped outside Claridge's, Karen felt immediately better. London was, for once, sunny and clear with a fresh breeze snapping the flags that hung outside the hotel. She turned right and began to walk, feeling the wind in her hair, breathing in the safe, sane surroundings. As she made her way across the first crosswalk, she noticed a Coffee Emporium to her left. She impulsively headed inside and ordered a double cappuccino. As she drank it peacefully, before long her thoughts turned to Nate Gregory. It was difficult to separate the man himself from the outrageous dangers they had shared.

She quickly reviewed the last few days, then went back further—to their first conversation. Now, weeks later, it was difficult to imagine how her life had been before she knew him. With a grimace, she remembered Sid's lame message. Suddenly she missed Nate and wondered if he was still asleep. She realized she hadn't left word for him about where she was going, and that he might worry about her. A warm rush flooded over her face and through her body—for the first time in years she felt like she belonged with someone, maybe even belonged *to* someone.

Like an emergency fire brigade, a hefty array of emotional defenses immediately tried to douse her warm thoughts with cold rationalization. *It's stupid to fall in love with a man just because you've been through some hard times together,* she cautioned herself. *Don't go there!* But the warmth wasn't easily extinguished.

Fears or no fears, trust or no trust, Karen knew there was more to Nate Gregory than a collage of drama and dangers they had encountered together. One thing she liked very much about him was his willingness to communicate. She also cherished his unequivocal acceptance of her—irrational fears, cynicism, doubts and all. Still another quality she treasured, perhaps most of all, was his faith, a quality she wished she shared; one she intended, somehow, to pursue. She remembered the night—it seemed like months ago—when she had emotionally melted down, calling out for some sort of help and then finding strength to go on. She also recalled, a little ruefully, a prayer that if she survived Nigeria, she would believe.

It was becoming clear to her that all the terror and trauma had cut deeply into her soul, creating a place for new ideas, feelings, and maybe even some kind of a personal faith in some kind of a personal God. She remembered the words, "Beauty for Ashes," a phrase she had seen carved into the wood of Nate's half-constructed church. Her eyes stung, as she suddenly grasped the ancient truth to herself. Ironically, the carved words had probably been burned to ash themselves, thanks to the rampaging jihad warriors.

Still thoughtful, Karen returned to her errands, completed her purchases. and got back to the hotel an hour and a half after she'd left. The red message light on her phone was blinking. She punched in the voice mail code, and heard Nate's concerned voice. *"Karen,"* he said, *"where on earth are you? I hope you're okay. I'm going down to the Lobby Bar for lunch. If you get this, come down and join me."*

The message had been left 15 minutes before. Karen brushed her hair, quickly applied some mascara and lip gloss, and hurried to the door. Cynical and untrusting she might be, but she really couldn't wait to see him.

Just as she turned the doorknob, the phone rang.

"Karen," a friendly voice said. *"You have no idea how glad I was to hear that you've made it safely to London!"*

"Sean Murray! I haven't talked to you for days. I thought you'd abandoned me!"

"Oh God, Karen, I would never do that. I only stopped calling you when I heard that the generator had broken down in Nigeria, and you needed to reserve the charge on your phone. In the meantime, I nearly burned my church down lighting candles for you!"

Karen closed her eyes and shook her head. *There's more than one good man in the world,* she thought.

"Have you called your mother yet?" Sean was asking.

"I tried to. She didn't answer, but she might have been asleep. Why do you ask?"

"Oh, I just wondered," he said, not mentioning that Ellen Burke had called him at least twice a day for the past week. *"Anyway, I was hoping that you and I could get together for lunch or dinner."*

"You mean in D.C.? I think I've got a direct flight back to LA.

"No, I mean here, in London."

"Wait a minute. You're in London?"

"Sorry, Karen," Sean laughed. *"I thought you knew that. I'm at Claridge's. I'm calling you from a phone in the lobby."*

Now Karen really did hurry. She wanted to see Nate. She

also wanted to see Sean. She quickly tried to call her mother before leaving the room, but once again she got voice mail. She left another quick message then rushed into the Lobby Bar only to find Nate Gregory, Sean Murray, and David Levine engaged in an animated conversation. She almost hated to interrupt, but once she appeared all three of them rose to their feet and embraced her, one after the other. Sean Murray left after greeting Karen and making her promise to have lunch with him the next day. Nate gestured for her to sit next to him in a vacant chair.

"So you two have finally met," she said, nodding toward David Levine.

"Thank God I got to meet him. I owe him my life. In fact I owe him double!"

"We've all got a lot to be thankful for," Levine smiled. "I've got a great team working for me. So do you think you'll be able to finish your book?" he asked Nate, then Karen.

"I haven't talked to Mr. Goldberg yet," she replied, "but depending on how much you will allow us to say, Mr. Levine, we've got an amazing story, especially if we can include Jumoke's rescue. It will be an awesome book!"

Levine smiled. "I think we can figure out how to tell the story without giving away too much. It's worth the risk to get some hard facts about militant Islam and Shari'a law in front of Western readers. How long will it take you to finish the book and get it in print?"

Karen swallowed and looked at Nate. He looked up at the Dale Chihuly sculpture on the ceiling. "I'd guess we can finish in three or four weeks once I get back," he finally answered. "Maybe less."

"And I'll do my best to get the book on a fast track with New York," Karen added. "I have a feeling that by now Mr. Goldberg will be more than happy to cooperate."

"You can remind him," Levine said with a quiet smile, "that this may not be the author's only book."

"What do you mean by that?" Nate's eyes widened. "No more adventures for me, thank you very much. At least not this week. I've been through enough death-defying escapes for awhile!"

"From what I hear, you're a very gifted writer," Levine said. "Suppose another story came along, with a different set of circumstances, but once again involving radical Muslims and their violent tactics. I can imagine that it might be resolved by a similar paramilitary mission. Maybe you could write it, Nate. And between us, I think we could make sure it got in front of a competent acquisitions editor. As a matter of fact, I've already raised the idea with Mr. Goldberg himself." Levine winked at Karen.

For a moment, she and Nate stared at each other in disbelief.

"Are you talking about something specific, Mr. Levine?" she finally asked.

"As a matter of fact, I do have something in mind." Levine sipped his tea and wiped his mouth. "I think you'll find tomorrow evening's get-together very instructive," he added, getting to his feet. "I look forward to seeing you both there— maybe we can continue our conversation then. Now if you'll excuse me, I have an important meeting to attend."

For several minutes, Karen and Nate sat together quietly, each of them lost in thought.

"Karen," Nate spoke first, "there are a million things going through my mind right now. There are some things I want to say to you, and I know I probably shouldn't say them until later, when we're out somewhere sipping wine, with music in the air and candles on the table. But I don't want to wait that long. Besides, I want to say it in broad daylight, so you can be sure I'm not moonstruck or drunk or something worse."

Karen's heart, which had done its share of pounding in recent days, was beating hard yet again. "Okay...what is it you want to say?"

"Above all else, I don't want to lose you," Nate told her quietly, placing his hand atop hers.

She smiled at him and without hesitation said, "I feel the same way about you."

"I have no idea what lies ahead, Karen, but I know one thing for sure..." He paused, searching for words.

Karen's eyes sparkled as she awaited his reply. This had to be good.

"First of all, like I said, I know that I don't want to lose you. The last few days have been crazy. Even being here in this hotel, it's like something unreal, something unbelievable. But we'll soon be home, and once we get there, and we get back to our normal lives, and get a handle on all that's happened..."

"Then what?"

"Then I...I still want to be your best friend. And I hope you'll be mine."

Karen felt slightly deflated. *Best friends?* "Okay, I like that idea, too."

"And I want you to trust me. I know it's hard for you, but I want you to learn to trust me."

She nodded. "I already trust you, Nate. How could I not trust you after everything that's happened?"

Their eyes were fixed on each other. Nate looked away briefly, gathering his courage. He squeezed her hand and gazed at her once again. "There's one more thing. It's been a long time since I've felt this way, and I'm not sure I've ever said this to a woman before. For a while I wasn't even sure it would ever happen again. But I want to make love to you, Karen. I want you more than I've ever wanted anyone, and definitely more than you can imagine."

The air between them was suddenly electrified. They were barely breathing. Nate fidgeted with a spoon, and seemed to be growing increasing agitated. Finally he asked, almost whispering, "Did you hear me?"

"Yes. Of course I heard you."

"So..."

"So...I'm scared. And I'm... But it's okay, Nate. I agree with everything you said. I want what you want. Scared or not, I want the same things. And I feel exactly the same way."

* * *

When Levine's "personal shopper" arrived in her room, Karen was fairly sure that whatever she ended up wearing to Levine's special dinner party the following night would be disappointing and maybe even embarrassing. She wanted to shop for herself, but right then she was really feeling terrible, broadsided by every kind of exhaustion in the wake of her recent exploits. To make matters worse, her ankle was starting to throb. Resigned to being immobilized for the rest of the day and evening, she gave the effusive man her dress and shoe sizes, her ideas about what would be appropriate, and the two or three colors she would prefer. He glided out of the room in delight.

He rang the doorbell at 4:30, breezed in with several shopping bags for her, and immediately called the room's valet to see that her clothes were pressed for the evening. For the next evening's big event, he had located a black, silk long-sleeved sheath to be worn with an exquisite handmade shawl, also black, embroidered with vibrant poppies in red, magenta, and purple. He presented her with a pair of amethyst and garnet chandelier earrings that sparkled with the shawl's colors. And, miracle of miracles, he had not only provided shoes for every other outfit, but had somehow managed to replace her lost Jimmy Choo shoes with an almost identical pair. Now if her sore ankle would just cooperate while she balanced herself on 3 ½ inch stiletto heels, she would be the belle of the ball.

Michael the shopper had also bought Karen a pair of jeans, a trendy leather jacket, and three silk shirts in different colors for her remaining time at the hotel and her flight home. He had added pointy-toed pant boots, a Coach handbag, and a pair of simple gold earrings. The man's taste was disturbingly identical to hers. She loved everything he bought, and better still, it all fit her perfectly. "Michael, you're the best," Karen told him as he left.

"Are you kidding? Shopping for you made me day," he twinkled. "Jimmy Choo shoes are to die for!"

Once Michael left, Karen pushed the do-not-disturb button next to her bed and fell asleep. She didn't wake up until 7:30 the following morning. Over breakfast she learned that Nate, too, had been outfitted with new clothes, although by a different shopper. Nate wasn't as ecstatic as she about his new acquisitions, however. He was still mourning the loss of his favorite jeans.

When the following evening arrived, the two of them met in

the lobby, both admiring each other and looking far better than they should have, considering the past week of their lives. Only the scratches on their hands and faces, and Karen's purplish, swollen ankle betrayed their recent ordeal. No matter. She was defiantly wearing her new Jimmy Choo shoes anyway.

The hostess ushered the two of them into a private area behind the Bar, partitioned off from the rest of the guests, where they found Joe Brac, his friend Kate Slagle, and Billy Jones enjoying a round of Glenlivet. "To Joe and Billy, our heroes, and to a job well done," Nate said, lifting his gin and tonic toward the two soldiers.

Just as they were about to strike up a conversation, Karen felt a tug on her arm. An attractive and cheerful middle-aged woman was smiling at her.

"Mom!" Karen cried in astonishment. "What on earth are you doing here? I thought you were in California. No wonder I kept getting a recording when I called you."

"This was Mr. Levine's idea," Ellen Burke beamed. "What a wonderful man! He knew how worried I was about you."

I'll bet he did, Karen thought. *He and everybody else.* Fortunately, she kept her thoughts to herself. "I'm so glad to see you!" she told her mother. "When did you get here?"

"I've been in London for a few days, touring with an AARP group."

"AARP? What's that?"

"American Association for Retired People or something like that. Some of them are a little, well, elderly you know. But it's been fun to see London anyway. And is this Nate?"

"Yes, this is Nate. Nate Gregory, my mother, Ellen Burke."

"It's a pleasure, Mrs. Burke. You have a wonderful daughter."

Mrs. Burke, who had felt secretly optimistic about her daughter's relationship with Nate, looked very pleased indeed when she saw how handsome Nate was, how polite, and how attentive.

The group grew larger, joined by several Nigerians who lived in London and were closely connected to an influential human rights organization there. A couple of retired American military officers appeared in uniform, one of whom seemed to know Joe Brac very well. At around 7:15, David Levine and Sean Murray arrived with a small man dressed in a black robe, a red cummerbund, and a small cap. He wore a large jeweled cross around his neck. He had an alert, intelligent face, and a ready smile. "Metropolitan Abel, I want to introduce you to my friends."

David Levine took a few minutes to explain that Father Abel served in southeastern Turkey as the spiritual leader of the Assyriacs, an ancient community of Christian Orthodox believers. Their population, he said, had been nearly decimated, along with Armenians and Jews, during a Turkish jihad in the early 20th Century. While Turkey was negotiating a place at the table in the European Union, the situation seemed to have improved for the few hundred Assyriac Christians who lived in the shadow of an ancient monastery less than ten miles from the Turkey-Syrian border. Their numbers had begun to grow again. They had called their Metropolitan back from his professorship at a university in Western Europe and asked him to be their spiritual shepherd.

"But now," Levine explained, "the situation is growing dark again. Radical Islamists find it all too easy to traverse the porous Turkish-Syrian border, and they are determined to wipe out every Christian within their reach. Since Father Abel was visiting with me today, I invited him to join us tonight. And I have asked him to offer a blessing on our little celebration. Father Abel?"

The priest adjusted his glasses, folded his hands, and bowed his head. "We thank you, our great and mighty God," he prayed in a powerful voice, "for the wonderful victory against our tormentors that we are celebrating tonight. We thank you for the release of a young woman who was unjustly sentenced to death. We thank you for the skill of the warriors, and for the protection you have provided to everyone involved. You, indeed, are the great warrior King, and we praise and worship you. Please protect our brothers and sisters all around the world. Guide our conversation tonight. Help us to speak and write the truth boldly. And may the words of our mouths and the meditations of our hearts be acceptable in your sight, O Lord, our Strength and our Redeemer."

The prayer gave Karen chills, and judging by the faces of some of the others, she wasn't the only one who reacted that way. After praying, the Metropolitan smiled broadly at everyone in the room, then rested his gaze on the Africans. "We have much to learn from you and your people" he said. "And we all have much to thank you for, sir," he said to David Levine.

With that, elegant flutes brimming with Dom Pérignon were distributed, and David Levine lifted his toward heaven. "Mission Accomplished" he said joyfully, and for the moment all eyes turned to Joe Brac and Angel. Then the toasts went on, "To Jumoke." "To Joe Brac and his team." "To Angel's Flight." "To Nigeria's courageous Christians." And on and on, repeated by everyone there, and accompanied by the almost continuous clinking of champagne glasses.

A hostess quietly informed David Levine that their table was ready. But before they all set down their glasses and filed into the Gordon Ramsey restaurant, Joe Brac managed to have the last word.

"Another battle has been won," he proclaimed, "thanks to you, Mr. Levine. Now with the help of God, may we continue to provide protection, defense, and freedom for those who cannot help themselves."

"Hear, hear!" several people responded.

"May we always give our enemies more than they ask for," Brac went on, "and stop them from killing the innocent before they can get started."

This time the whole group loudly concurred.

"And may we not only continue to win the small battles," Brac concluded, his fist clenched in the air, "but may good people be victorious in the great war against evil and injustice that is raging all around the world. *De Oppresso Liber!*"

About the Authors

Lela Gilbert is an award-winning writer who has authored or co-authored more than sixty books. A Christian who has resided in Israel since 2006, her most recently published non-fiction work is the critically acclaimed Saturday People, Sunday People: Israel through the Eyes of a Christian Sojourner (Encounter Books, 2012) which, although authored by a Christian, was listed as one of the 20 best non-fiction Jewish books of 2012 by J.G. Myers in Jewish Ideas Daily.

Gilbert also co-authored Persecuted: The Global Assault on Christians with Nina Shea and Paul Marshall (Thomas Nelson, 2013).

Lela Gilbert is a contributor to Fox News, National Review Online, Weekly Standard Online, Lapidomedia (UK), Jerusalem Post, Huffington Post, Ricochet and other publications.

She is a Fellow at Hudson Institute, a public speaker, and is frequently interviewed on television and radio. She is also active on Facebook and Twitter.

Jack Buckner was Deputy Commander, Combined Joint Special Operations Task Force - Afghanistan (CJSOTF-A): Deputy Commander of all Special Operations in theater. He served as the principal adviser to the Commander in all matters pertaining to the training, organizing, supplying, and deployment of all CJSOTF-A assets, to include over 1500 U.S. and Coalition Special Operation Forces Personnel, and in the absence of the Commander served on numerous occasions as the overall CJOSOTF-A Commander. Was deployed to many remote fire bases, under often times hostile conditions, to personally assess the combat and environmental conditions facing the combat soldiers on the ground. Served as the CJSOTF-A Program Manager and successfully managed and executed a SOF Command Operating Budget of over 5 million dollars.